opportunity
rings

opportunity rings

sheryl steinberg

KEY PORTER BOOKS

Library and Archives Canada Cataloguing in Publication

Steinberg, Sheryl
    Opportunity rings : a novel / Sheryl Steinberg.

ISBN 978-1-55470-158-2

    I. Title.
PS8637.T4373O66 2009   C813'.6   C2008-906740-1

THE CANADA COUNCIL | LE CONSEIL DES ARTS
FOR THE ARTS | DU CANADA
SINCE 1957 | DEPUIS 1957

ONTARIO ARTS COUNCIL
CONSEIL DES ARTS DE L'ONTARIO

The publisher gratefully acknowledges the support of the Canada Council for the Arts and
the Ontario Arts Council for its publishing program. We acknowledge the support of the
Government of Ontario through the Ontario Media Development Corporation's Ontario
Book Initiative.

We acknowledge the financial support of the Government of Canada through the Book
Publishing Industry Development Program (BPIDP) for our publishing activities.

Key Porter Books Limited
Six Adelaide Street East, Tenth Floor
Toronto, Ontario
Canada M5C 1H6

www.keyporter.com

Text design: Martin Gould
Electronic formatting: Sonya V. Thursby / Opus House Incorporated

Printed and bound in Canada

09 10 11 12 5 4 3 2 1

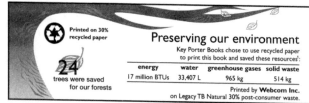

Printed on 30%
recycled paper

24
trees were saved
for our forests

Preserving our environment

Key Porter Books chose to use recycled paper
to print this book and saved these resources[1]:

energy	water	greenhouse gases	solid waste
17 million BTUs	33,407 L	965 kg	514 kg

Printed by **Webcom Inc.**
on Legacy TB Natural 30% post-consumer waste.

[1]Estimates were made using the Environmental Defense Paper Calculator.

FSC

Mixed Sources
Product group from well-managed
forests, controlled sources and
recycled wood or fiber

Cert no. SW-COC-002358
www.fsc.org
© 1996 Forest Stewardship Council

for my dad

If you have good bandwidth:

(a) the 3 mm diamond eternity ring on your left hand is the perfect complement to the three-carat rock on your right

(b) you can get away with not washing your mane for a day, especially if you got your hair band from Lululemon Athletica (along with a new hoodie and pair of yoga capris)

(c) you are part of a good band with, well, what every good band has—lots of drugs

(d) you can send loads of photos from the cam on your mobile without so much as a hiccup

chapter one

I hunger for a rose.

These are not the words of Geoffrey Chaucer, a lonely spinster, or a sappy greeting card writer. I mean, I actually want to eat a rose. It's Wednesday afternoon, just shy of 2:30 and I am so hungry I could eat a horse—nothing proverbial about it. However, in light of the fact that (1) I have a scheduled meeting with our corporate publicist in two minutes, and (2) I gobbled up the last of my granola-bar stash last Wednesday, a rose or two will have to suffice.

It's not so bad, I convince myself, sizing up the bouquet of sweet marshmallowy white blooms sitting well within reach on my office credenza. Roses, after all, *are* edible flowers. And I'm almost certain Martha Stewart once topped a salad with rose petals instead of croutons. Or were they pansies? Oh, who the hell can remember?

It was long before she was incarcerated. Can't be too picky at a time like this.

Dani will parade in here any minute raving about her restaurant du jour with a morsel-by-morsel account of lunch (neglecting to mention, of course, the two glasses of red wine she routinely orders despite company policy) as my hunger pangs play out Beethoven's Fifth.

Determined not to inadvertently orchestrate a concerto in my empty belly, I plan an impromptu lunch. For my appetizer, I decide on a single snowy white petal, shucked and served on the half leaf. I'll follow that up with an organic blossom hand salad, nice and light without dressing. The Naked Chef couldn't do better under the circumstances.

I close my eyes and inhale the bouquet like an overindulged blueblood named Frederick sizing up a fine wine. *Mmm.* Pomegranate meets jellybeans—how divine. I wonder if Jamie Oliver has ever done a *Naked* floral cuisine show as I take a bite of my fluffy meal. Er, maybe not. It's horribly bitter and has an unpleasant gritty texture. Yuck.

I should have known better. I hate Fredericks. Swishing, sniffing, and swigging their wines like they actually know what they're doing when everybody knows it's not about the wine. It's about the pretense. Isn't everything these days, I think, forcing down the less-than-savoury bite.

"Knock knock," chirps Ms. Well-Fed Publicist at my door as I innocently rearrange the roses in the vase and force down the last of my lunch. "Erica, have you tried the grilled fruit and greens at the Blue Ruby?" she asks snidely, knowing full well I rarely leave my desk at lunch.

I smile back, teeth clenched, as she takes a seat by my desk and continues on. "The fruit is so juicy you don't need dressing, though I did order it on the side, just in case. At first I thought the chef just had a knack for picking good melons. But did you know he actually marinates the fruit in honey and sesame oil for a good two hours before? And he removes any trace of seeds. Uh, speaking of which, you have an apple seed in your teeth."

Chalking up my obviously tipsy publicist's remarks to two too many glasses of shiraz, I check my reflection in my polished chrome desk lamp and do a double take when I spot the decapitated ant lodged between my two front teeth. Clearly, Dani needs glasses, though I'm not about to suggest it. No, that would be rude, I think, as I quickly grab a tissue to remove the poor little bugger and envision a giant hot fudge sundae to stop myself from gagging.

"They also make a great rare seared yellow fin tuna," she steamrolls on, clueless to the fact I might vomit any minute.

If only I could. Truth is, it's been seven hours since I finished my buttered bagel at breakfast—the only real food I've eaten today. So besides those petals, half an insect, and a couple of breath mints, I have nothing to heave except air.

Dani moves on to desserts as I wipe my sweaty brow. "I really wanted the molten chocolate lava cake. You know, the one where the chocolate oozes out? But I couldn't justify the hundreds of extra calories, not to mention the twenty-minute wait time...."

Breathe, I tell myself. *Relax. Focus.* I put on my Anthony Robbins hat and give myself a pep talk: *You are Erica Swift, the quintessential modern woman. You're only thirty-five and already the marketing director of Rockit Wireless. You came up with the idea of dressing cell phone towers like rockets to launch Rockit Talk 'n Text smartphones (despite opposition from the Chief Technical Officer) and made the cover of* Modern Marketer *magazine. You manage a multi-million-dollar budget and a team of nine. You can certainly stomach a little bug, right?*

Inaudibly, I scream "yes", praying ants aren't like those parasites people get from eating bad sushi. I'm kind of phobic about that.

"...so if you're in the mood for something sweet but not too heavy," Dani finishes, "you've got to try the mango crème brûlée."

"Sounds good," I respond, not missing a beat. "So, how are our media impressions for January? Our numbers should be up, especially with that Associated Press feature." *Rrraawwwwl*, my stomach rumbles. "It ran in every major market."

Rraawwlawaaraaw. Beethoven's Fifth, my ass. I've got friggin' Hurricane Katrina in my belly. There's no way Dani could not have heard or felt the natural disaster waging its war inside me. She doesn't miss a thing (except ants in my teeth it turns out…).

Oh my lord. Maybe she saw the bug and was just politely thinking on her feet like all great publicists. Jeez, this is awkward. I don't know whether to hide under my desk in shame or give her a raise. That apple seed line was brilliant.

Then again, I shouldn't expect anything less. Danielle Carou (Dani to her close friends and me) always says and does the right thing. You know the type: all hair, teeth, and boobs, perfectly packaged in Prada, Burberry, and Tory Burch and doing that double-cheek kiss thing like Baroness Schraeder in *The Sound of Music*.

My ancestors must have been peasants because, in my humble opinion, unless you're an aristocrat that sort of public display of affection is as phony as a paint-by-number *Mona Lisa*. That might explain why Dani claims that her maternal grandfather, Louis ("pronounced Lou-ee like Louis Vuitton and not Lou-iss like the St. Louis Cardinals," or so she says) was a duke who owned a winery in Bordeaux many moons ago.

A little far-fetched, although she does have an almost genetic attachment to red wine. Perhaps I'm a bit naive but I'm going to give Dani and her dubious pedigree the benefit of the doubt anyway.

Whatever the truth, one thing is for sure: Dani is a female Frederick. If she wasn't so good at generating positive publicity for Rockit and keeping me up to date on gourmet cuisine and company gossip, I'd have to hate her.

"Want some chips?" Dani offers. Suddenly I want to hug her.

"Don't tell anyone but I couldn't resist them at lunch." *Real food, thank you, thank you, oh great and wondrous chip god.*

From her black leather tote she withdraws a makeshift picnic sack made from a knotted blue linen napkin. "They're made of taro root, much better than common corn tortillas," Dani whispers as if the restaurant Gestapo has wiretapped my office.

Frankly, at this point I wouldn't care if the chips were made of sweet gherkins, which by the way—along with sweetbreads, venison, and rabbit—are on my Foods to Avoid list. I just want to stuff my face and feed Katrina before my intestines are thrown into a tailspin.

Counting what adds up to twenty-six salty brown Doritos, I guesstimate I could fit four in my mouth at a time without looking like too much of a pig. That makes six helpings of four chips each for me, and two leftover singles for Dani in case she needs a little mid-afternoon snack.

Before I can reach for the chips, she hands me her latest public relations status report, forcing me to suspend my hunger and scan through the eight pages nicely bound in a red Rockit folder. "Not only did that smartphone etiquette wire story run in the majors, smaller dailies picked it up, too. And almost everyone wrapped their story around a photo of a Rockit. Not bad, *n'est-ce pas?*" Dani says, scooping a large handful of chips.

Wait a—didn't she just come from lunch? What happened to the grilled fruit salad and bloody mango custard?

"Magazines, radio, TV. *Tout le monde.* It generated over 300 clips in total and that doesn't even include pickup online." She beams and bites into a chip.

That was downright rude. She heard my stomach roar. The building wobbled, for crying out loud. Why else would she have pulled out the chips? *They're for me. For ME!*

"If you turn to Appendix A, you'll see our year-on-year coverage is up 15 percent from last January."

"Nice job, Dani." *Now move away from my chips or I will call the chef at the Blue Ruby and snitch.* "Now we've just got to develop an equally compelling story for the new product launch in June and we're laughing." I smile and nonchalantly drag the napkin with the remaining chips directly in front of me to avoid any ambiguity as to ownership. "That is, if we're still on schedule."

I rethink my portion strategy and decide that eating fourteen chips individually will keep me chewing longer and will, as a result, seem more filling. I gobble down my first chip, then another and another, etcetera, etcetera, licking the excess salt off my fingers. They must use sea salt. These are excellent. Dani was right.

I catch her stare and remove my fist from my mouth. "Uh, I'll check with Teddy."

I inhale the last of my chips, pick up the phone using my dry hand, and speed dial the extension of Teddy Francesco, Rockit product manager extraordinaire and more times than not, my saviour. *Voice mail. Screw that.* I hang up and send him an instant message from my computer. He'll get it no matter where he is.

```
launch still on 4 june?
             yep
  get some face time?
             yep
       4 today?
             yep
```

I sense a pattern. He must be in the thick of a meeting, texting me while reviewing the production schedule with our offsite engineering team again. Teddy's not one to waste words, especially when he's thumb typing on his Rockit. And I'm sure that of the dozen messages he's received in the last two minutes, mine are the only ones he's answered. After all, we go way back.

I interviewed him four years ago when I managed the direct and interactive marketing department at Go-Go Mobile and needed a tech-savvy assistant because, although I could sell stilettos to a nun, I also thought that bandwidth referred to wedding rings and not cell phone data plans. Not exactly something to brag about when you work in the wireless biz.

I lucked out with Teddy. His résumé said geek all over it. Valedictorian at one of the country's best technical colleges, he ran the computer lab on campus to pay his way through school and was a card-carrying Trekkie. Could he be more perfect for the job? As it turns out, yes.

At the start of his interview, I tried to print a computer aptitude test from HR but nothing happened. I clicked on Print again. Still nothing. I decided to waste time while I figured out what was wrong and get to know Teddy at the same time, so I made small talk about *Star Trek*.

Teddy declared Spock to be the king of characters because not only did his logic always prevail, but he arched his left eyebrow at the end of nearly every episode. How could I argue? In way over my head, I nodded and tried to hold my own as a transient Trekkie. I mentioned that I admired the Starfleet commander for his fearlessness and steadfast search for justice. I couldn't possibly tell this serious propeller-head the truth: that my love for young, dreamy Captain Kirk was really only based on how hot he looked in his skintight polyester suit.

Anyhow, I must have clicked Print a dozen times to no avail. I had no clue what was wrong with my printer. I had also exhausted my limited knowledge of *Star Trek* trivia. Seeing no solution but to run to HR for a hard-copy quiz, I was about to excuse myself, but Teddy wouldn't let go of our obviously deeply stimulating conversation.

"I think it was one of the most creative shows ever written. Did you see the one where Scottie had to replace the dilithium crystal to get the warp drives to work?"

Dee-the-hell-what? Oh lord. Why me?

"It wouldn't have had nearly the same effect if, say, Scottie had said 'The *Enterprise* needs more go-go juice' or 'The printer needs more toner.'"

Why that little… My eyes met his, expecting an arrogant know-it-all stare. But all I saw from behind those bronze wire-rimmed glasses was a twenty-six-year-old propeller-head talking in code. Teddy left a couple minutes later without taking the quiz. He didn't need to. I hired him on the spot and was never out of toner again.

We clicked right away. The more I got to know Teddy the more he reminded me of a big kid, namely my little brother, Jack. They were roughly the same age and had the same innate kindness. Physically, they could not have looked more different. Jack has fair skin and green eyes like me. Not Teddy. Except for his Old Navy wardrobe, he's Italian through and through, with olive skin and hazelnut eyes, usually hidden by his glasses and overgrown, curly, dark brown hair. Like I said, he's a big kid.

In no time, we established a relationship that complemented each of our strengths. I gave him advice on clothing and dating and he penned the technical aspects in my marketing briefs— telling me as much as I needed to know without putting me to sleep. It was a genius plan and no one was the wiser.

Naturally, a year later, when Brett Lawrence, the thirty-year-old dot-com hotshot who bought Rockit Wireless, began wooing me to run his marketing division, I made sure Teddy received an offer he couldn't refuse. Now he's my numero uno, most trusted business confidante and friend. Plus, every Monday, he's my resident lasagna pusher (his mom has the best recipe this side of Sicily). If only today was Monday. I wouldn't have tooth-butchered one of Mother Nature's innocent creatures.

"Assuming no sudden production delays," I tell Dani, confident that my stomach tremors have subsided, "we've got about five months to coordinate the June launch. After my meeting with Teddy, I'll have what I need to finalize my marketing brief." (*Translation: All the tech stuff spelled out in plain English.*) "I'll email it to you tomorrow so we can regroup on Monday. In the morning. First thing. So our brains are fresh," I say, telling a little white lie. Under no uncertain terms will I subject myself to another one of Dani's post-lunch restaurant reviews—even if I've just returned from an all-you-can-eat buffet and she has the judges from Zagat in tow.

"I'd like to start brainstorming today if possible, Erica. Without getting too technical, what can you can tell me about the new generation of smartphones?

Like everyone else, Dani assumes I'm a she-geek so I oblige her request. "In a nutshell, we're giving it more memory and more bandwidth... Oh wait, too geeky, I mean it will be able to work on the next generation data networks and will have more room to store files, photos, and video," I explain in a matter-of-fact tone as Dani types onto her Rockit.

"No, I mean, are we still targeting thirty-plus businessmen and women wearing Hugo Boss and Armani?"

As little as I know about tech, Dani knows less. Yet she never seems to be fazed or intimidated by it. In fact, whenever we announce a new product, I'm amazed by the intensity of Dani's interest. It's not as if we work at Burberry and are announcing a new plaid.

I've always wondered why she's not working at some fashionista brand. She would be a natural at plugging the Prada phone.

Why are you here? I think, half shaking, half nodding my head at Dani. "Yes, we will definitely be targeting our existing professional customers and trying to get them to upgrade to the new phone."

"Got it," Dani says, tucking her phone into her bag. "See you Monday. Ciao for now."

"Bright and early. We'll work up a good appetite for lunch," I reply, but she's gone. Every trace of her, except for the stolen blue napkin and a few taro root chip crumbs, is gone.

A few hours later, Teddy darts in with a plate of lasagna. "It's not Monday. Is it?" Could my lack of sustenance be bringing on delusions?

"I broke into my reserves at home after you emailed me what happened," Teddy says. "I always have extra in the freezer for emergencies. Like when I go to customer dinners and they only serve Peking duck." I've never had duck but all I can think of are feathers and paddling feet. Better add it to my food avoidance list. "To be honest, this is my first bug-on-an-empty-stomach emergency."

"Very funny. Hand over the lasagna or this could get messy. I'm starving!"

Teddy's mother's lasagna is the Sistine Chapel of pasta. It's a masterpiece. A towering three-inch skyscraper al dente, reinforced with homemade chunky tomato sauce and four cheeses. The Louvre should at least serve it in its restaurant—it's that impressive. However, I haven't the strength or willpower to gawk at noodles—no matter how artistic—at a time like this. No, this afternoon I am a Hoover.

"So how's your little piece of Italy?" he asks as I scrape the last of the melted mozzarella from the plate.

"Going straight to my butt, but it's worth it. Thanks."

"So you wanted to talk earlier? About the launch I'm assuming," Teddy says. For the next hour, he updates me on Rockit's new smartphones, with specifics on everything from minor engineering changes and service plan restructuring to the availability of product evaluation units and dealer training. I brief him on scheduled meetings on dealer incentives, consumer promotions, advertising, and, of course, PR.

"How is the duchess, by the way?"

"She's our same quick-thinking, double-kissing Dani, only now she's added chip-hogging to her list of endearing qualities. She's a great publicist but she's no Beth."

Beth Gordon is my accountant and, in my opinion, Teddy's ideal woman. She's brilliant (got me a $5000 tax refund last year), super sweet and a card-carrying Trekkie (wouldn't you know she hosted a Halloween party last year wearing Spock ears!). I set them up on a blind date three months ago and aside from the fact that it turns out Beth is lactose intolerant and will never be able to enjoy Mrs. Francesco's lasagna, things seem to be as spicy as her sauce. They're going to make great godparents when I decide to activate my ovaries and have baby Riley someday (girl or boy, it doesn't matter. The name is foolproof!).

"We broke up."

Mental note: Keep eyes open for new godmother/girlfriend.

"Sorry, Teddy. I had no idea."

"Forget it. It ended last month. She's moved on to a dentist."

"Maybe he can fix her beaver teeth, the wench."

"Love your loyalty—" he smiles "—but I dumped her. No sparks."

"You seemed so happy."

"Didn't wanna hurt your feelings. You put so much into our relationship. By the way, thanks for those tickets to *Dr. Phil*. Beth learned a lot."

Right. As if it helped.

Mental note: Deduct $200 from next tax return bill.

"Cheer up," Teddy says, reading me like a book. "Drinks are on me."

"I could go for a marketing brieftini—light on the geek, heavy on the vodka."

"Done."

I glance out my third-floor window at the evening gloom as I pack my bag, wondering where the superficial glow of the winter sun went. It seems like only minutes ago that it was light out. It's a shame it's dark already. This is the first time in weeks I've skipped out of the office before 7 p.m.

As Teddy and I walk down the corridor I confess that I feel a bit guilty leaving at six even though, with the exception of the cleaning staff, we seem to be the last to leave. It's ironic. As a technology marketer, I promote the freedom and flexibility of being able to work wherever you want, yet the instant someone offers to buy me a chocolate martini and co-write my marketing brief I suffer from an acute case of office separation anxiety.

"You need to get out more. Stop and smell the ros— I mean, daisies. Maybe go out for lunch with Dani sometime," Teddy prescribes.

"I get out," I say sheepishly.

"Like today?"

"Well, as a matter of fact…" I stop myself. "You're right."

As a matter of fact, he is wrong. Dead wrong. I did get out today and had something even Dani would envy. Grilled fruit and greens is nothing compared to having sex every Wednesday for lunch. But I can't tell Teddy that. There are some things even he doesn't need to know.

If you're an expert in disaster recovery you:

(a) could replace Stacy and Clinton on *What Not to Wear*

(b) know the difference between a black box and a BlackBerry

(c) probably work in crisis communications

(d) are better than the guy who couldn't fix Carrie Bradshaw's MacBook

chapter two

Lunch Sex on Wednesdays. Sounds like the name of a book or movie. A cross between *Breakfast at Tiffany's* and *Tuesdays with Morrie* with some added nudity and scenes intended for mature audiences only. Maybe I should register it as a trademark—you know, in case I ever write my memoirs.

Despite how it may sound, I am not sleeping with my boss. I am doing the exact opposite, actually. I'm having an affair with my husband to help jazz things up a bit.

Don't get me wrong. Being married to Lowell is great. We both love sports, business, and sleeping in late. He gives me the space I need to work my way up the corporate ladder, which is perfect for a cosmopolitan woman like me, and he sees me as his equal though I don't see why that should make a difference when it comes to holding the door open for me. We once debated that particular point for a whole day. It's not about being equal, I argued. It's about chivalry and treating the woman you love with courtesy and kindness.

Debating. That's another thing Lowell and I both love doing; not philosophically like I did in college but real-life, good-for-something, practical debating. It's become part of our morning routine. When your schedules are as tight as ours, it's far easier to squeeze in a good early-morning debate over your breakfast than, say, find the time to see the Broadway touring production of *South Pacific,* which by the way, is one of the issues we are currently debating.

A couple of months ago, however, I realized that aside from debating and sleeping in on Sundays, Lowell and I hardly did anything together anymore. We shared a bed but were so exhausted by the end of the day we had nothing left to share. Our marriage was in a slump. We had turned into roommates.

That's when I came up with the whole Lunch Sex on Wednesdays concept. It seemed like a brilliant way to spice up our relationship. After all, anyone can roll in the hay after work, but how many married couples have a secret rendezvous in between meetings?

Aside from the obvious pleasurable benefits, it's practical and way cheaper than a marriage counsellor. Both our offices are relatively close to our house, so we don't even need to pay for a hotel. When I propositioned Lowell a few months ago, none of that mattered anyway. Sex is always an easy sell. I don't need any TV shrink to tell me that.

Like clockwork every Wednesday at 1:00, I dash out of the office as if I'm on my way to a media luncheon at the Four Seasons. I'm like a serious actor in that respect. I totally get into character. It's not too difficult, mind you. I've attended more ho-hum marketing presentations over the years than I care to remember.

My normal industry seminar ensemble consists of black pants and matching vest over a white Club Monaco T-shirt, a pair of shiny black patent oxford lace-ups with a slight heel and my shoulder-length sandy blond hair, neatly pulled into a classic pony. One time,

I put it up in a chignon but quickly abandoned the look because it got too dishevelled while we were doing the horizontal mambo and one of the bobby pins stabbed Lowell in the arm.

I make sure the event is officially entered in my Rockit calendar to make my alleged luncheon appear authentic. Sometimes, for effect, I even give feedback to my snow-globe-obsessed assistant, Tory, sending Hawaii (one of the two dozen or so kitschy tourist bubbles stationed on her cubicle shelves) into a blizzard as I express my concern over a daily rag's declining readership figures.

Today, I attended a fictitious free luncheon sponsored by the Direct Marketing Association. I quite enjoyed the keynote speaker, a forty-something strategist from the south. Don't remember much about him but I liked what he had to say, something or other about using social networking to expand into new markets. Unfortunately, the meal didn't live up to the same standards. I could barely cut into my beef tenderloin. Tender? Ha! That's today's official lunch story, anyway.

The secret rendezvous version went a little differently. I arrived home at 1:10. Lowell's racy new red Audi convertible wasn't in the driveway, so I decided to plan a welcome-home surprise. I unlocked the front door and threw off my coat, unbuttoned my vest and draped it over the brushed nickel door handle inside. I kicked off my shoes and watched them catapult three feet in the air before thudding into my white wall and leaving an ugly black smudge. Not exactly according to plan but no one said spontaneity and spotlessness went together.

I advanced up the cream sisal staircase runner, peeling off my socks and trousers, and made a mental note to wash the wall later. Off went my T-shirt and lacy nude bra, which I festively wrapped around the banister as if it were Christmas garland. Finally, I shimmied out of my black satin panties and left them by our partially opened bedroom door.

Inside, I put Marvin Gaye on Lowell's CD clock radio. *Ooh, baby.* Nothing like a little "Sexual Healing" to make the workday productive in a whole new way. *Baby, I think I'm capsizing. The waves are rising and rising. And when I get that feeling. I want sexual healing. Sexual healing is good for me...*

Lowell would be arriving any minute. In all my naked glory, I strutted into the bathroom for what I like to call aroma control: a splash of mouthwash and a spritz of my new perfume. Now for body language.

Like Catwoman, I crawled onto our puffy king-size bed and struck a seductive pose on the cream-and-beige-striped duvet cover. I laid on my side with one hand on my hip; the other tucked under my ear on the pillow. I gave my best Halle Berry meets Angelina Jolie pout. Lowell wouldn't know what hit him.

"Ah-ah-ahchoo!" In a matter of seconds, my centrefold stance was reduced to an awkward sprawl across the bed. Then the next track started to play. Where the hell was Lowell?

I turned my attention to "Ain't Nothing Like the Real Thing" playing on the clock radio. How could anyone get turned on by this crap? I mean, if you're celebrating your parents' silver wedding anniversary, "Ain't Nothing" is lovely. But for Lunch Sex on Wednesdays, it ain't no "Sexual Healing."

I reached over, programmed the CD player to repeat "Sexual Healing" and returned to my seductive pose. After the third song repetition, my arms were cramped and I was starting to get worried. Ever since he bought that sports car, he had been racing through the city, racking up speeding tickets like crazy. He was already thirty minutes late and he always texts me if he's going to be late.

Wait a sec, where was my Rockit? I remembered hanging up with Tory as I pulled onto our street. He probably left me a message saying he was running a bit late but couldn't wait for lunch. I must have left it in the car. Should be fine. I locked the car doors.

But what if some thug broke in and stole it? Last time that happened it took three days to replace the window. It wouldn't have been so bad if they'd given me a rental car. But I had to rely on Lowell to chauffeur me to and from work. My God—Lowell. Where was he? The way he drove, he should have been home by now.

My imagination got the best of me. I sat up cross-legged and grabbed the cordless phone off my nightstand. There's nothing wrong with seeing if any accidents have been reported. If my personal life were a corporation, the move would be considered prudent and fiscally responsible. I dialed 9-1-1. That's when I heard the front door slam shut.

I hung up and dashed down to the foyer, colliding into Lowell. Unscathed, love of my life, short, pale yet handsome Lowell. He grounds me. Makes me think things through—although the thing I was feeling most at that point was discomfort. His navy tweed blazer might as well have been steel wool the way it scratched against my bare breasts, already sore from running downstairs without a bra.

"I was worried," I said, trying to snuggle inside his jacket. I was getting cold.

"Sorry," he said, distracted. "It's that damned Harris project. He said he needed twenty minutes to review one little change to the program. I left a message on your Rockit saying I'd be a bit late. But when I got to his office, he orders turkey sandwiches and walks me through six pages of changes. Before I know it, it's 1:30 and I'm late."

"You're here now." I stroked his chestnut sideburns and noticed his skin seemed paler than usual. He'd been so stressed at work lately. And I knew how much he hated turkey. "Forget about Harris." I nibbled at his clean-shaven neck.

The phone rang.

He pulled back. "The phone."

"Don't want to talk. It's lunch. It's Wednesday." I unzipped his pants. The phone rang again.

"I've got to meet my boss at two."

"I need you more than your boss," I whispered back, easing his pants down to his knees.

"I can't be late."

"I can't wait for you to operate," I sang along with the music coming from the CD upstairs. "When I get this feeling, I need sexual healing."

"There's no time," he whimpered.

He was putty in my hands. "Shhh. I've got it all worked out," I whispered. "A quickie. Right here on the stairs. Like when we got married."

Staircase sex. I remembered it like it was yesterday. Actually, it wasn't that long ago. Two years less a month to be precise. We had a small wedding with thirty of our nearest and dearest at The Pines, Lowell's parents' country club. Everything very tastefully done in the tone-on-tone ivory private dining room overlooking the lush green golf greens below. It was beautiful, though I would have been just as happy at a tacky wedding chapel in Las Vegas.

I've never been one to get caught up in planning a wedding. As a girl, I didn't have a fantasy dress etched in my mind. I didn't imagine a cake nor did I have the time or inclination to stop and smell any roses, calla lilies, or stephanotis for the bridal bouquet. I was too busy playing baseball and road hockey with my brother and his buddies.

Even twenty-odd years later, after puberty, dating, graduating, entering the workforce, accepting Lowell's marriage proposal, and losing my virginity (not necessarily in that order), the only thing that had changed was that I played with a marketing budget instead of a glove and stick. It didn't matter where we got married as long as we got married.

I gladly left all the wedding coordination details to our mothers, who couldn't have been more delighted. They had far more fun than

I ever could. Besides, I was more interested in planning a relaxing, romantic honeymoon.

Originally, Lowell and I envisioned sand, sea, and sex (not necessarily in that order) at a secluded, all-inclusive beach resort tucked away in the Caribbean. We found the perfect place but were a bit dismayed at the fact that the only fish on their menu was red snapper. Nothing wrong with snapper—it's nice and mild—but every night? The resort was on an island, for crying out loud. Surely another species must swim by every now and then.

Then I found this unbelievable private beach villa for rent in St. Kitts. It came with a charming housekeeper/cook/gardener named Millicent to take care of our every whim during the day. Sheer heaven.

I imagined we'd wake to the smell of homemade ginger tea every morning at precisely 10 o'clock and stroll into the kitchen to find a note from Milli wishing us a good morning and informing us that she'd left for the market to buy lobster for dinner but had whipped us up some chocolate-banana pancakes for breakfast from bananas she picked earlier down the road.

Then we'd hike into town to explore and work off some of our breakfast. By the time we arrived home, we'd have just enough time to take a dip in the ocean before our late lunch on the terrace. Milli would cut up fresh papaya and mango in the shapes of miniature island flowers and use them to garnish the crab cakes and chicken coconut salad she'd prepared. Then we'd frolic on the beach afterward and catch up on a few dozen novels we had been meaning to read back home.

By five o'clock, we'd take a little nap, made all the lovelier thanks to the bedside tropical flowers that Milli cut from the garden. When we woke from our nap at eight, there would be another handwritten note from dear Milli, resting alongside our grilled lobster dinner. It was the honeymoon of my dreams.

But every dream has its price. And the price for this one—Milli and all—was $10,000 a week. For the same money, Lowell argued that we could buy top-of-the-line stainless steel appliances for the kitchen. Besides, Lowell gets sunburned even thinking about the beach. Goodbye, island. So long, villa. Thanks anyway, Millicent. In the end, we decided it didn't matter where we went, as long as we were together.

We didn't go far. We spent the entire week christening every room of our house. When we ran out of rooms (it's only a three-bedroom house), we improvised. On the staircase. In the crawl space. Even in the linen closet (the key is to first remove the shelves). We couldn't do that in a one-bedroom villa, certainly not with Millicent fluttering about. It was the right decision. Lowell was right.

Then again, Lowell is always right. He's so sensible and level-headed—like one of those financial experts CNN interviews to keep you from investing in the Enrons of the world. He actually looks more like an accountant because he always wears a navy blue suit and prefers KitchenAid to St. Kitts. But he's not in financial services at all.

Lowell is a systems engineer (whatever that means) at a software company, though for the life of me, I can't tell you much more than that. Not because it's top secret or because he hasn't explained it to me but because it's really not that interesting. Really, it's not. He's always talking about his job at dinner parties and barbecues but somehow the hostess always needs my help in the kitchen. Really.

When it comes to Lowell's professional life, all I need to know is that it's technical, which is a big plus for me because when I take my work home Teddy's not around to help. Aside from being the love of my life, I've come to regard Lowell as my personal IT manager. Just last week he installed new antivirus software on my computer, did something with a modem, and well, you know, stuff like that.

Some girls get diamonds and rubies, I get all the bits and bytes I could ever want. I'm extremely lucky in that respect, I thought, glancing at my blingless fingers grasping the white painted spindles on the staircase.

"Hang on, this step is killing my hip," I panted. "Move up to the left."

We synchronized our way up the stairs like Siamese twins fused at the waist, wriggling ever so delicately until we found the right position. *Ahh, much better.* My hip no longer felt like it was being crammed in a vice and my head conveniently found itself on a crumpled black pillow, formerly known as my trousers.

I grabbed a higher pair of spindles and braced myself. Lowell steadied himself over me and away we went, carpet burn and all. *Helps to relieve the mind, and it's good for us. Sexual healing, baby, is good for me....*

The rhythm was intense. No offense, Marvin, but we were making our own music. The phone had finally stopped ringing and Lowell was hitting notes most of Motown wouldn't dare make—not in public anyway. I wasn't doing too badly myself. I've never been much of a screamer but Lunch Sex on Wednesdays had liberated my libido. I couldn't help but scream.

Then, all of a sudden, an axe came splitting through the front door. I'm not being poetic. Our front door was literally under attack. No longer in the throes of passion, my screams took on a totally different tone. "Hellllllllp!"

A squad of burly charred khaki uniforms barrelled toward us. What the hell was going on? They grabbed Lowell by his jacket collar, his boxers still dangling by his ankles, and forced him against the wall with the smudge like he was a criminal. Why were they after Lowell? I scrunched my body into a ball, using my knees and trousers to hide as much skin as possible. Everything was happening so fast.

"It's all right, ma'am," said Firefighter #1, looking off to the side and handing me his forty-pound hero jacket. "He won't hurt you anymore."

"Huh? He's not hurting me!" I said.

"But…didn't you call 9-1-1?"

Holy backdraft. How awkward—and I'm not referring to the Kevlar-reinforced, mother of a jacket swathing me. "But I hung up before anyone picked up. It was a false alarm. I thought my husband had been in a car accident."

"Ma'am, the call automatically registered with Dispatch. And then nobody answered the phone. Is this man your husband?"

I nodded, realizing the gravity of the situation.

"Well, then. Seeing as how you both appear to be, uh, safe, our job is done. I'll just need my jacket back."

Firefighters #2 and #3 released Lowell, freeing him to pull up, zip up, and offer me his scratchy tweed jacket so I could return the firefighter's—except he didn't. He just excused himself and ran upstairs, jacket and all. Not exactly chivalrous behaviour, but given the circumstances, I didn't think it wise to debate the matter.

Nope, this turn of events called for some internal PR upstairs. I initiated a four-step action plan: Take responsibility, apologize, kiss, and make up. Lowell took it all rather well. I acknowledged it was my fault and that I was sorry for putting him in a compromising position. I planted a single soft kiss on his lips and sealed the deal with a long hug. Typically, the plan would have involved make-up sex, but that would have been overkill.

I felt so exposed on my drive back to work, thinking about all the gossip that could happen when you're caught with your pants down. The public can be downright cruel when it comes to these sorts of things. I mean, accidentally calling firefighters into your home while you're in the missionary position is nothing like making a celebrity sex tape, but I could see how people might get the wrong idea.

I could picture it already. Nosy neighbours and gossip mongers making clever, backhanded compliments—saying that our marriage is so hot we needed a fire department to put it out. Teasing that we give a whole new meaning to the term "Third Watch." Not that I thought things would come to that. Firefighters have an unwritten hero–victim confidentiality agreement, don't they? I started feeling around the passenger side of my hybrid sedan for my missing Rockit, thinking I should call the station and chat with the chief just to be sure.

I heard a familiar *Jeopardy* ring tone coming from the floor by my seat. "I'll take 'Annoying Callers' for 500, Alex," I said aloud, reaching beneath my knees. Got it.

"Hey, Tory," I answered on hands-free, thinking I should have picked another category and should really give my regular callers their own ring tones. "Tiny Bubbles" seemed like a good pick for Tory; "Rocket Man" for Teddy. My gut said forget about "Sexual Healing" for Lowell. How about the *Love Boat* theme song? I dunno.

"Just wanted to let you know that Lowell called to say he just found out about a dinner meeting and would be home by nine. And, Erica, you're meeting with Dani in five."

"Right. Thanks, Tor. I'll be up in a minute. I'm pulling into the parking lot as we speak." *Nice touch, Lowell. Tory had no idea you were my luncheon.*

I searched my glove compartment for something edible and found half a roll of Mentos. Not the grilled eggplant on toasted focaccia I had hoped might magically appear, but they'd do. They're bound to have some nutritional merit. At the very least, I would have fresh breath for my meeting with Dani.

If you're running wireless, you are:

(a) jogging without boob support

(b) answering the front door in Velcro versus hot rollers

(c) sitting on the toilet, applying your makeup, and sending email at the same time

(d) having a good time with your battery-operated vibrator

chapter three

There's no sweeter way to end the workday than to indulge in a chocolate martini. You get all the benefits of a chocolate bar with only a tenth of the fat and ten times the buzz. Any woman who doesn't agree is either lying through her teeth, anorexic, or travelling on a one-way ticket to menopause.

Now that's a scary thought. Where was I? Oh yes, Martini Heaven. *Mmm.* I finish sipping my drink as Teddy enters some final technical points in the marketing brief he is, by and large, ghostwriting for me. I'm not sure whether he's a really quick thumb typer or I'm just a really slow sipper. What I do know is that we've been at the Sweaty Duck pub for about fifteen minutes and, with the exception of having to throw in some marketing blurbs later, my work is done.

"On its way over," Teddy says with the click of a button on his Rockit. "Tell me when you get it."

As I retrieve my phone from my bag, I bask in the glory of

being so accomplished in the art of delegation. I look around to see if anyone from work is likely to discover my little secret. Except for our server, Phyllis, and a bartender preoccupied with counting bottles, we're the only ones in the dimly lit, amber room.

I shouldn't be surprised. It's Wednesday and there's nothing remarkably remarkable about the Sweaty Duck except that it's down the street from our office and has somehow managed to stay in business as long as Phyllis, a sixty-something Peggy Lee lookalike, has been dyeing her hair platinum.

The Sweaty Duck's your basic pub and grub, heavy on the grease, light on the fibre. Even the salads are oily. No chance of bumping into Dani and the others, which is why Teddy and I always hold our covert marketing meetings here. Besides, the chicken wings are the best outside of Buffalo.

My phone starts to vibrate, triggered by the arrival of Teddy's email. Perfect. Smooth sailing ahead. "Got it. Want to share a bucket of wings? My treat."

"Don't you have to go home?" Teddy asks.

"Lowell has a dinner meeting. He'll be home by nine so we can install our wireless network."

"So *he* can install your wireless network," he clarifies.

I hate quibbling over minutiae. "Your point?"

"Just making conversation," he says. "Actually, I could go for some wings. Extra spicy?"

My day has been spicy enough, thank you very much, I think. "How about mild with extra spicy sauce on the side?" I suggest. "And I get dibs on the drumsticks."

"Only if I get your carrots," he counters, giving me a sudden image of a brace-faced, fifth-grader Teddy trading lunches.

"Deal." I smile and wave to Phyllis.

"What'll it be, kids?" she says in her husky chain-smoking voice. The years and cigarettes have not been kind to Phyllis, chiselling deep lines into her cracked porcelain face and dulling the sparkle of her hazel eyes. She could have been Peggy's twin, though there's no beauty mark on her right cheek. She didn't need it. She used to be stunning.

The pub is full of old black-and-white framed glossies of Phyllis from the late 1960s when she and husband Vic Duckman opened the place. The Sweaty Duck was hot in its heyday—he called (and poured) the shots while she crooned to a full house every night. Local legend has it that early one morning Vic left with an unidentified floozy and had a massive heart attack at the wheel, crashed into a tree, and died instantly. Phyllis never sang again.

After she takes our order, I decide to check up on Teddy. "So how are you doing with the whole Beth breakup?"

"Fine. Quit worrying."

"I'm not worried. I have someone else for you."

"Not interested."

"Her name is Macy Wagner. She lives next door to my mother and she's perfect for you. I don't know why I didn't set the two of you up in the first place. She's the anti-Beth. Hates doing her taxes and has phenomenal teeth. Did I mention she's a budding actor? Just got the lead in *Peter Pan* at the City Playhouse."

"Erica…."

"I know what you're thinking but she doesn't look like a guy so relax. She's not as flat-chested as she looks on stage. She binds her boobs before the show. It's incredible, really. You'd never guess she's a 34D."

"Still not interested."

"Did I mention her 34D chest?"

"Er, I'm too busy to date right now. Unless it concerns the launch, I'm not interested in anything or anybody."

Teddy's so stubborn sometimes. "Fine, then let's discuss your wardrobe—for the launch. Chuck the baggy cargo pants."

"You're the one who told me to buy them."

"Four years ago. You've moved up in the world. Keep your cargos for watching football. At work, you've got to walk the walk in a pair of distressed jeans. I promise you'll like them. They're not tight, just fitted." I decide to reply to Teddy's email with URLs to Rock & Republic and True Religion Jeans.

```
thx 4 making me look god in briefs
    here's the lest i can do 4 u
```

"How's your thumb typing practice coming along?" Teddy smiles, looking up from his phone.

Oh crap. My thumbs must still be churning out typos despite the fact that Rockits have predictive text built in to help thumb-skulls like me type better and quicker. Of all the thumbs I know, mine are the most inept—and that's not counting all the nimble knuckles outside our company.

The other day I read about the National Texting Champi-onships in a trade rag I grabbed from Teddy's office. One of the finalists, a thirteen-year-old girl from Pennsylvania, "trains" (as if she's in the Olympics or something) by sending 8,000 text messages a month. Seriously. Talk about thumbs working overtime—and this kid isn't even old enough to land a job anywhere other than an illegal sweatshop in India.

Eight thousand text messages! Where does that leave time for homework and hanging out with friends? I'm no child psychologist, but Houston, we may have a problem. I know we're trying to make the world a more productive place, but aren't we going a *tiny* bit overboard? This girl is going to get arthritis before she starts dating.

As a member of the human race, I'm outraged. But as head of marketing for Rockit Wireless, I'm dying to know if she uses a

Rockit. Furthermore, as a ham-fisted thumb typer, I'm considering hiring her as my tutor.

When I first joined the company, I likened my thumb-typing condition to stuttering, only instead of my mouth moving too fast for my brain, it's my thumbs that jump the gun and make errors in the process, like when I sent an email to my boss after he got strep throat.

heard u were adick

feel wetter

Thankfully we laughed about it later, though his politically correct keener of an assistant, Joyce, went out of her way to tell me people don't stutter anymore. "It's called disfluency now," she explained in her nasal academic voice.

"So you're saying I have disfluent thumbs?" I asked.

"I doubt there's anything wrong with your thumbs or any other limbs on your body. Just slow down and proofread before sending."

That worked for a while. The next day, however, I was back to my old tricks, juggling budget reviews, ad layout approvals, and employee performance reviews—all before noon. Who has time to proofread emails and text messages? Give me a break.

Mental note: Get Rockit engineers to enhance spell-check on new product.
P.S. Dig up more info on texting prodigy.

"Here you go," Phyllis announces, to my delight. "One order of Sweaty Duck wings."

Teddy and I dig in. I go for the mini drumsticks, he goes for the carrots, dip, and the—I haven't the foggiest idea what you call the hinged part of the wing. The flapper maybe? Well, whatever it is, that's what he goes for. The point is, we both get what we want. Everybody's happy.

"So you were going to tell me about thumb-typing practice?" he repeats.

"Right," I respond. "Haven't offended anyone this week."

"It's only Wednesday."

"Ye of little faith."

"Don't play the religious card. I've seen your handi—or should I say thumb-work. Emailing Lowell that you were taking me condom shopping."

"I don't know how that *m* got there. Anyhow, I thought we put that whole incident behind us. Lowell said he liked your new place. And I know he's not threatened by you or our friendship anymore."

"He thinks I'm gay. What about last month when you emailed Tory from New York asking if your dealer had delivered your LSD yet?"

"A bit awkward, but clearly an accident as Abe 'my middle name is monitors' was quick to point out when he delivered my new LCD flatscreen. Hey, did you see the Trump snow globe I got Tory? Donald's comb-over shakes, too."

"Erica, you've got a problem."

"Yep, and it's called 'I've got to get my wireless network up tonight.' Lowell's going to be home soon so I better split. Still love me?" I ask, as we settle the bill and walk out, best friends and partners in crime.

"Thumbs and all."

Pulling into my empty driveway at home, I make sure my Rockit's in my bag. History will not repeat itself today. *Oh damn.* I missed a call from my brother. He's been roaming the globe for months, incommunicado for weeks, and when he finally sends me a message, where am I? My Michael Bublé tunes must have been jacked up too high. Of course, singing at the top of my lungs in the car couldn't have helped either. Okay, Jack, where are you now? Like magic, I get a text message from him, too.

alli— chiang mai rox
got job feeding elephants
— croc

He's called me Alli since he was six and it was cool to say, "See ya later, alligator," and even cooler to reply, "In a while, crocodile." Our nicknames just sort of stuck. Almost three decades later and they still suit us just fine.

Now if only he'd come home. I miss him a lot, but not like Mom. Her whole world crumbled when Dad died four years ago, and she clung to Jack and me tighter than plastic wrap. Things got better when she joined a widows' support group and made some new friends with women who were travelling down the same path. She even formed a book club and now goes out on Saturday nights with a few of them. I'm proud of her. I can't imagine having to build a new life after thirty years of marriage, but Mom's strong. No question. Even so, I know how much she'd love Jack to come home.

u bananas
have gun!
come home soon — alli

Send. *Oops.* Proofreading might not be such a bad idea after all. Oh well, I'm sure Jack will know I meant 'have fun' and wasn't insinuating he should hunt exotic animals. He knows how much I loved *Dumbo* as a kid.

Inside, the first thing I see is the huge wall smudge from lunch. Standing four feet away, it reminds me of a contemporary art exhibition I saw last month. There was this one piece called "Kids," which was basically a gigantic, picture-less stainless steel frame with tiny pink and blue fingerprints all over it. The critics called it a brilliant post-modern interpretation of the effect child rearing has had on our current generation of would-be art collectors. *Duh.*

If they liked that, they'd love my shoe smudge. I call it "Kick," abstract drywall commentary on the effect that long work hours can have on productivity-driven married couples trying to squeeze in sex during the lunch hour. Jackson Pollack, eat your heart out.

My glance turns to my recently patched front door, another addition to the collection of modern art in our home. Plywood nailed into oak, I call this original piece "Axe." It's a testament to the strength and virtue of the unsuspecting artists/heroes who created it.

My foyer is a mess but, on the positive side, I have my health, happiness, and a home improvement store five miles away. I'll handle the smudge and new door later. Right now, I've got a wireless network to get ready for.

I set up my new laptop on the kitchen table and get it ready for Lowell. It's got a built-in wireless network card so all we need is the connection thingy Lowell was going to pick up at the electronics store today.

Just imagine. In no time, I will be able to get in my pajamas, hop into bed with my laptop, finish my marketing brief, and email it to my team from under the covers. Maybe once I'm done I'll even browse eBay for a bedside laptop organizer. It's going to change my life. I can't wait!

In actuality, I am going to have to wait. Lowell won't be home for half an hour. No matter, I'll just adjust the sequence of my wireless events and work on my brief, pre-jammies.

All I need to do is copy the technical points from Teddy's email and paste them into my document and I'm done. Two tiny problems: (1) I forgot my connection cable so I can't download the notes from my Rockit to my laptop, and (2) my laptop can't access the Internet until Lowell installs our wireless network.

Okay, so I'll wait. Twenty minutes will breeze by. I watch the seconds change on my digital sports watch. There's got to be something better to do with my time. What if I download Teddy's email on Lowell's computer upstairs? Then I could save the file on a USB flash drive (the geeks call it "the new floppy drive") and pop it in my laptop. I'd be finished my brief in ten minutes tops. Plus I'll be able to give Lowell and our network installation my full attention. Sounds like a plan.

Besides a 5" × 7" framed photo of Lowell and me on our wedding day, a couple of Miles Davis jazz posters on the wall, and an oversized L-shaped cherry wood laminate desk, there's not much to look at, which makes waiting for the computer to boot up seem even longer than normal. Finally, I connect to the net and log on to my Rockit account. Man, Lowell's system is so slow. I click but nothing's happening. *What happened to high-speed Internet? Jeez, this is painful.* I give a few more clicks but still nothing. Maybe the system is frozen. I click on a few more icons and then, thankfully, a new screen pops up.

Huh? I must have clicked on Lowell's email button. *Whoops.* I'll just close it and—that's when I see the new message.

```
From: Meryl Wynter
Subject: Did you tell her yet?
```

Tell who? Me? Meryl is the forty-seven-year-old president of Lowell's company. What could she possibly want Lowell to tell me? Omigod! He's finally got the big promotion he's been gunning for! That's it. That's why he's put up with the long hours and stressful projects. And as a special bonus for putting up with Mr. Turkey Sandwich, Meryl is sending us on an all-expenses-paid, second honeymoon! Lowell must have told her about cancelling Millicent. This just keeps getting better. I can almost taste the chocolate-banana pancakes. I could care less about my marketing brief right now. St. Kitts, here I come!

"What are you doing?" Lowell pops in the room with his brief-case in his left hand, a gadget with some wires in his right.

I throw my arms around Lowell. "You don't have to tell me, honey. I figured it out and I just want you to know how much it all means to me."

Lowell's not hugging me back. He's never been overly affectionate, but still, I would have expected a little squeeze, maybe a peck on the cheek. Something's not right. He's entranced by something on the screen. Something I've missed.

When he turns to face me, he suddenly seems different. I mean, he's always been a little nerdier than the other guys I've dated but he seems different than his normal nerd. "I'm sorry, Erica."

"What? We're not going to St. Kitts?"

"We're not going anywhere. I'm… I'm…"

"You're what?"

"I'm with Meryl now."

"Get out of here," I laugh. There's no way. Meryl is old and she's a shark. Kind of like *Jaws*. Lowell's trying to play a fast one on me. Firefighter payback.

"You're right," he says, clearing his throat. "I should leave. I'll send for my things later."

"Okay, ha ha, you're hilarious. Joke's on me."

But Lowell's not laughing.

"Come on. You and Meryl? You… You're having an affair with her?"

No response.

"Be serious."

He sighs. "I am. I'm in love with Meryl."

"I don't believe you."

"I swear on my mother's life," he says.

"Why not just swear on Meryl's life? She's old enough to be your mother!" I scream and throw our wedding photo at his head. He ducks. Sadly Miles Davis doesn't have the same quick reflexes. The corner of the frame pierces his ear and falls to the floor. So do I. "How could you, Lowell? How could you do that to us?"

"It just happened."

"That's your response? Lowell, if our marriage has problems, let's sort them out."

"We're past that point."

But," I say, shaking my head, "you love me. Don't you love me, Lowell? Why are you doing this?"

"I'm sorry."

"You're sorry? That's it?

"It's the right thing to do."

"All of a sudden you have a moral compass? Where was it pointing this afternoon on the stairs?"

My head is throbbing. I get up and massage my forehead, trying to collect my thoughts and make sense of all this. I turn back to the computer and see that Meryl's email is date-stamped today, 11:34 a.m. Oh my God. He was going to tell me at lunch, but instead he… That's so wrong.

Lowell's eyes bob around the room randomly, stopping at his computer. At his chair. Everywhere except at me.

"You were supposed to end things at lunch, weren't you?"

He sends a quick nod to poor Miles Davis and starts to say something, but I can't make anything out. He sounds like a human garburator, his words reduced to disjointed goobly-gook. I can't believe this is happening. I don't know what to do. I have no crisis communications plan in place for this. I never expected to be the crisis.

My brain, which must be communicating with my nostrils, lungs, and heart because I am still breathing and haven't had a coronary yet, subconsciously instructs my arms and legs to move. Without thinking or saying a word to my two-timing, boss-loving, letch of a husband, I run down the stairs, grab my laptop and bag, and run out my good-for-nothing, ugly, plywood-patched front door.

If you need your handheld:

(a) you've been dealt a royal flush at Caesar's Palace but you have to pee

(b) you're giving birth but your partner is #!@&! stuck in traffic

(c) you electronically schedule your day to drive carpool, "bring home the bacon and fry it up in a pan," and still manage your family's social calendar without missing a beat (or appointment!)

(d) you are trying to whip up meringues but your prosaic whisk won't cut it

chapter four

TEDDDD LOWWO HAVIN AFAIR COME 2 SWEATY DICK 4
DRUNK... ERIA

I've got the equivalent of a chocolate martini catamaran sailing through my bloodstream. I know, at a time like this I should be drinking the hard stuff. Whiskey... Turpentine... Trouble is, I can't stand the former and the latter is out of the question since I've never been the martyr type. What's wrong with a chocolate martini or five, anyhow? Truth is, the way my luck is playing out, I'm bound to get PMS any minute. So really, I'm killing two birds with one delectably intoxicating stone.

He is leaving me for his boss. I can't believe it. I mean, she's almost fifty. Almost half a century, for Christ's sake. Sure, she may be attractive in a matronly sort of way but she's no Demi Moore—or maybe she is.

Maybe Lowell is her Ashton Kutcher. I've read about women like Meryl. Older female cradle-robbers; "cougars" they call them. There's Courteney Cox, Susan Sarandon, and God knows how many thousands of beautiful forty-plus women using their experience, power, and money to lure younger men into their dens. It's happening everywhere in Hollywood. It's practically an epidemic. But how could it happen to me?

I've got a good head on my shoulders. I'm not the president of my company, but I'm doing okay. I've been told I'm attractive. Not drop-dead gorgeous but definitely girl-next-door material. I've given Lowell the best two years of my life. I once ate sushi for him against my better judgment. I've been giving him Lunch Sex on Wednesdays (which he willingly accepted, I might add) for months. I even exposed my sorry self to some of the city's finest firefighters today. And for what?

What happened to our plan? It was perfect. We were going to get pregnant in the next year or two. My ovaries were ready to get cracking. I was supposed to be a mother to Riley. We were going to live happily ever after.

I was going to redecorate Lowell's home office and work for Rockit from home. I would tote Riley and my laptop to the backyard and stay connected via our wireless network. Now, even that's gone. How could he do this to me? What the hell am I going to do now?

"I'll have another," I call out, raising my glass for effect, not that anyone at the Sweaty Duck notices. Phyllis has disappeared into the kitchen and I'm invisible to the handful of people here now—except, that is, for Cam Keon, the sportscaster who has just started flirting with me from within the jumbo screen TV.

I love how even though he's talking hockey, he doesn't take his dreamy baby blues off me. He's got lovely irises, I think, as I count the pixels surrounding his pupils. One, two, nine, twelve—God that kills. Maybe I should just sit back and enjoy the scenery.

"With less than five minutes to go, the Toronto Maple Leafs and LA Kings are tied at two," Cam says with a secret lover's wink as he cuts to a commercial. I'm barely separated and I've already bounced back with someone better looking, who adores me and has a job that actually makes for enjoyable dinner-party discussion.

See, Lowell, I am desirable. Sexy. Smart. Um, intelligent. Quick-witted. And sexy, too. Yep, I've got the whole package. I was the best thing to happen to you. Who else would give you Lunch Sex on Wednesdays, huh? Meryl?

Oh. My. God. Meryl. Maybe she's Mr. Turkey Sandwich. It's all starting to make sense. Lowell running late at lunch…. Pulling back from sex… A last-minute dinner meeting... Debating every-thing—even which light bulbs to buy. The writing was on the wall. Question is, where was I?

"We've seen a much younger Leafs team than we've seen in years," dreamy Cam says. "They're skating hard and passing well but they're going to need more than that to outplay these veteran Kings." As I sink lower into my cozy, chenille club chair, I decide to root for Toronto and order another drink.

"Are you okay, Erica?"

I gaze at the TV in awe. Kismet. He even knows my name.

"I am now, Cam."

"Who?" Teddy slides into the chair beside me, lightly nudging my shoulder. "Got your text."

"I'm sorry." I try to sit up and compose myself. "Didn't know what to do."

"Hey." He turns to me. "This is me. I'm always here for you. What can I do?"

"Beat him to a pulp. Or find a butcher looking for a spineless pig," I say, waiting for a reaction. Nothing. Just silence and his trademark boyish smile. I should have known. Teddy's too nice. Or maybe he's just too tired. It's almost midnight and I'm too drunk to tell the difference. I am certain, however, that if he's not going to hop on my Lowell-bashing bandwagon, the least he can do is fuel my fire with another drink.

As Teddy flags down Phyllis, I suddenly feel a kinship with her that didn't exist earlier. Then again, I was a different woman earlier. Less than five hours ago, I felt sorry for Phyllis. But now I feel her pain as only another woman scorned could. Even as she serves me with a smile, I can tell it's a façade.

I give her a slow, knowing nod as a sign of unity and sisterhood. "I'm here for you, Phyl," I whisper into her ear. "We're two peas in a pod." I lightly rap my chest twice and point to her in solidarity.

She looks a bit dumbfounded by my appreciation of her situation but rather than make her feel more self-conscious, I turn my attention to the latest notch in my martini belt. Loaded with chocolate shavings on top, I decide to down it in one shot.

"How was it?" Teddy asks as Phyllis walks away.

"Best one yet."

"Well, ya know what they say about drinking with friends."

"I mean, it's got more chocolate than all of my other drinks combined."

"Oh. How many have you had?" he asks, assuming I've kept track.

"Why is it that no matter how much chocolate they put in my glass, half always sticks to the glass?" I reply, changing the subject. "Murphy's Law? Nope. Gravity? Maybe. Punishment? Bingo! Whaddaya think: finger or tongue?"

"S-sorry?" Teddy stammers.

"Fingering is easier but it's so uncouth," I continue. "Tongue, on the other hand, takes longer and requires skill. On the upside, it could be considered foreplay." *Hmmm*, I think, my eyes fixated on my hunk of a TV sportscaster. "No brainer." I proceed to fish out every last sliver of chocolate with my tongue. "I think Cam wants me," I whisper.

"How many martinis?" he presses like a police officer. You know, if he didn't have such a good head for IT, he'd make a great officer of the law. He always goes by the book and he'd automatically get a new, blue wardrobe.

Mental note: Get Teddy a cop costume for the Halloween party. Correction, make that a firefighter costume. I could borrow gear from the local station. Surely they'll remember me. And they'll come to my rescue once I tell them what Lowell did. What Lowell did... I still can't believe what Lowell did...

"Hey." Teddy interrupts my trance with a snap. "How. Many. Drinks?"

"Doesn't matter," I snap back. "What's done is done. I'm done with buying appliances instead of honeymoons. Done with sushi. Done with Lowell Green and done counting drinks, okay? I'm done!"

My rage passes as quickly as it came. I didn't mean to lash out at Teddy. How could I? Aside from Jack, he's the only guy I still trust. My eyes start to well up. I wish my dad were here. He'd know what to do. He wouldn't even need words to put me in a better place.

I can almost feel his great big arms comforting me, rocking back and forth and stroking my hair when I lost my first little league baseball championship game, striking out at the plate with the winning run at third base. Dad was the one who met with my junior-high principal after I was suspended in eighth grade for telling my home economics teacher she looked like Albert Einstein (she insulted me first, saying the apron I made was the worst in the class and, to be fair, Mrs. Gaston's salt-and-pepper frizzy hair was in dire need of a comb-out). When I didn't get into Princeton, it was Dad who wiped the tide of tears that kept rolling down my cheeks and soaking my shirt.

Truth is, I miss him more than I thought I would. And not just in bad times. At my wedding, he wasn't there to walk me down the aisle. He couldn't take his rightful place on the dance floor after Lowell's and my first dance. As a little girl, I may not have dreamed of my wedding gown but I couldn't have dreamed of Dad not being there. That was supposed to be a given. But nothing's absolute anymore other than that his absence in my life makes happy times less happy and sad times almost unbearable. I try to convince myself he's my guardian angel, looking down on me and guiding me from above. Most of the time, I buy that because it helps me get by. But right now, I just wish I could feel his strong arms around me one last time, making everything better.

I turn to Teddy, remembering Dad saying he liked him, after Teddy brought me to the hospital to visit. Teddy was just supposed to drop me off but the two of them got into a long discussion about the pilot episode of *Star Trek* (Dad wasn't a Trekkie, he was just a TV junkie). It was good to see Dad smile; the chemo took so much out of him. Even so, I could feel my sinuses tingling, tickling my tear ducts. But I couldn't cry. I needed to stay strong.

As I held him, emaciated to a fraction of his once hefty self, and kissed his forehead, I bit my two front teeth into my tongue, hard—not enough to cause bleeding, just enough to distract my tears. I aged a generation in that visit, knowing the tables had turned. Dad would never hold me again.

Now, almost half a decade later, losing Lowell pales in comparison, but still, I feel alone and self-conscious. I'm starting to doubt my sense of self. Maybe my independent yet pro-chivalrous ways pushed Lowell into Meryl's den. Maybe I am incapable of being loved. Maybe I'm destined to end up like a tragic character in a Tennessee Williams play. I hope Teddy doesn't think any less of me. I couldn't bear that, too.

Then something magical happens. He looks at me with those sweet Italian eyes and calls my soul sister Phyl for another round. Three more lovely chocolate martinis later and I find myself in uncharted territory. Drinking five ounces of vodka in one night is a big deal for me normally. But twelve ounces in two hours? Let's just say it's Monty Hall huge.

Hell, with all the alcohol circulating in my system, I'd either fly or float away if not for my constant trips to the washroom. I've never been known for my great bladder control. Once during college, my best friend, Sloane, and I took a four-hour flight to Aruba. She drank at least five glasses of water plus two bowls of consommé soup during lunch without a single dash to the stainless steel cell of a cubicle they call the restroom. Not only did she not use the airplane restroom even once, but she showed absolutely no struggle holding it in. No shifting side to side. No pee-pee dance. Nothing. And if that's not impressive enough, when one of the flight attendants fell ill somewhere over Jamaica, Sloane filled in serving drinks and had absolutely no trouble pouring liquid.

I, on the other hand, who peed twice before we boarded, drank only half a glass of water and gave Sloane my soup. I couldn't even look down at the ocean for fear of bringing on a gusher. Plus, I shimmied down the aisle so often I was on a first-name basis with several passengers on the flight.

My point is this: In this great big world, some of us are born with the bladder of a ten-hump camel and some of us have one the size of a goldfish. It's just unfortunate I don't live in a bowl of water.

On my way back from my umpteenth trip to the ladies' room at the Sweaty Duck, I somehow lose my bearings. I stop in front of a table of beer-bellies wearing matching orange bowling shirts and hairlines, all of which seem to be receding as fast as the Arctic ice cap.

"There's only one minute left in the game!" one of the follicle-challenged triplets screams. "Get your fat ass out of the way!"

Jerk. I'll show him. I haul my slightly enlarged ass—damned lasagna—up to the TV and change the channel, confident Cam will forgive me in the name of chivalry. "Oops! I'm sorry," I shout back. But I'm not. Especially when I see Gloria Gaynor with her disco-loving bosom shimmering in a billowy black chiffon pantsuit on the big screen. I love her!

She may be old enough to be a cougar but she would never pull a Meryl. She knows what it's like to be on the receiving end, dumped like a stinkin' green garbage bag.

Mental note: Google Gloria's personal life, just in case.

As I hum along, I can feel her pain.

"First I was afraid, I was petrified. Kept thinking I could never live without you by my side. But I spent so many nights thinking how you did me wrong…"

I listen and take stock of her words, leading me down the path of enlightenment.

"Go now go, walk out the door. Just turn around now, 'cause you're not welcome anymore. Weren't you the one who tried to hurt me with goodbye? Think I'd crumble? Think I'd lay down and die?"

Why didn't I see it earlier? Carrying on, holding her head up high, she will survive. It's a sign. Telling me I'm going to be okay. I'm relieved by this onset of good news, of course. I will survive. I will reinvent myself. I will become stronger and wiser. I'm not exactly sure how, but I know when I call Sloane in the morning, she'll have a brilliant plan. In the meantime, I've got reason to celebrate.

And celebrate I did, or so I think. After my survival epiphany, I don't remember a single thing.

~~~~~

I wake up with what feels like a sledgehammer pounding my skull into a thousand little pieces. I can barely open my eyes—with the morning sun blazing into the room as if on a religious mission to convert the dark floor under the small, lumpy bed on which I find myself.

Leave me alone, stupid sunshine. I close my eyes and apply pressure to my forehead to alleviate some of the pain. Ooooh, I just want to sleep. But then I hear footsteps and it occurs to me that not only do I have no clue as to whom the footsteps belong, I have absolutely no idea where I am, other than not the Sweaty Duck. It pains me to open my eyes and look around the happy, golden room, especially when I realize it's my childhood bedroom, complete with all the trimmings: my faded daisy wallpaper, frilly yellow gingham curtains, and matching quilt on my twin white canopy bed.

Oh crap. Teddy must have brought me to my mother's. What must she think of me? Her only daughter on her way to getting a divorce and becoming an alcoholic. How will I ever face her?

"Rise and shine, dearie!" chirps the same voice I heard every morning for over half my life. "I've got a fresh pot of coffee on— and I'm whipping us up some pancakes!"

Is it possible she doesn't know? Maybe he made up a story about Lowell being away on business and me losing my key. That would explain needing someplace to crash—but what about my intoxication? My mother's always led a sheltered life, but is it possible she failed to realize I was more drunk than free bottled water during a heat wave?

"Erica dear, are you okay? I've also set the table with a banana milkshake, tomato juice, and aspirin."

Damn. She knows. Guess I might as well face the music. With my hand still plastered to my forehead, I get out of bed, peeling my eyes open just enough to make out where I am going, and stumble past the poster of Kirk Cameron (pre-ordination, of course) on the back of my bedroom door into the kitchen.

"How many pancakes—two or three?" she asks, like we've rewound my life and I'm thirteen again. "I mixed in cinnamon the way you like."

Ugh. I haven't the stomach for much of anything except crawling back under the covers for a few months. "Maybe later, Mom," I whisper, reaching for the small red-and-white painkiller bottle calling my name. "Not hungry."

"Of course you aren't. Try the milkshake, anyway. It's one of the best hangover cures around. Did you know the body loses a lot of potassium when you drink?"

Who is she? Friggin' Bill Nye the Science Guy? I'm not sure her claim has any validity but she sounds very convincing and I don't have the strength to argue so I pop my pills and take a sip.

"Better, see? Don't you worry, sweetie. I'll help make everything better. I called Lowell and—"

"You what?" Both my hands hit the wooden kitchen table with a bang, causing further damage to my delicate skull.

"I hate seeing you like this, honey. I thought you could get a good counsellor, maybe try more together time."

"Together time? Mother, he's having together time with another woman! The only together time I want with that dirt bag is in court."

What was she thinking, I wonder. I mean, I know she always compared Lowell to a matchbook that brought stability to my wobbly restaurant table, and though I never really much appreciated being compared to a table, she does have a point.

Growing up, I was little Miss Spontaneous, go-with-the-flow, roll-with-the-punches, there's-nothing-I-can't-do Erica. Talk about determined. I remember the look of fear in her eyes morning after morning, telling me she was certain I would join a cult and move to a commune in the desert and she'd never see me again. She wasn't delusional. Dad said she was having nightmares, and the fact that I shaved my head probably didn't help any. What can I say? I was young. And if Sinéad O'Connor could be sexy bald, so could I. That, and I was determined to win the air band contest at school.

Seems like an eternity ago. Then, I was Erica, young and naive. Now I'm Erica, old and—let's see, I thought my husband's boss was sending us to St. Kitts when she was really sleeping with him—ah yes, still naive. What a winner.

"I know he hurt you but he doesn't love her. He loves you! You're the one he's going to retire with and move to Arizona. Did you know there's a cryonics lab in Scottsdale?"

"Mom, don't you understand? He left me!"

"Lowell said you walked out."

Coward. He's right, technically, though for the record he was about to leave before I had my mini breakdown. And emotionally he left me whenever he took up with that Botoxed bimbo. Either way, I don't want to talk about it anymore. "Mom, please. Just leave it alone. I'm a big girl; I'll figure this mess out one way or another. In the meantime, can I stay here for a bit?"

"Stay as long as you like, dear. I'd love the company. We can catch up, do our nails, you can even join my book club. I know—why don't we have a girls' night tonight? I'll order a pizza from Marcello's and we'll watch a movie. Have you seen *Chinatown*?" her voice chimes.

Dumbfounded by her ability to skip out of the room like a pony-tailed schoolgirl on her way to cheerleading practice, I realize I haven't seen her this cheery in I don't know how long. That aside, I know deep down she's all torn up about my situation.

~~~~~

"That's the most vile thing I've ever heard," Sloane consoles me later on the phone. "How could he leave for someone of her vintage?"

"Enough about her. I need your help. I don't know what to do."

"First, we're going to sue the bastard for everything he has."

"Before that. I mean, what should I do right now?"

"Take more Tylenol. Wash up and come borrow some clothes. You'll feel much better. Besides, I'm having a dinner party tonight and one of Wes's colleagues is coming alone. He's perfect: Single, rich, and the youngest lawyer to make partner."

"Slooooooane?"

"Where is my head? Oh right. He likes sports, too."

"I'm not interested in lawyers, doctors, or millionaire playboys, Sloane. I don't know where to live or what to do. Christ, I don't even know who I am anymore. I heard my mom mention something about buying matching bikinis for a mother–daughter Caribbean cruise she wants to take me on, and the scary part is it doesn't sound half bad."

"Erica, you are an independent, modern woman. You can do anything you want. I'm on my way over and we'll come up with a two-part plan."

"Two-part?"

"There's nothing wrong with planning ahead. How do you think Elizabeth Taylor managed to win two Academy Awards and five husbands before she hit thirty-six?"

You are a product of social engineering if:

(a) your best friend set you up on a blind date with a billionaire

(b) a fraudster pretending to be your help desk fooled you into telling them your password

(c) your roots date back to Nazi Germany

chapter five

I have no idea who started the rumour around the office but it seems I became an alcoholic when I found out Lowell left me for an eighty-year-old man. And while Meryl probably does have the balls of an eighty-year-old, I am far from becoming a drunk. Every single one of my drinks was watered down with a tonne of crème de cacao. (Anyone who really knows me knows I can't stand straight vodka.)

Then again, I hadn't the faintest recollection of what happened after my Gloria Gaynor epiphany at the Sweaty Duck until my mother revealed the actual turn of events to me the following morning (as if I wasn't humiliated enough) as she flipped her flapjacks.

Even though she assured me there was nothing to be embarrassed about ("These things happen to everyone," were her exact words), I hid the best I could behind my banana milkshake hangover antidote—but it was no use. It wasn't that large a glass. Plus, when she recounted the few facts Teddy told her a few hours earlier, I nearly fell off my chair.

Turns out that as much as belting out "I Will Survive" did wonders for my inebriated self-esteem, it did a number on my inhibition. Hoisting a faded Phyllis photo that I grabbed from the wall, I apparently rallied the few patrons remaining in the bar to help me restore her glory days and persuade her back on stage. When she refused, I proceeded to pay homage to her personally by delivering my own artistic interpretation of "Fever." My voice was a bit off-key but no one seemed to notice. After all, no one tried to stop me—not even Teddy before he went to the men's room. Then again, he told Mom, he never expected me to strip down to my panties.

It took me a few days before I could look him straight in the face. Thank goodness for modern technology. It's brilliant for avoiding people. When I finally returned to work a few days later, I decided I didn't have to face Teddy at all. We would simply communicate via text messaging and email.

My plan worked perfectly for a good half of my first day back until I realized that as brilliant as modern technology is, it's also a curse. You can't escape when you're connected. No matter where you are, they'll find you. I was in the sick room, working remotely from a bolstered, black vinyl daybed. And wouldn't you know it, by lunch Teddy had found me.

```
                 r  u  hidng?
             bo just busyyy
     r u in sick room 4 brkn thumb?
```

Oh crap, he really found me. Did he secretly equip my Rockit with a bloody GPS tracking device?

```
   mayb contagious> don't rant to nfect anyone


wll rsk it. ive got lazgna. btw yr thumb typng
                  stll scks.
```

Five minutes later we were sitting on the daybed, twirling our forks around stringy mozzarella and discussing the new Rockit launch as if nothing had happened. As if he never saw me strut my nearly-naked stuff on stage. As if we were still the same people we were the week before.

Dani is another story.

"Mmm, that smells divine!" she exclaimed the next day in the lunchroom as I made some tea. "I never took you for a lemon fan, Erica."

"There's a lot you don't know about me," I mumbled.

"Lemon is soothing to the soul. Helps heal emotional wounds. Good choice. I'd recommend chamomile when you finish the lemon," she continued in her best Dr. Phil-meets-Frasier Crane psychobabble.

I glanced at the stack of twenty-odd packets of lemon tea in the dispenser. I guess my deep wounds were still showing. Or maybe I've just been eternally typecast as an unfulfilled workaholic who drove her husband to switch teams—and generations—for no good reason.

Around me she pretends to care about "my situation" as she puts it—imparting tea trivia along the way. But here's the thing: if I really cared about soothing someone's soul, I'd at least offer to make them a cup. Oh well, no biggie. Can't teach a duchess new tricks.

"This bra is so you," Sloane argues, handing me the size 32B lace push-up bra she picked up for me.

"But I'm a 32C," I say, tucking in as much breast as possible.

"All the more to push up."

Whatever. I'm not really into this blind date, or the three others she's set up over the past month. Be that as it may, my best friend/marriage broker is determined to find me a new husband, a better husband, a richer husband, and she's got a slew of eligible doctors, lawyers, and business tycoons all lined up for interviews despite the fact I told her I wasn't hiring.

"There's a reason HR departments accept résumés when they're not looking," Sloane replied. "Besides, think of all the fabulous restaurants you'll be wined and dined at."

She has a point, though not in the way she thinks. Since I moved back home, my mother has been driving me absolutely insane with her theme nights. The worst: Lambada lessons. I can't believe I dirty danced with my mother. Thank goodness she forgot her camera. She may be having the time of her life, but I need to escape. I'm starting to feel like an incestuous mom-dating lesbian, destined to end up on a really bad reality show (is there any other kind?).

I'm not even close to my mid-life crisis years and my world is already going to pot. Where did I go wrong? One minute I'm the girl in high school voted most likely to cure cancer, the next I look like a loser who wants to get it on with the very woman who gave birth to her thirty-five years ago. Talk about a change of fate.

I stare at my reflection in the mirror, barely recognizing myself. My breasts are spilling out of the scant black chiffon La Perla cups trying to hold me in. All I can say is we better not be going trampolining. No, that would be tomorrow night. With my mother.

Mental note: Wash heavy-duty iron-clad sports bra before bed. Hide camera.

Now just slip on my heels, paint on Sloane's low-cut black linen cocktail dress and I'm ready. I have to admit, for a happily married woman, she's got a great dating wardrobe. My cleavage has never looked better. Then again, I've never worn La Perla or Oscar de la Renta before. I've never worn 99 percent of the labels I've worn as of late. All courtesy of Sloane Couture.

"Your body looks like a dating machine," Sloane says, admiring her handiwork.

"I guess so, but my heart's still in mourning."

"Nonsense," Sloane snaps. "Your marriage never should have happened. There's nothing to mourn. Case closed."

There's no point arguing. Sloane never liked Lowell and Lowell never liked Sloane. They both thought I could do better.

"Reynolds Ault is 200 billion times better," according to Sloane. President of Woodwynn Financial. Responsible for over $200 billion in assets. Patron of the arts. Harvard graduate. Online bridge buddy of Bill Gates and Warren Buffett. And the best part? Sloane says he's newly divorced, though I happen to think the fact that he plays cards with two of the most brilliant business minds of our time trumps his marital status any day of the week. That said, I have never met the 200-billion-dollar man, whereas Sloane and her husband Wes golf with him regularly at their country club.

"It's sad really," Sloane told me the other day. "All that charm"—translation: money—"and he plays golf on his own. Naturally, I took it upon myself to find him an appropriate partner. Just think, Erica, we could be a foursome!"

Honestly, that girl has a one-track mind. Besides ensuring that I remarry well, all she seems to think about these days is her role as a country-club trophy wife. She's capable of so much more than lounging, shopping, and creating the perfect home for Wes and her seven-year-old twins Molli and Maddi. Especially since she has two nannies and a cook. She could be raising millions for cancer research or some other charity. There's got to be something better to occupy her time.

The former Sloane Walden could do anything she set her mind to. It's like she's pre-wired for success. I knew it the minute my sixth-grade public school teacher Mrs. Hartsfield introduced her to our class for the first time. I had never seen an eleven-year-old wear a black suit to school before. Certainly not one who curtseyed.

Everyone (Mrs. Hartsfield included) thought she had just come from a funeral. We didn't find out until later that her father was a successful menswear designer. Though he travelled most of Sloane's childhood and wasn't around much, she always clung to his advice, namely to match your socks to your pants and wear black for a slimming silhouette. (The only cardinal rule I remember my dad ever sharing was, when batting, never swing at the first pitch.)

It's amazing that two people so different could end up being best friends. In college, we travelled in totally different circles. Sloane spent the majority of her time on Greek Row planning socials and charity fundraisers with her sorority sisters. Not me. Eating the occasional chicken souvlaki was about as Greek as I got, though between you and me, I once slept with a varsity second-baseman named Stavros.

Hanging out in pubs and at sporting events was more my speed in college. In fact, next to Sloane, my best friend at school was the captain of the football team, who was also Sloane's boyfriend. One of them, anyway. Among her string of college boyfriends: the son of a senator, a dot-com boy wonder, department store heir, and a campus hotdog vendor (I always wondered how he made the cut....), all doting on her like fairy god-boyfriends.

Some girls have all the luck. Then again, Sloane doesn't need luck. She is more focused and disciplined than anyone I know. When she sets her sights on something, she devises a plan and goes for it. She graduated at the top of her class and, professionally speaking, could have been anything she wanted. She opted for law, not because she sought justice or a six-figure salary. Law school and law firms, she contended, were better breeding grounds for prosperous marriages than say, med school, hospitals (who has time to date when you're saving lives twenty hours a day?), bars, or online dating services (guess I should have listened better).

Like with everything else, Sloane was bang on. Within six months of joining Schiffer, Smythe & Prusky, Sloane had accumulated almost 2000 billable hours, not to mention a three-carat diamond engagement ring, courtesy of senior partner Wesley Schiffer III. It was the best work she had ever done.

Mental note: Find Sloane new project. Maybe crusading against land mines for the Red Cross. No one seems to care anymore since Princess Di.

Personally I have nothing against country clubs, except the elitist ones. Nor do I have anything against country-club trophy wives, though to be honest there's little room for advancement (unless you're looking for a richer husband on which to advance).

The truth of the matter is that I simply have no desire to join their ranks. That's not to say I'm opposed to playing the odd round of golf—providing I can drive the cart. It's not to say that I wouldn't look gosh-darn-swell on the arm of Reynolds or any other Richie Rich. I mean, I may not be Melania Trump but I used to be confused for Renée Zellweger quite often during her *Jerry Maguire* days (once I even signed autographs for a busload of Japanese tourists, amazed at their good fortune to find Dorothy Boyd-Maguire waiting for her luggage at the airport).

I guess I've just always wanted to contribute as an equal and make my mark in the world. I'm not an extreme feminist. (I still maintain Lowell should have held the door open for me.) I'm just an equal opportunist is all. Not that I should be bragging. Look where it got me.

No sense worrying about my sorrows when I can drown them. I'm currently sipping a glass of wine that costs almost as much as one of my shoes. I can't believe I'm at the Dove Supper Club. Dani's been trying to get reservations since it opened last week. Wouldn't you know, Reynolds makes one call from his tinted, jet-black Mercedes and we've got a primo window table in the VIP Room.

It's ironic. Dani would kill to be dining on the white truffle risotto, organic greens, and pistachio-crusted rack of lamb I just ordered. I'd sooner be having wings at the Sweaty Duck. Scratch that—I just noticed Kevin Costner sitting two tables over. Make no mistake: I'm still grieving my marriage but Kevin's no fly-by-night fantasy. I've loved him for years. Those tender eyes. That soothing voice. That great *Bull Durham, Field of Dreams, For the Love of the Game*, good old-fashioned baseball-playing ass.

Reynolds starts asking me about Rockit and where I see wireless moving over the next decade. I may have been right about this date feeling like a job interview, only it appears I'm not the one doing the hiring and I may as well be wearing a three-piece suit.

I start mechanically spewing out memorized facts and figures about smartphones and amazingly he seems really interested. Almost too interested. If I didn't know any better, I'd say he was about to invest in the industry and saw me as free market research. So even if the date didn't pay off at the end of the night, he'd at least get his money's worth in business intelligence over dinner.

The thing is, I know he's got financial analysts and other hired guns more qualified than me to get him the information he needs. Plus, I can downright guarantee Bill and Warren know more than I do. As I look across the table at this seemingly kind, intelligent, older man (by his thinning greyish hairline I'm guessing he's pushing fifty), I decide to give him and his interest level the benefit of the doubt. Kevin, on the other hand, has barely even noticed me, although I've indiscreetly looked his way several times.

I look to the right one last time. *God, no.* He couldn't have left. But, alas, all that remains at the table are some nothing-special, dirty, white-and-gold dishes. Where did he go? I didn't even get a close-up view of his ass. Isn't that one of the perks of dining with the stars?

"*Bull Durham* or *The Bodyguard*?" Reynolds asks.

Ouch. Caught red-handed.

"Was I that obvious? I'm sorry," I respond awkwardly, quickly looking down to make sure my cleavage hasn't jumped out of my dress to chase after Kev. "I can get a little star struck."

"You should see me around Katie Couric." He smiles.

Not Angelina Jolie or Halle Berry but Katie Couric. Girl next door meets Walter Cronkite. There's something about this man I'm starting to like.

"I once read a poll that showed most women preferred *The Bodyguard* over *Bull Durham*. What's your vote?"

"You'd be hard pressed to find a woman who wouldn't want Kevin Costner guarding her body. Still, I like his baseball films best. Must be the sports fan in me."

"Sloane said you were a tomboy. That reminds me, how's your swing?"

Before I knew it, Reynolds had asked me out again. Golf at the country club, next week. Somehow though, by the way he looked at me as we each sipped our lemon herbal tea, I knew it had little to do with my golf handicap and even less with my wireless knowledge.

In your world, patches are:

(a) very hip and retro fashion accessories in a Sonny and Cher kind of way

(b) the best cure for butting out your nicotine habit

(c) saviours when it comes to protecting your computer against viruses

(d) where you (and Linus van Pelt) wait for the Great Pumpkin to appear

chapter
six

One minute Sloane's ecstatic about Date #2; the next, she's devastated.

"But I have to be in San Fran," she gasps when I call her from work in the morning. "Can we move it a few days ahead? That should work with Wes, too."

"Whaddaya mean?"

"He *is* part of our foursome. I'll call you back to confirm."

"Wait!" I barely beat her hang-up. "Reynolds is going out of town for a couple weeks."

"Then I'll just cancel my trip. I won't let you down, Er."

"What about your cousin's wedding?"

"Step cousin *by marriage*," she clarifies. "*You* are my sister. Besides, Kiki doesn't need my help getting to the altar."

Meow. Ouch. What exactly is my so-called sister trying to say?

"Sorry, Er. What I meant to say is I'm committed to helping you get back on track."

"That's more like it. Listen, I've got a meeting but why don't we play nine holes after work tomorrow and you can give me some pointers?"

"Only if you promise to text message me from the greens on D-Day."

It's just like high school (without the golf and text messaging of course), I think, shaking my head as I hang up my office phone and rush to the boardroom, first to arrive.

I take a seat and dare to imagine a new life, far away from Rockit. Jet-setting off to Seattle for tea at Bill and Melinda's. They tell us how they're starting to make a dent in the AIDS epidemic in Africa. Reynolds, of course, commits many millions for a new vaccine and, with my encouragement, recommends Sloane to chair society galas in New York and LA. After tea and the back and forth of intelligent banter, we play a little bridge, telling Warren via webcam how unfortunate it was he couldn't pop over from Omaha for even an hour.

"*Waah-waah, waah, waah, waah, waah.*" I may as well be Peppermint Patty. Only I'm not tuning out my grade school teacher. Standing in front of me is our head of engineering, Dr. Jade Haiku, addressing the Rockit launch team now gathered around the boardroom table.

"*Waah-waah, waah, waah, waah, waah,*" she continues, as I recall how much I used to love Charlie Brown. "*Waah-waah, waah, waah, waah, waah.*" How the *Peanut* peeps ever came up with that wonderfully infectious boob-tube dialect for their holiday TV specials, I never found out, though not for lack of trying. As kids, Jack and I spent countless hours after every new *Peanuts* TV special plugging our noses and honing our *waah-waahs* as if we were practising for a studio audition in Hollywood. And why not? If you're going to pretend, you might as well go big.

As soon as the *Peanuts* score and credits were over, we'd haul out the clunky Sony cassette tape recorder from our fake-wood-grained bookcase in the den. It was the same drill every time. Sitting on the orange shag rug in front of the TV, I'd begin the proceedings by simultaneously squeezing my nostrils and pressing a Record button the size of a black piano key. Jack and I took turns belting out our best *waah-waahs* into the giant silver lollipop-like microphone, working hard to outdo each other and getting louder with every turn.

Like clockwork, Dad would banish us from the room so he and Mom "could watch *M*A*S*H* in peace." (I didn't get it at the time but, looking back, I can see that he was quite the comedian. Suffice it to say, his dry sense of humour was wasted on us, a pair of pipsqueaks with pinched red noses and a penchant for making silly noises. Thankfully, Mom, his consummate fan, could always be found smiling nearby.)

Following Dad's orders, we "skedaddled" to the basement with recorder in tow, leaving the grown-ups to watch their favorite show. Downstairs, we could get as rowdy as we wanted with little chance of getting in trouble from the parental units, glued to the goings on of Hawkeye, Hot Lips, and Hunnicutt.

We took creative liberties one might expect from a couple of Snoopy groupies and took the *waah-waahs* where nobody dared take them before. Jack invented the caveman *waah-waah* (much raspier, less nasal) and the wrestler *waah-waah* (very abrasive and performed with a full body fall). My trademark was the granny *waah-waah*, which when played back on tape, sounded more like a dying sheep. As much as we laughed our heads off, we took the whole thing pretty seriously. Why else would we have mailed our tapes to Charles Schulz?

"*Waah-waah* Rockit *waah-waah* productivity *waah-waah* faster *waah waah waah*." I remember it like it was yesterday. Only it's a quarter of a century later and there's not a teacher in sight.

Dear, sweet Jade. Too intelligent for her own good, our company lunch meetings are the extent of her social life, Dani once told me. She practically lives at work, constantly developing new smartphone features so, ironically, our customers can work conveniently from a golf course, spa, dance club—anywhere but the office. Jade, Dani went on to say, knows all the night cleaning staff by name even though they all wear the same drab blue uniforms. The way she said it, it wasn't exactly a compliment.

"Our new Rockit 2200 smartphones will offer more multimedia functionality than previous generations of Rockits," she says with slightly more enthusiasm than a dead leaf. With a surname like Haiku, you'd think poetry would just ooze out, but no. This is brutal. Her name might as well be Jade Instruction Manual. "Plus, we're designing a version that supports multiple wireless data technologies."

No disrespect to Dr. Jade but at this rate, I'm going to drift back into animation land. I casually slide my binder a few inches closer to me on the table so it hangs over my lap just enough to hide my text message to Teddy, sitting across the table.

sos

huh?

zzzzzzz

huh?

if prod anyhinge like jades delovery, we r doa

prdct gr8 not 2 worry

2 late dying of beerdom

u o me $80

Teddy winks at me like we're playing poker and he's just cleaned up. We may as well be. I play poker as badly as the game Teddy suckered me into. It's called Thumbs Up and it's supposed to train me to "up" my typing skills and become a more careful communicator.

Abbreviated words and emoticons are fair game. But each typo costs $20, so you can see how things can add up. I'm already in the hole for $680 and we just started the other day. Any fear of becoming addicted to chocolate martinis has vanished. At this rate, I'm not going to have any money left for food or drink, though, come to think of it, we never formally negotiated currency or payment terms. I'm crossing my fingers (thumbs, too) we're only playing for Monopoly money.

I pretend to ignore him and focus my attention on Dr. Jade. It's a shame really. She's one of the nicest people working at Rockit; she has a pretty face (think Kristi Yamaguchi, add glasses and 20 pounds, then subtract the ability to do triple axels and talk easily in front of millions of people), she's financially independent, and she's brilliant. Anyone would be lucky to have her. Even me. Given my current situation, why not? Not as a lesbian (I do not swing both ways and I know absolutely nothing about the direction of Jade's pendulum) but as a friend. I could use some more friends. Besides, I bet she could install a wireless network with her eyes closed.

Mental note: Invite Jade for dinner in new apartment.

First, I have to move in. That is, once I break the news to Mom.

I've dreaded telling her I'm moving out since I signed the lease last week. She's put so much into planning our latest mother–daughter outings (badminton night, guitar lessons, and go-carting), I have no idea what moving out might do to her.

With the exception of going to her book club meetings, she rarely sees her fellow widow friends anymore. It's like she's reverted

69

back to the way she was before Dad died, and I've become his stand-in. I know she misses him. We all do. But I don't think I realized how much she misses the old her. With Dad, she had someone to take care of. Someone to watch TV with. Someone to be a couple with.

With Dad gone, Mom began drifting from their lifelong "couples" friends because, quite simply, most of them were still couples. Can't blame them for that, but Mom said she felt like a third wheel. That, or a charity case. If you ask me, they were just being nice by picking up the restaurant tabs but Mom's got her pride. She learned that from Dad. How can I argue?

The truth is I've enjoyed hanging out and getting to know each other better as grown women. In many ways, I have been given a gift. We both have. Most adult mothers and daughters don't spend this much time together until they have no choice, and by then it's no fun.

I remember in high school when Sloane's grandmother moved in with her family. She had just lost her third husband and had nowhere else to go but a retirement home. Feisty woman would hear nothing of it; she had all her senses intact and could hardly be classified as an "old folk."

Sloane and I would chat at length with her after school about everything from the weather and current events to what was going on in school. She would tell us how the world had changed since the Great Depression with our microwave ovens, VCRs, and TV converters, all of which she used proudly. The conversation would always come back to how happy she was now that she could see her only granddaughter every day. But in all those times while we ate her homemade poppyseed cookies at the kitchen table, not once did she ever mention anything about her own daughter. Certainly not about doing fun things together like going trampolining or go-carting.

Like I said, life with Mom over the past three months has been fun. The fact that she also makes most of my meals is an added bonus and a real money-saver.

I haven't ordered takeout once since becoming a single woman. Tonight, we're having chicken scaloppini, basmati rice, and steamed asparagus, followed by popcorn and an encore performance of *Something's Gotta Give*. We both adore that movie. Maybe I'll spill my news to her after the movie. She'll be feeling like Diane Keaton and in a good mood.

"What would you do if I brought home Jack Nicholson?" I ask as we munch our popcorn in our matching pink-and-taupe-striped flannel pajamas (she bought them at Sears for our mother–daughter movie nights and washed them before I could demand she return them).

"Jack? Or his character Harry?"

"Does it matter?" The way I see it, they're both old.

"It matters, Erica. Soulful or not, I could care less about meeting an overaged, overindulged bachelor like Harry Sandborn. But ever since *Easy Rider*, I've always dreamed of meeting Jack."

I don't have the heart to point out the obvious. *Easy Rider* came out in 1969. I wasn't even born. She's been pining away for a long time and if her fascination with Jack is anything like mine is with Kevin, this could be serious.

"Well, just don't hold your breath, Mom. I don't exactly travel in the same circles as Jack. But you never know, I could start dating an older man," I say, thinking it might be time to broach the subject of Reynolds with her.

"Or younger, dear. I think Diane Keaton may have had the right idea with that virile lad of a doctor," she says, just as the screen shows Harry's ass sagging from behind his hospital gown. Instinctively, we both stop eating.

"Indeed." I decide to postpone debriefing her on my dating life and secretly hope Reynolds' ass is holding up better. Not that I have any right to be so superficial or picky. Over the last few years, I myself have gone a few rounds with gravity and have noticed my breasts starting to go downhill. Literally.

We watch the rest of the movie, hanging off every word, knowing full well the outcome of each scene but, hey, it's a modern classic. We're hooked. Romantically speaking, Mom and I agree that Diane ending up with Jack makes for a happy ending but we still give her decision a major thumbs-down (that, my inept thumbs can handle).

As I get up and collect our bowls, empty save for granules of sea salt and a few unpopped kernels, Mom asks what movie we should see next week.

"Actually, I don't think movie night's going to work."

"Plans with Sloane? Another night then," she replies. "How's Thursday?"

Boy, this is tricky. "It's not Sloane. It's not the night. It's just not going to work out anymore."

"It's the pajamas, isn't it?"

"Mom, the pajamas are great. I'm just..." How do I put this? "I'm moving out."

"Who are you, Billy Joel? Erica, this is your home. Stay as long as you'd like. Bring home Bob Barker for all I care. Just don't leave. Please."

I'm starting to feel the guilt. I can see my leaving is going to hurt her, but staying isn't going to help me. "Mom, you know that going through my breakup hasn't been easy. But what you might not know is that without you, it would be a thousand times worse. You've helped me get this far. But I need to take control of my life and I need to take care of myself. We're putting the house up for sale and I've rented my own place. It's time I learned how to cook my own meals. Program my DVD player. Get a PVR, maybe even a GPS. But first, I'm going to install my own wireless network."

"I see."

"Please, don't be upset, Mom."

"I'm not. I'd just like to know how you're going to do all that on your own."

Join the club. What the hell am I getting myself into?

If you've heard about Blu-ray:

(a) you'll be relieved to hear he's taking antidepressants

(b) wait till you see Red-ray

(c) you know it's the newest version of Bluetooth wireless technology

(d) you know it's the best format for watching action flicks

chapter seven

It's no Buckingham Palace but it's all mine. For the next six months anyway. I glance around my new furnished apartment, a compact, 800-square-foot loft with wide plank floors, ten-foot windows, an exposed brick wall, and a few pieces of modern furniture in black leather and chrome. In design-speak it's called minimalist. I'm pretty sure everyone else calls it cold and sparse but it's clean, centrally located, and has everything I need. Everything except, wouldn't you know, a wireless network.

I rented the place on a short-term lease from one of Sloane's country club friends whose banker husband bought it (and another like it) as an investment. Reynolds and I were paired up with them for our golf date. I assumed it was random, but I think Kendra and Marc Canard were flies on the wall for Sloane—she didn't exactly fess up, but I eventually put two and two together.

When Sloane returned from Kiki's wedding, she knew *way* too much about my date. Silly little details I didn't include in my text messages. Not because I didn't want her to know but because they were, well, silly. Sloane couldn't possibly have known about them unless she had someone on the inside working for her.

Kendra was as inside as the yolk in an egg. I had a feeling she was watching us flirt from behind her tinted Gucci sunglasses across the fairway. I figured her note-taking had little to do with golf but I assumed she was spying on Reynolds for some of the divorcées at the club.

I can only imagine what she might have thought when I bent down in our golf cart to retrieve my fallen water bottle. My earring got caught on the bottom of Reynolds' argyle cashmere sweater. Careful not to tear his sweater or my earlobe, it took a few minutes to become unhooked. It was silly and Reynolds and I laughed about it after. But it didn't take long for Sloane to call and advise me that giving blow jobs on the golf course went against club rules.

Publicly, she was disgusted with my behaviour. However, between the two of us, she admitted she was downright thrilled. Things were moving faster than even she could have imagined. Reynolds would soon be mine, she said. Of course, she reminded me, when we go out as a foursome with her and Wes, I'll have to control myself. She wouldn't want Wes to get any ideas about her following suit. It's simply out of the question. She is, after all, already married.

When I finally convinced her that nothing inappropriate took place, she was seriously disappointed. We'd have to work harder to stay on schedule, she said. I knew Sloane was determined, but a critical path for dating? And spying on me? I never would have expected that from her. If anyone was going to spy on me, I'd expect it to be Lowell, especially since I dropped Reynolds' name (translation: ego-boosting therapy) when I called him to set the listing price of the house.

But I haven't heard boo from him other than a couple of text messages, which I personally found terse and aloof (he could have picked up the phone or thrown in a happy-face emoticon; it's not as if we're strangers, we did have some good times) but I can take it.

I'm a lot stronger now that I'm past the honeymoon stage of separation, so to speak. I've weaned myself off chocolate martinis (daily helpings of chocolate biscotti with my tea have helped) and stopped crying at the sight of babies—though all those diaper commercials were a nightmare for a while.

Mom was a great help, keeping me distracted when I wasn't at work, as did Sloane and her unofficial dating service. I've gone from shocked to drunk to hurt to angry to anxious to getting legal representation, which is where I am right now.

Mental note: Ask Sloane to recommend an attorney.

As far as I'm concerned, Lowell and his cougar can run free, climb trees, and have wild animal sex in the Appalachian Mountains. I've moved on in the kingdom—and can't wait to sell our house of lies to someone else. But if he thinks he's getting our stainless steel appliances, he's got another think coming. No way in hell is he getting our honeymoon. Of course, I didn't use quite those words when I told our real estate agent she should include them in the listing.

The good news is, the house is finally about to go on the market. We had the front door replaced, walls painted, and the whole house professionally staged by a designer who even stocked the closet with women's clothing to replace all my stuff. ("It's no one's business it's a Splitsville Sale," our agent said with her arm around me. "Besides, you'll get more money.")

"The more the merrier," I replied without even the faintest bit of sorrow. "The quicker the better." I used to love that house. I used

77

to love Lowell. Once upon a time. The end.

Now I've got this great loft all to myself. I can do whatever I want, whenever I want. I can stay out till the wee hours of the morning. I can invite gentleman callers up for a nightcap. Heck, I can even host an orgy. Of course, with Reynolds out of town and no other prospects to invite, it's unlikely. I'm just saying.

I haven't seen Reynolds since our second date over a week ago. I have received voicemail messages from Tokyo, London, and Berlin. He sent me flowers Monday morning at the office ("To start the work week off right"), but I want more. A ring? Heck, no. I don't work that fast. I'm not even looking for a commitment.

All I want is a little love—or a reasonable substitute—to get my blood flowing again. I haven't had Lunch Sex—or any sex—for months and it's starting to affect me. I've been sensing my blood sugar rising. Mind you, I have been devouring a lot of chocolate. Helps alleviate my sexual anxieties. The odd thing is, I'm no nympho. Seriously. Just ask Lowell. I can usually go for months without sex, no problem. Something else is going on. But what, I have no clue. I'd better call Sloane.

"It's a classic case of emancipation," she says.

"Pardon?"

"You've been set free from Loser Lowell. You are no longer tied to his nerdo bedposts."

That only happened once and I didn't tell anyone. How did she know? "What are you talking about?"

"I'm saying, spiritually, that dim-wit held you back. So you held back in the pelvic Olympics."

Why does everyone want to be my shrink? First Dani. Now Sloane. Who's next, my Rockit? *Hmm.*

Mental note: Talk to Dr. Jade about integrating therapist software.

"The good news is you're with Reynolds now, Er, so you can peak. In more ways than one," she chuckles. "He is so good for you. Did he send flowers?"

"White roses." I beam.

"But I don't understand." I can hear the frown in her voice. "Why would he dump you?

Dump me? But we had good chemistry, I think, baffled.

"White flowers are the kiss of death," Sloane continues.

"But I told him I love them."

"Are you crazy? White means purity—that is hardly the message you want to be sending. Tell him you meant red roses and do it quick. In the interim, there's one more thing you can do to improve your situation…"

I can't believe I'm shopping for a dildo. On one hand, it's kind of exhilarating. On the other, I feel like a gutter: low-down and dirty. Of course, I can't take any credit—or blame—for this sudden transformation. It was Sloane's idea.

Here I am, bright and early on Saturday morning in aisle three at LoveBurst, an adult toy store on the edge of town. I see their TV commercials whenever I can't sleep at night, but I never imagined I'd ever set foot inside. Why would I? a) I'm just not that kind of girl; and b) Even if I decided to become that kind of girl, LoveBurst has an online store "for the ultimate in convenience and discretion."

I went to the website last night without so much as even trying to make a purchase. With over fifty vibrators to choose from, it was worse than trying to order dinner at The Cheesecake Factory (another place that only offers guilty pleasures in large portions). I put on my baseball cap and sunglasses and went to the store incognito.

"Erica? Is that you?" I hear Dani's voice calling out from the end of the aisle. Damn. This is worse than the time I bumped into Teddy at the pharmacy while buying a case of Monistat 7 for my reoccurring yeast infections. Teddy doesn't gossip; Dani spills like a glass of milk. Maybe if I pretend like I don't hear her, she'll assume mistaken identity and move on. Without moving a muscle, I fix my eyes on a rubber-ducky vibrator, astonished that anyone would think of putting something so *Sesame Street*-ish well, you know, down there. I continue scanning the Animal Life section: rabbits and monkeys and bears, oh my!

"Erica?" Oh crap, she's coming closer. This is bad. "Funny bumping into you here!" she chirps with about as much genuineness as a Canal Street Gucci bag.

"I'm a regular," I reply sarcastically.

"Really? This is my first time. I heard they might have a good gag gift for my brother's forty-fifth surprise party. He's single, a workaholic, doesn't get out much, you know the type." What's she insinuating? "*Très* appropriate, *n'est-ce pas?*"

My eyes turn to the inflatable doll she's carrying, hers survey the dildo zoo before me, neither of us able to look each other in the eye.

"Well, gotta run," Dani says as she skips down the aisle. "Tons of errands!"

And off she flies like she's Wonder Woman and I'm Horny Girl drowning in a sea of vibrators.

Another five minutes trying to decipher product packages and I'm no further ahead. I get the obvious differences between slim and chubby and smooth and ribbed. But I'm not sure why I'd buy one with flashing lights. (If I wanted a light show, I'd go to Las Vegas.) And what's the deal with the pink beaded butterfly unit. Beaded? Really. I may be new to all this, but it seems to me there are better places to flash your baubles.

"Can I help you?" the guy from the commercial says with a smile. I assumed he was just a model on TV. I must admit, he's hotter in person—his face tanned with dimples, long blond hair, and big brown eyes I could easily get lost in. His badge says Hank, Employee of the Month. I'll bet he is.

Red in the face, I grab the vibrator closest to me—a huge green silicone cactus prickler. "I'll take this one," I tell Hank and run to the front of the store to pay.

I did it. If I wasn't walking out of a virtual orgasm factory, I'd be shouting at the top of my lungs. I am an independent woman ready to conquer the world. Feeling very "Helen Reddy: I Am Woman," I slip behind the wheel of my car and place my large green friend on the passenger seat. Precious cargo, indeed. I can't wait to get home and formally introduce myself.

In the meantime, I have some more conspicuous consuming to do. I don't care if it kills me, I'm not going home without a wireless network router. I walk into Best Buy and am relieved I only have to choose from six devices. Quickly, I scan the packages—no beads or lightshow—easy, breezy, piece of cake.

Okay, let's see: `802.11n with MIMO technology and WPA2 and SPI firewall`. Sounds vaguely familiar. I'm sure I've heard Teddy use those terms. I pick up another technologically advanced looking blue package with a nice white font. `Smart antenna technology with Wireless-G 802.11g and WPA2`.

Not sure what WPA2 is about but both routers have it so it must be good. As for 802.11n or 802.11g, I haven't decided, though *g* definitely rolls off the tongue better. Better check another package to be sure. Majority always rules.

"Can I help you?" asks the overzealous sales guy currently invading my personal space. His shiny, clean-shaven head barely reaches my armpits. And he smells like—oh my—I didn't think they made English Leather anymore.

"No thanks." I step back and smile confidently. "I work in tech."

"Sweet." He steps forward with his ear-to-ear grin and resumes his front-row position under my chin. "My name's Oliver—I'm nearby if you need anything."

A little too nearby, thank you very much. I've always been overly sensitive to strong smells and my nasal passage has started to do Kegel exercises. If I don't leave quickly, Oliver will soon feel like he is on a *Maid of the Mist* ship in Niagara Falls, only he's not wearing one of the blue rain slickers they give for protection. It could get messy.

"Thanks," I reply, dashing down the aisle to sneeze and examine the third router package, now covered in spit. I give it a wipe and examine the product specifications: `2.4GHz router with 54 Mbps high-speed throughput, 802.11g connectivity. Backwards compatible to 802.11b.` Whoa— who said anything about *b*?

I pull out my Rockit and dial *T* for help. One minute later and I've plunked an 802.11n router Teddy recommended (apparently it's faster) into my basket. En route to the checkout, I stop at the Rockit display area to tidy up the mess of product brochures strewn across the counter.

"Need a smartphone? We've got good deals on Palm Treos." Oliver reappears under my jaw.

Treos? If he's not careful, I'm going to bite off his little ear. "Covered, thanks." I hold my tongue. "I have what I came for." I swing my basket toward him, forcing him to retreat a few steps. I decide to use the basket as a human force field and keep him at bay.

"Need our Geek Squad to install that?" He tries to come closer.

"No thanks," I reiterate, jabbing him with my basket. "I work in tech."

"Oh yeah, I bet you have every gadget in the book," Oliver says in awe.

"Well, I did." I tell a little white lie to maintain my dignity. "But I left all my things with my ex and I'm starting over." No lie there.

"Blu-ray?"

"Yep," I respond without thinking. Sounds like one cool laser gun.

"Heart breaker," he sighs.

Personally, I can't see the big deal about losing a video game gun controller but some guys never grow up.

"C'mon, I'll show you what we have in Blu-ray. We'll get you all fixed up."

"Shouldn't I get a video game system first?" I ask.

"Good thinking," Oliver says. "PlayStation 3 comes with Blu-ray built in."

Huh?

He leads me over to the other side of the store to the gaming section. Things sure have progressed since Pong. I mean, I've heard about the video game revolution but I've never really looked at the actual games that closely. I watch a couple of boys with brush cuts play basketball and can't get over how realistic their players look onscreen.

"We's got it going on," one says—clearly some slang I've never heard before. "We's like sooo wicked!" adds the other.

"We's selling like gangbusters," Oliver says, obviously trying to fit in. As we walk, he motions to a white-and-grey box with W-i-i spelled out. *Right, Wii.* Cool name unless you're an elementary school teacher. Talk about screwing up the English language even more. "The game controllers are sweet. They're virtual reality. So let's say you're playing your favourite sport which is—"

"Baseball," I say, not missing a beat.

"Okay, so you're playing baseball. Instead of swinging the bat by pushing buttons, you swing the controller as if you're actually at the plate."

"I'll buy one."

"What about the PlayStation 3 with Blu-ray?"

"No biggie. I'm not into guns and violent games."

He gives me a funny look and starts saying something about game titles when he's paged over the loudspeaker. As soon as he's out of sight, I pull out my Rockit and search "blue ray" on the web.

```
Blu-ray is a type of disc that uses a
blue-violet laser to read/write high-data
storage density. Blu-ray discs store more
data than DVDs because of the shorter
wavelength of the laser blah, blah, blah.
```

Sounds fascinating. And quite different than a laser gun, I might add. When Oliver returns, I tell him I'd like a PlayStation 3 with Blu-ray so I don't blow my cover.

"What about games?" he asks.

"Surprise me," I say. "But no violence."

The games aren't the only surprise I get before I leave the store. Turns out I'm a techno-junkie. I have the stash to prove it.

New toy	Why I need it
Wireless router	To use laptop in bed or on balcony. Especially on work-from-home days.
55" LCD HDTV	Always wanted a huge TV. But Lowell always said no.
PVR	Hate commercials. Plus working late means I keep missing *Grey's Anatomy*.
PlayStation 3	Can play games vs. Enid (imaginary PS3 lesbian pal from Liverpool) if dating thing doesn't work out. Can use it to watch Blu-ray movies!
PS3 games (5)	Duh. See above.
iPod	To inspire me to start jogging. To listen to "I Will Survive" while

	jogging.
	To watch movies if/when I ever travel for work.
iPod speakers	To listen to "I Will Survive" out loud at home.
iPod alarm clock dock	To wake up to "I Will Survive".
iPod car dock	To listen to "I Will Survive" in car.
Satellite radio	To make daily commute therapeutic. To listen to Cosmo radio, E! radio, CNN radio when sick of "Survive."
GPS	Much cooler than a road map. Heard Meryl has one in her car (what's good for the goose is good for the gosling).
Digital camera	To document life as independent modern woman. To start photojournalism hobby. To take perfect self-portrait with rotating e-view finder.
Robotic vacuum	Someone has to clean floors in loft.

I'm not sure what I was trying to accomplish but I can tell you it wasn't to become Oliver's biggest sale. I went in for a $100 wireless router and, in just under an hour, I spent a whopping $8300 plus shipping (it wouldn't all fit in my car). On the up side, in just under forty-eight hours I will be the epitome of the so-called modern woman. I will eat, breathe, sleep, even clean high tech. I can hardly wait.

In the meantime, it's noon and I'm back at the loft. I'm alone, I'm exhausted, and I have absolutely no plans till Monday. As I crash on my firm leather sofa, it becomes painfully clear that it wasn't purchased for comfort. Ouch—it's not just hard as stone, it jabbed my left butt cheek and sent me flying. Wait a second. There's nothing sticking out from the couch. As my hand reaches back to rub my maximus bruisiest gluteous, I discover the source of my pain—a large, plastic tube hiding inside my jacket pocket—and suddenly I'm healed.

"Hello, sailor," I say, pulling my shiny new cactus out of the package. "Where have you been all my life?"

If you like to duplex, you:

(a)   have a thing for small, low-rise buildings

(b)   are one efficient, paper-saving tree-hugger

(c)   probably also like Pyrex

chapter
eight

New toy	*Why I am returning it*
55" LCD HDTV	Large-screen TV that came with loft isn't high-def but good enough for watching doctors get medical with each other once a week.
PVR	Can catch missed McDreamy episodes for free online. Hello, handsome!
PlayStation 3	Who am I kidding? With product launch on my ass, I don't have time to pee, let alone play games (nothing personal, Enid)
PS3 games (5)	See above.

Satellite radio	Love morning show on local station, which btw, has no monthly subscriber fee. Besides, only in car 10 mins at a time.
GPS	Must stop comparing self to Meryl. Rarely drive anywhere except to work, Sloane's, and Mom's and could do that blindfolded. Besides Rockit has it built in.
Digital camera	Rockit has integrated camera.
Robotic vacuum	Tripped and nearly killed myself walking to the bathroom last night.

I'm on hold with Best Buy waiting to speak with a manager. Tapping my fingers to a jazzed-up rendition of "Fire and Rain," which has removed all of James Taylor's soulful anguish to put me into the happy-go-lucky mood for buying consumer electronics, I look around the loft. Not the minimalist space it once was.

There's a giant wall of boxes in the hall blocking the doorway to my bedroom. Everywhere else: Styrofoam blocks and oddly shaped slabs scattered on the wood plank floor, black leather sofa, cherry dining table—even on top of the stainless steel fridge. (Must have put it there during a double chocolate fudge chip ice cream break.) I know they're all supposed to fit back in the boxes but achieving that degree of precision is totally beyond me.

If that's not enough, a few pieces of foam have disintegrated into a million tiny static-charged evil snowballs that cling to everything. And I mean everything. Trying to sweep them up has only made matters worse. Now I'm covered in them. Wearing my favourite black sweater, I look like a giant domino. Kendra would be appalled, that's for sure—though whether she'd be more offended by the state of her condo or my new yin-yang fashion statement is a toss-up. Either way, I've got to clean things up before I head back to work tomorrow.

"Laurel speaking, may I help you?"

"Hi, I have a lot of returns."

"No problem. Just bring them in with your receipt."

"I can't. They won't fit in my car. Your truck delivered them."

"Is this Erica Swift?"

"Uh-huh." I nod as if she can see me through the receiver. I feel my face go red and close my eyes.

"Oliver spoke very highly of you. You're his favourite customer."

"Oh, yes, um, well about that. I went a bit overboard. I don't need most of those things. And as it turns out, I didn't get the one thing I could really use right now."

"No worries, Erica. I'll take care of everything."

A few days later, I walk into the gadget Mecca over my lunch hour only to be greeted at the door by a somber Oliver in a yellow polo shirt.

"Welcome back to Best Buy," he mutters without the slightest trace of enthusiasm. Somebody sure took the air out of his tires.

"Hi," I say, retreating a few steps just in case he tries to pop into the crook of my neck again. But this Best Buy boy may as well be a mannequin. There's no popping, no moving, nothing. "Thanks again for all your help the other day," I continue with a smile.

"I should thank you. Everyone started to take me seriously because of you, even if it was just for a day. I was a selling machine, not the manager's numbskull kid cousin."

I flash back to me running away from Oliver. I'm just as bad as his colleagues, pegging him as the Herb Tarlek of high tech—a nice guy who's in the wrong job and tries too hard to fit in. I bet he'd make a great accountant.

Mental note: See if Beth needs an apprentice.

"Listen, Oliver. The truth is I only came in for a wireless router. But you made everything sound so fantastic. I had to have it all. You're a hell of a salesman."

"Really? Thanks," he says, brightening.

"And for the record, I didn't return *everything*," I carry on. "I also kept the iPod."

"How's the workout coming along?" he says, stepping closer and poking my bicep.

"I'm a new woman," I respond, only half lying. I mean, I am a new woman, that's 100 percent true. I'm independent, sexually satisfied (thanks to Mr. Cactus), and jogging three miles a day—but I've been putting that MP3 music mileage on my Rockit. My mom, on the other hand, hasn't stopped thanking me for the iPod gear. She's the hit of her widows' group, which started a music club to share their favourite iTune songs and YouTube videos.

If I were a betting woman (which I have not been since college when I lost my shirt—literally—during a late-night poker game with my football team buddies), I'd wager they'll be back to reviewing books after the novelty has worn off. But you never know, video games could be next. I picture Mom and her friends thumbing it out in militia war games while munching canapés. *Oh look, I found a chainsaw bayonet! Maya, be a dear and pass the mini-quiches, they look gorgeous.* I actually read something about how women are poised to become bigger gamers over the next few years, but this may be a stretch.

Telling Oliver about giving Mom my iPod will only complicate matters and could gouge his re-inflated tires, sending him into a depression I haven't witnessed in retail since I saw John Cusack in *High Fidelity*. Somehow I feel responsible for Oliver's current disposition. Until his shiny, bald head tries to re-enter the no-fly zone otherwise known as my personal space. Quickly, I step back and turn to my left. "Is Laurel around?"

I head over toward the petite curly coiffed brunette helping an older man under a big Customer Service sign. Laurel is the plainest of Janes, wearing a blue polo and khakis. Standing in line, I watch her listen to the Water Matthau look-alike (think *Grumpy Old Men*) with great interest and I can't help but listen, too. It's not that the conversation is so compelling, it's just pretty impossible not to hear, given that the guy is hollering.

Seems after forty-two years as a women's shoe salesman, Walter retired to travel the world. To celebrate, he bought a new digital camera and photo printer against the advice of his wife, a 35mm photography purist. But for the life of him, he can't get it to print a thing and he wants his money back.

"Let's see," Laurel says, removing the pint-sized printer from the box. Next she removes a wafer-thin data card from the camera and inserts it into the printer. All of a sudden, an image appears on the LCD display showing the man and his wife riding a camel. "Nice shot."

"Nicer if I could print it." He scowls.

This is the point at which I would have told the guy to stick it where the sun don't shine. Not Laurel. She ignores the old cranker and presses some buttons on the screen. It makes some noises but nothing happens.

"Told you. Broken," he says. He makes a *hurrumph* sound unique to old men with irritable prostates.

Laurel lifts the printer cover, removes the ink cartridges and turns them upside down. Not to give them a shake, as I would have thought (had I not worked in tech), but to remove the factory tape covering the ink nozzles. "Let's try again," she says as she shuts the cover and prints the photo.

What a pro. I wonder if she has worked in PR?

Mental note: Get her résumé.
Still have a hunch Dani applied to the Prada phone people.

Laurel has no clue who I am but she gives me a big smile. Dani would never do that unless she wanted something. "Hi there. Return?"

"Oh. No. I'm Erica. We spoke on the phone? I just wanted to thank you personally for your help the other day with the returns and the truck. Oh, and the turbo vacuum you shipped. Sucked the foam right out of my hair without tangling or splitting my ends. Much better than the robotic vacuum."

"Glad it all worked out." She nods with another smile.

"Thanks to *you*. Anyhow, I thought I could make your life easier." I hand her a gift bag with a Rockit smartphone. "It has a year of free voice and data."

"Thank you. But I couldn't," she says.

Did she just turn down free airtime? My jaw drops. (Good thing Oliver isn't here, I could have bruised his forehead.) "Company policy?"

"Personal."

"Does your husband work for Apple?"

"Nothing like that. It's just too generous a gesture."

"It's not so generous," I lean forward and whisper. "I work there. I get a good discount."

"Even so."

"An amazingly good discount. Huge," I say, explaining I won't leave without repaying her kindness.

"It's really not necessary, Erica."

"There must be something," I think aloud. "Coffee?"

She shakes her head.

"Tea?"

"Sorry. I had my one-cuppa-lemon quota this morning." She shrugs.

Lemon. Well, whaddaya know? Laurel and I were meant to be friends. One day she'll realize that, too. But for now, I'll just skip over to Starbucks to get her a not-too-generous gift card to make her next few months of mornings easier.

In a nearby constellation, Sloane is on cloud nine. "Erica, honey! I scheduled back-to-back facials and massages for us both—5 p.m.?"

"Sorry, can't make it. Launch stuff," I say into the phone, as if there's any point. What Sloane wants, Sloane gets.

"Of course you can. You're an executive. Delegate."

I hate it when she tells me what to do. Okay, so that's not entirely accurate. When it comes to my personal life, I often rely on her to tell me what to do. This isn't one of those times. A product launch isn't personal. It's business, my business.

"It is soooo not business," she contends. "It's quite personal. Ren's flying back today and he can't wait to see you."

Now I'm really steamed. Sloane can spin it any way she wants but she has stuck her perfect, dainty nose into my business life one time too many. Not only that but if "Ren" (when did he become Ren?) wants to see *me* so much, how come she got an email from him? I've received nothing but a few voice mails these last two weeks. I have no time for these games. I need to work on my marketing campaign and install my wireless network when I get home. I tell Sloane as much.

"Honestly, Er, you're blowing things way out of proportion. We need to get you ready for dinner at the club. Ren invited me and Wes along, too."

This just keeps getting better. My Daddy Warbucks of a boyfriend comes home and summons me to dinner through my best friend, and it's not even dinner for two. And he actually expects me to show up? He may know how to manage money but he's not too sharp when it comes to women. And Sloane? Is she serious?

"The timing is perfect. I figure you'll be betrothed within a year. Mrs. Erica Ault. You have to admit it has a nice ring to it."

"I'll never change my name. Besides, aren't you forgetting about Lowell?"

"A minor technicality—which ironically enough sums him up quite well. My lawyers are working on it. Expect a call."

"Slooooane." It's all I can say without going into a frenzy.

"Sweetie, you sound awfully tense. The massage will do you good. I'll see you at the club at five. Oh and don't worry about what to wear for dinner. I have the perfect blue macramé lace sheath dress to show off your gams and bring out your eyes. It's Valentino. Ren won't know what hit him."

Him? If Sloane's not careful, she won't know what hit her. The left side of my brain is ordering me to punch her lights out; the right side is working overtime trying to calm me down. I've never worn Valentino before.

I may not be the first woman to install a wireless network, but how many do it in Valentino? This dress is the single most stunning piece of clothing I've ever worn. And when I pry my swollen feet free from the matching Jimmy Choo three-and-a-half-inch slides, it's even as comfortable as any one of my Lululemon yoga outfits. Okay, that's a lie, but I can't change my clothes yet. Tomorrow the dress goes to JetSet Drycleaners before finding its rightful place in Sloane's treasure chest of a closet, while *poof!* I return to work wearing my trademark black pants, white T-shirt, and vest.

Happily, that's not for at least nine hours and I'm not the least bit tired. Sloane was right. After the massage, I felt like a million bucks. And after dinner with Ren, Sloane, and Wes, I felt like a billion bucks. Seems Ren's daily emails (fourteen in total; Sloane only got two!) were intercepted by Rockit's anti-spam software, which of course I verified during dinner by calling Teddy from the restroom and having him log in to the system.

"Who's Reynolds?" he asks.

"No time. Gotta go."

"Wait a sec, Erica. Who does this spamster think he is? Inviting you to Bill Gates' house? Unbelievable."

Speechless, I walk out of the restroom hardly believing it myself. I wonder if Warren will be there. I wanted to ask Ren about our pending getaway to Seattle but there just didn't seem to be a good time. He was telling us about his trip across Europe, meeting with high-net-worth customers in Paris, Milan, Monte Carlo, and then some.

No one was mentioned by name but I suspect at least one of them was a royal because he mentioned something about doing yoga in a castle. Sloane interjected about how the twins have been imitating her doing yoga, but all I could think about was how my boyfriend did yoga with the Queen and my upcoming trip to the Gateses'.

"Normally I would never condone that behaviour from Molli or Maddi. I am not raising mimics. But watching them in downward facing dog was positively enchanting," she giggled. "And it worked! They were both so relaxed afterward."

Is she for real? I'm no child shrink but aren't seven-year-olds supposed to be relaxed? I mean, they don't have the stress of a job or a cheating husband for Christ's sake. Talk about being out of touch with reality. Good God.

Then, for what seemed to be hours, Ren and Wes talked polo

while Sloane quizzed me on the life and times of Elizabeth Taylor, secretly acknowledging the power of our plan. While our Liz quiz-fest was riveting, as you can well imagine, I found myself eaves-dropping on the guys—especially when they were talking about polo ponies.

"In England, a small thoroughbred stallion called Rosewater is the foundation sire for most of their ponies," said Ren.

My ears were being pulled in two directions but it was bearable until Sloane started reciting lines from *Cat on a Hot Tin Roof*. "You can be young without money, but you can't be old without it."

I couldn't take it anymore—so while Sloane was being Mag-gie/Liz, I turned to Ren and did the unthinkable. I knew Sloane would think asking Ren to dance was bad etiquette but I didn't care. Thankfully, neither did Ren. As he held out his hand and led me to the dance floor, I could feel everyone's eyes on me, especially Sloane's, but I was determined not to look back. Instead, I did the only thing I could at a time like this. I twirled like I had never twirled before.

Lowell, more of a side-to-side swayer, had no interest in ex-ploring the virtues of ballroom dancing, as I discovered when he didn't show up at the Arthur Murray–certified dance lessons we got as an engagement gift from Aunt Ida. He, of course, always had a good reason for missing class and, in the end, pairing up with our teacher Mr. Valorzi had its benefits: he coached me far more than the other students. Then again, he pinched my ass more than he did theirs, too. I thought about lodging a formal complaint but I de-cided against it since he was in his eighties and was about as harm-less as lukewarm water. Not only that, I won the star student award.

Reynolds was as skilled a dancer as Mr. Valorzi. Unfortunately, he didn't pinch my ass—on the dance floor or off. On the drive back to the loft, I invited him up for a drink. I whispered in his ear. I placed my hand on his thigh. I even intentionally tried to get my earring stuck on him again. But he dodged all my manoeuvres, insisting his jet was waiting to take him back to London. Like I haven't heard that line before.

"Before I go, I have something to ask you," he said, gazing into my eyes, still holding the hand he removed from his thigh.

As a rule, you're not supposed to sweat in Valentino. I'm told you're not supposed to do anything but look fabulous. But I was in way over my head. Everything was happening much quicker than Sloane's most aggressive predictions.

Women on the receiving end of a marriage proposal should gaze lovingly into their special someone's eyes. Not me. All I could do is sweat—even my eyelids were getting clammy so I shut them tight. But that wasn't helpful either. All I could see was the face of a stern, bald state judge shaking his finger in disapproval and it occurred to me that there might be legal implications of becoming engaged to one man while still married to another. I mean, this isn't Utah.

"Will you go to Seattle with me next month?" Reynolds asked. I unclenched my lids and expressed my delight, squashing any fear of committing a social sin. I waited for him to swoop me up in his arms and kiss me like I was Scarlett O'Hara (before she alienates Rhett of course).

Alas, we can't all be drama queens and smooch Hollywood-style. And there's nothing more respectful or character-revealing than when a man plants a soft, gentle kiss on your hand. I felt like a royal after yoga class. Besides, it's given me one more thing to look forward to. Talk about having a lucky night.

Back up in the loft, I am as charged as one of the few remaining Styrofoam balls still clinging to my espresso twill curtains. I am determined to finally install my wireless network. I take the box in my arms and twirl on the plank floors. I have a good feeling about this.

An hour later, I'm not feeling quite as good. I haven't made much progress unless you count the crossword puzzle I completed while I made lemon tea. I don't get why it won't work. I inserted the start-up disc and did exactly what it said. I took the cable that normally connects my laptop to the broadband modem on my desk and inserted it into the router. Then I took the cable that came with the router and plugged it into my laptop. Router in the middle! Then I opened my web browser like I have done a thousand times before, only this time nothing happened.

`404 not found`

No signal. No nothing. I must have missed something, so with great patience, I do it again. Same damned thing. My first instinct is to call Teddy. No, scratch that. My first instinct is to stomp my Jimmy Choos all over this good-for-nothing, crappy, little silver box and fling it out the window—my second instinct is to call Teddy. But I resist, for I am not the helpless, dependent woman I used to be. And deep down, I know I can do this. Undoing everything I just did, I reconnect my laptop directly to my broadband modem and I'm back online.

`SEARCH: wireless network setup`

Fast forward ten minutes and fourteen websites: Forget about the router; now I want to throw my laptop out the window. It's as if the World Order of Geeks got together and pledged to make it as difficult as possible for normal people (I consider myself in this group) to install a wireless network. WEP? WPA? TKIP? IPFADM? Does anyone speak plain English anymore? WTF? Isn't there someone who can make things easy? Like the Naked Chef—I mean, I'm no cook but he makes cooking great food easy. If only he did a

show that substituted a modem, router, and laptop for veal, mushrooms, and marsala wine. Wait, that's it.

SEARCH: vidcast wireless network setup

I don't know why it didn't hit me sooner. I recently met with
someone about sponsoring some podcasts and vidcasts. There are
a ton of podcasts out there, broadcasting to anyone who'll listen,
and it won't be long until the really good ones add video. There
are already some good vidcasts on the web. Question is, are there
any that can help me install this piece-of-junk wireless network?

**Lab Rats! A vidcast about technology
you already own.**
Episode 7 — Set Up a Wireless Home Network.
www.labrats.tv/episodes/ep7.html

Bingo.

If you contract viruses daily:

(a) horizontally speaking, you really get around

(b) you work with kids and should really think about taking a good multivitamin

(c) you are undoubtedly pissing off everyone in your email address book

chapter nine

I'm fairly certain these so-called "lab rats" escaped from the World Order of Geeks because they helped me install my wireless network in forty minutes flat. Unlike the rest of their evil species, the pair of madcap techies named Andy and Sean welcomed me into their world and made it seem relatively easy. Sure, there was the odd moment of boredom (it was inevitable) especially when they got super nerdy, gabbed about network security, and dished out jargon, like SSID or something. But here's the thing: after they got over themselves, they took the time to explain everything and make it meaningful and relevant.

I now know that SSID stands for Service Set Identifier, which in a nutshell is the name you give your network (I named mine Valentino). I also know that I am not the only one who gets confused with what the rat named Andy called, "all the 802.11 nonsense out there." Believe it or not, I found the propeller-heads mildly entertaining—duelling scissors and cutting up a computer cable and book on Internet security.

"Good for you!" Sloane exclaimed over the phone line when I told her about my Mount Rushmore of a technological breakthrough. "Wes named our home network Bimmer after his car. In your infinite wisdom and new-found fashion sense, you have stood up for fashionistas everywhere."

I told her that she was missing the point. That I had finally installed a wireless network on my own. That I could do anything I put my mind to.

"Of course you can, Erica. Tell me something I don't know. Like what happened with Ren after you two left the club? You looked positively perfect together on the dance floor."

When I told her about my pending Seattle trip, Sloane started updating her calendar with new projected timelines for Ren's marriage proposal. "Three months, six months, I can't say for sure. What I do know is it won't be long till you have Ren eating out of your hands."

Eating or kissing? I decided against telling her about the kiss on the hand. If the white rose incident outraged her, I could only imagine how she might react to my latest brush with virginal symbolic gestures. Not that I much cared right at the moment. Even though she was being wonderfully supportive on the phone, I was still a bit annoyed at her.

Last night was supposed to be about me—but it's almost impossible for someone like Sloane to play a supporting role even to her best friend. She's used to playing lead. That's just always been her reality. When she walks into a room, everyone stares. When she speaks, people hang on every syllable. When she smiles, they're enchanted by the sparkle of her emerald green eyes, exquisitely framed by her shiny long black hair. And if that doesn't blind them, her picture-perfect, bleached white teeth always do.

Sloane is the stereotypical It girl. Always has been, always will be. I accepted that long ago and normally that suits me just fine.

But for once, I was starting to feel like the It girl. And even though Sloane is orchestrating this big plan to remarry me off and wipe Lowell off my radar screen, deep down I'm fairly certain she'd prefer to be standing in the spotlight than doing a Ron Howard and directing it.

Oh well, not to worry. Right now, the spotlight is nowhere in my vicinity. Ren is halfway around the world and I'm still in bed. Good news is I'm not alone.

I don't know how I ever used my laptop anywhere else but in bed. I have more freedom than the women you always see hiking in tampon commercials. I've been super productive—catching up on some work, emailing Jack in Thailand, Googling Reynolds, and bidding on some Valentino dresses on eBay (not necessarily in that order)—and it's not even noon.

Busy Saturday morning indeed, I think, as my Rockit rings again. It's Nick White, a smooth-talking lawyer with Schiffer, Smythe & Prusky. Right. Sloane said to expect a call but I never expected service this fast. He wants to meet as soon as possible. Now that Lowell and I have listed the house for sale, I do, too.

"How's tonight at eight?" Nick White asks.

"Uh, fine," I answer, a bit overwhelmed. I wouldn't have thought it possible to get same-day service especially on the weekend, but hey, Sloane has pull. I wonder if she can get me a friends-and-family discount. Even his voice sounds expensive.

"Excellent. Have you been to the Dove Supper Club?"

Oh no…if he thinks we're going to meet at one of the ritziest restaurants in town so he can have a great meal and expense it back to me, he's got another think coming. I know all about these high-roller lawyer types. If I'm going to pay, I'm going to pick the place.

"How about somewhere more casual," I suggest, giving him directions to the Sweaty Duck and patting myself on the back. Let it be known the new Erica Swift is no pushover.

I'm barely off the phone when I get an instant message from Teddy. I'm starting to feel like Grand Central Station.

```
gates invite sounds fishy investigating
            reynolds ault
    fake name if ive evr herd 1
        has he askd 4 $ yet?
```

Has *he* asked *me* for money? Ha! That's a good one.

```
whoa cowboob! heez friends with bill gates
    for real and heez my new boobfriend
```

Oh crap, something's wrong with the *y* key on my Rockit. Not only do I now owe Teddy another $40, but all that thumb-typing practice seems for naught.

```
concrnd bout yr boob obsession
    meet u @ strbcks in 45
        btw ur buying
```

So there I am, waiting for Teddy, curled up in a plush purple velour club chair enjoying my tea, when I notice Laurel Jenkins sitting across the room. She's sipping a giant steaming cup of something (lemon tea I'm guessing), nose-deep into a two-inch-thick red paperback. I try to catch her glance a few times but there's no competing with her book. Even the kicking-and-screaming toddler at the table next to hers doesn't seem to interrupt her headspace. I, on the other hand, am fifteen feet away and ready to shove my chocolate-dipped biscotti down his throat. I mean, the little angel looks famished.

running 18 b ther soon
strt w/o me T

"Laurel, right?" I take a seat at her table and catch a quick look at the book cover: *Gone with the Wind*. Another sign that we have a lot in common—that is, if you count the movie. I never actually read the novel.

"Right. Hey, how's the vacuum?"

"Still sucks. Get it?" *Oh my God. I feel like I'm on a first date. Stop trying to impress her,* I tell myself. Act normal. "Actually, I've been putting the wireless network hub to greater use. I installed it last night."

"Yourself?"

"You sound surprised," I reply, unexpectedly confident.

"Gosh no, I didn't mean it that way," she says, putting down her book and motioning me to join her. "It's just, besides you, me, and a handful of female IT administrators, I don't know many other women who spend their Friday nights getting technical."

"You forget I work in the tech industry."

"Of course." Laurel nods like a politician. "Actually, it wasn't so long ago that I didn't know a wireless network from a wireless bra."

Turns out Laurel and I have even more in common than lemon tea and Scarlett O'Hara. Up until two years ago, Laurel knew diddly about technology. Then again she didn't need to—or so she thought.

A librarian at a public library for almost a decade, she knew the Dewey Decimal system inside-out and could pinpoint the location of any book without even thinking. She was old school through and through, leaving the library every afternoon promptly at 4:45 to test out one of the new *Good Housekeeping* recipes she picked up during her break in Periodicals. Eggplant parmigiana, sole almandine, braised duck—as a young woman from a tiny midwestern town, she was taught they were all secrets to a man's heart. She believed it, too, until her husband, Thom, started returning home from work later and later and eventually started missing dinner altogether.

Then again, when you're an entrepreneur like Thom, trying to get your toy sales agency off the ground, you have to pay your dues, roll up your sleeves, and put in extra hours. The sad part is that while Thom and his sleeves were busy putting in extra hours designing a corporate website, it was Laurel who ended up paying her dues. Big time.

Thom left her for his twenty-five-year-old web designer, iRene Stromoulogolousi. Seems she legally changed her first name to have the look and feel of an iPod. Seems reasonable for an overaged adolescent but personally, Laurel and I agree, if she was going to change anything, it should have been her surname.

"I may not have met iRene but I know exactly who she is," I say to Laurel. "She's one of those adorable cubs you want to pet at the zoo. 'Come here you furry-wurry, little-bittle baby bear—you wouldn't hurt a fly, would you, until you sink your teeth into my husband and leave me out to die.' My point, Laurel, is that iRene is a baby Meryl. Neither of us saw them coming. And even though I can't say whose teeth are sharper, I can tell you our kingdom would be a lot safer without cubs or cougars roaming around."

"Here, here," Laurel concurs, tapping her paper cup lightly against mine, careful not to spill.

"So why'd you leave double D for double B?"

"Double what for what?"

"Dewey Decimal for Best Buy?"

"Ah. Creative. Well, mostly, I couldn't take all the whispering. I know there's bound to be gossip whenever something like infidelity hits. But in a library, you can't escape the whispering; that's the culture. Every time I saw my colleagues whisper, I was convinced they were talking about me. Every time I saw Mrs. Young whisper to little Robbie…"

The reference prompts me to take a fleeting look at our little stroller screamer, now throwing Cheerios on the floor as he sucks from his sippy cup. "You thought little Robbie knew?"

"It sounds crazy, I know. And that's why I had to leave. I was on the verge of having a nervous breakdown."

"But why the tech biz and not some other library?"

"Whispering knows no boundaries. I needed someplace loud where I had no past. I knew nothing about technology, other than using the library's computer system to check out books. Guess what? Check-out computers and wireless routers aren't so different. I worked my way up from cashier to manager and learned a few things along the way."

"And look at you now." I smile, impressed.

"What about you?" Laurel asks me.

"Well, I haven't encountered any whispering. Blatant patronizing, backhanded compliments, and avoidance tactics—but no whispering."

"Isn't it difficult to work with everyone?"

"Oh no, that's just my publicist. Everyone else is super supportive."

```
        sry stil tied up
dins on me + frget bout $40 T


        no can do
meeting divorce lawober 2night
        what $40? lol
```

Good thing I don't owe him the money, I'm going to need as much as possible to get through this damned divorce. Not that Lowell and I have many marital assets to divide but I've heard how legal fees can snowball out of control.

As I walk into the Sweaty Duck and catch my darkened reflection in the mirror over the bar, I flashback to the last time I was here, wearing noticeably less. Tonight, I am a fully clothed woman forgoing my newfound love of designer garb. Ta-ta for now, Valentino. See you soon, Armani. Hello, loyal tight, faded jeans and vintage Dr. Pepper tee. Mustn't give Nick White the impression that I spend mega money on haute couture, expensive restaurants, and even more expensive divorce lawyers.

Seeing as how I told Nick White I'd be the one with dirty blonde hair and chocolate martini, I sit myself down at a table and wait for someone to take my order. Over comes a cute new waiter with brown curly hair and chiseled cheekbones wearing a Red Sox shirt. "Can I have a chocolate martini, please?"

"You can have anything your heart desires," the Adonis responds, holding out his hand. "Nick White."

Nick White is nothing like I expected. If he wasn't my attorney, I'd jump him. He loves chicken wings and is a huge fan of baseball and virtually every other sport ever invented (did you know they have Beard Olympics in Austria?). "Thanks for picking this place," he says, waving Phyllis over. "The Sox are on a winning streak."

"My pleasure," I say, beaming that I outsmarted him at his own game.

"Hi, kids. What'll it be? Your regular?" she asks, not even realizing it's not Teddy.

"What's our regular, hon?" Nick White whispers in my ear with a chuckle. Hardly appropriate behaviour for my divorce lawyer. I'll have to set some ground rules.

"Mild large bucket with hot sauce on the side?" I ask him.

"Perfect. Oh and can I have a gin and tonic?"

"Chocolate martini for me," I chime in, only to get a concerned look from Phyllis before she heads back to the kitchen.

"So, why's a nice girl like you getting a divorce?"

"A not-so-nice husband. Tell me, Mr. White—" I begin.

"Nick, please. Mr. White's my father."

"Okay, Nick, since there aren't any assets to squabble over other than the house, how long should the divorce take?"

"I would guess about a year, perhaps, but I'm no expert."

"I appreciate your modesty," I assure him, "but being a divorce attorney would make you an expert."

"No argument there, hon, but I'm a criminal attorney. I don't get involved in divorce disputes unless he hit, punched, stabbed, or shot you."

I don't know what to say other than after tonight, I may need a criminal attorney. I'm going to kill Sloane. This is no meeting; I'm on a goddamned blind date. How dare she set me up and not let me in on the whole thing? Why happened to Ren, and the plan? And who the hell is my divorce lawyer and why hasn't he or she called?

"Take him to the cleaners," Nick says, reaching for my hand. "Sloane said I would like you."

I down my drink as soon as Phyllis serves it. "I'll have another."

"Easy, girl," she warns. "I'm watching you tonight."

"Me, too," says Nick, caressing my arm.

I swear if Phyllis was a little old lady with an umbrella, she would have swatted Nick off his chair. It had finally dawned on her that he wasn't Teddy.

"And you are?" she asks Nick, hands on her hips.

"Good question," pipes in a familiar voice from behind. I

swivel my chair only for effect. I already know exactly who's standing behind me and what he must be thinking.

"Hi, Teddy."

It didn't take Teddy very long to see the humour in the situation.
Me? That's a different story. "How could you, Sloane!" I yell into
my Rockit while driving home after dinner.

"How could I not?" she yells back. "Nick is the hottest attorney
at Wes's firm. I may be married but I can at least live vicariously
through you."

"What about Ren?"

"What about him? Has he mentioned exclusivity?"

There's no need for me to respond. We both know the answer.

"Sweetie, Nick's a great fallback if we don't get that commitment from Ren. He's the second part of our two-part plan. He's
backup."

"But two guys? I'm still legally committed to a third."

"That is a problem. I'll remind Wes to assign you a divorce attorney pronto."

"Thanks. And Sloane?"

"Yes?"

"Please make it a woman."

If you know all about Trojan horses, you:

(a) know that next to Mongolian wild horses, they're the most challenging to ride

(b) could write a book on Greek mythology

(c) have been infected with a sneaky virus

(d) have been watching too much porn

chapter
ten

What's with all the whispering? You'd think our office was a library. Now I get what Laurel was talking about. I needn't get a complex, though—I'm old news. Everyone already knows Lowell left me for an older woman. Maybe Brett is sleeping with the new reception-ist. Whatever it is, I haven't the time or the energy to figure it out. I've just come in from an offsite lunch meeting and I've got a PR meeting in fifteen minutes.

Speak of the devil—Dani is staring at me from across the of-fice as she escorts a short, chubby man down the hall, out to front reception. He looks very familiar but I can't place him for the life of me. Must be a reporter. Walking into my office, I start to vibrate.

```
chez me asap T
```

Sounds serious. If I didn't know any better I'd think I was in trouble, though I can't imagine what for. Why would Teddy be calling me into his office? Could he have finally figured out that I borrowed the last of his secret lasagna stash (it's marked Peking duck) in the staff room freezer?

"What's up?" I say innocently, turning the corner into his office. He's sitting motionless at his desk. "Close the door." I have obviously underestimated his love of lasagna.

I shut the heavy birch door against the whispering coming from the outside cubicles and take a seat. I don't know what to say, partly because I still have no clue what's going on, but mostly because he looks like hell. He's never been Mr. GQ but he never comes to work looking like he just rolled out of bed, either. His shirt has more wrinkles than a bulldog's face. His eyeballs have retreated so far into his lids that I'm surprised he can see anything. And then there are the bags under his eyes; airlines charge extra for baggage that heavy. He's a mess. No, this is bigger than lasagna.

"Did you find a flaw?" I ask.

"A what?" he says, rubbing his eyes.

"A flaw. Is launch being delayed because of a product flaw?"

Propping his heavy head on one hand, Teddy opens his mouth a few times attempting to speak but nothing comes out, at least nothing I can hear. I get the sense he is having quite a detailed conversation with himself, making hand gestures and facial expressions that paint a pretty bizarre picture. If I didn't know any better, I'd say he was losing it. *Omigod, the whispers are about Teddy.*

"Whatever you did, it can't be that bad."

He's looking at me like I'm crazy. "Whatever I did?"

"It'll be old news tomorrow," I try to console him. "They'll forget all about it. Take it from me. I know."

"It's online. Haven't you seen it? Accounting has. So has HR," he says, shaking his head and pushing his laptop toward me until it tips off the edge of his desk. Being a former little leaguer, I make the catch before it hits the ground. I nearly drop it, though, when

I catch a glimpse of what's onscreen: a blurry photo of Teddy fondling some woman's breasts from behind. *Yikes.* Who knew Teddy had a secret life?

I close the laptop and place it back on his desk. It doesn't matter, I decide. Teddy's still one of the most incredible people I know. Whatever he does in his own time is his own business. He's always been there for me and I'm going to be there for him.

"Teddy." I put my hand on his. "It seems bad right now but you will get through this. Remember when Hugh Grant got arrested with that prostitute? It's ancient history now. No one cares anymore. He ended up getting lots of great roles afterward. You'll be fine, too. Besides, it's not as if the police caught you with a hooker. So you like strippers. Big deal."

"That's no stripper," he leans toward me, whispering. "That's you."

"No way." Jumping to my feet, I re-open the laptop and study the image of the woman. A mess of long, sandy blond hair is covering her face. It could be thousands of women. "That is so not me."

"It's you. The night you found out about Lowell and Meryl. You were drunk out of your mind. Didn't your mother tell you you did a strip tease?"

I look at the screen again and spot my triangular-shaped birthmark under one of the breasts. *Oh. My. God. My hair may be covering my face but it's me all right. What the hell went on that night? Why don't I remember?* "She didn't tell me you were part of the act."

"It's not what it looks like, Erica. I was trying to get you off-stage and cover you with up with my jacket but it slipped."

I look a little closer at the screen, zooming in on where my nipples would be had his hands been airbrushed away—or amputated, depending on how this all turns out.

"I didn't touch you, I swear. It's a bad camera angle."

That's an understatement. Because in my heart of hearts, I

know there's no way Teddy would ever take advantage of any woman, least of all me. I'm like a sister to him. Not only that, Beth once told me that Teddy refused to kiss in public. Onstage breast molestation is just not his style.

"I know, Teddy. When I find out who took that photo I'm gonna…" I stop to think. Who else was there that night besides Phyllis and her staff? It was pretty empty except…wait. Those balding bowling bozos yelling at me to move my fat ass. As if they were anything to look at. Holy crap—the reporter—he's one of the rolypoly guys from the Sweaty Duck that night.

"Did you get a look at the reporter who was just with Dani?"

"Reporter? That's her older brother."

"Knock knock!"

"Come on in. Have a seat," I tell Dani a few minutes later in my office.

"Is Teddy okay?" she asks overdramatically, handing me her status report. "I hear he's having a meltdown."

"He's fine. What's our ratio of positive vs. negative vs. neutral news coverage this month?"

"I'm not sure Brett would agree with you on Teddy if he saw that photo," she says smugly, sitting on the corner of my desk like she owns it. "He might ask Teddy to take a little break, to clear his mind so to speak."

I can practically feel smoke shooting through my flaring nostrils. "I wouldn't do that if I were you." I glare at her.

"Of course you wouldn't. Because he might ask you to leave, too. Once he knows how close you two *really* are," she sneers as she pushes up her breasts with her hands. "If I were you, I'd leave on my own and spare Teddy the humiliation."

What the hell does she think she's doing? Staging a coup? She has no idea who she's dealing with. Throwing Teddy's humiliation (and her breasts) in my face like that. With every ounce of composure I smile sweetly. "Brett's not getting rid of anyone around here so quickly, except maybe you. You better talk with that troll of a brother of yours about what really happened that night. And clean up this mess fast or I'll find legal cause to have you fired."

I lean back in my chair and stretch my legs out onto my desk, pushing her off the edge. "I think we're done talking status for now."

"You're going to let that little Jezebel get away with it?" Sloane says after I give her the lowdown on the phone a few days later. "I'd bury her."

"I'm on top of it but I've got to be careful. If I fire her or go to Brett, the whole mess could resurface. Things are finally getting back to normal, including Teddy. The photo has been removed from the web and *someone* started a rumour that it was a fake, doctored by the competition to make Rockit look bad. Totally false, but everyone's buying it."

"If she tries anything else, let me know and I'll get Wes on it."

"One lawsuit at a time." I smile. "Thanks, by the way, for hooking me up with Bettina."

Bettina Glazer. Divorce attorney extraordinaire. Woman. "We only spoke briefly to set up a meeting for next week but I have a good feeling about her."

"She's the best for nailing philandering losers."

That Sloane, always the jokester.

Right now, all I want to do is slip into my jammies and catch up on some work. I look at my checklist: pull up competitive product data, approve our advertising spending, and review PR. Easy, breezy—especially in my warm, snuggly bed.

All right, just log in and away we go. While my laptop is booting up, I run into the kitchen and start the kettle. In just a few minutes I'll be working in bed with a nice cup of tea. How perfect is this? Not so perfect, I realize, when I return to bed. My laptop's still booting up. Something must be wrong. I tap on some keys hoping to trigger something and thankfully it takes me to my start page. My laptop is acting like Grandpa Simpson. Slow doesn't begin to describe it. I'll have to get it checked out at the office tomorrow. In the meantime, it takes me six minutes to open my research report and then out of nowhere an animated jumbo carrot wearing a blue satin smoking jacket pops onto my screen carrying a banner that says "BUY VIAGRA."

I know I'm alone in my bedroom (except for orange Hugh Hefner) but I can't help but feel like I'm on *Candid Camera*. This kind of thing doesn't happen to me every day. I call Laurel.

"It happens more than you know. You must have adware on your system."

"How? I didn't install it."

"It was probably a Trojan," Laurel offers.

"A condom?"

"A virus," she giggles. "Have you been surfing beefcake? Don't answer. Just tell me this: Do you have antivirus protection on your computer?"

"I think I made a mental note to install that later."

"You're very vulnerable, Erica—and I'm not talking about your love life. Something has poked its way into your system. It probably installed spyware and is snooping on you."

"My bad."

"It's not pretty, especially if you bank online. Disconnect from the network right away and scan your system to make sure it's clean."

"Gotcha. Goodnight, Laurel."
Goodnight, Valentino.

If you haven't heard about OLED:

(a) you haven't flipped through an IKEA catalogue lately

(b) your command of Spanish isn't as good as you think

(c) your co-worker might not have been rolling a joint after all

chapter eleven

There's nothing like sushi for fixing your laptop. Raw fish does nothing for me personally but Jade loves the stuff. And she's so adept at using chopsticks she can stick-handle salmon sashimi and simultaneously clean up my computer without a second thought. I'm just fortunate that a) she offered to help me and b) SushiMobile also has honest-to-goodness real cooked food on its menu for sushi-phobes like me.

Watching Jade maneouver her wooden chopsticks without getting so much as a splinter in her lip confirms that I have absolutely zero Asian blood in my body. (Not that my fair skin, green eyes, and blonde hair would suggest otherwise but you never know; my great grandmother's maiden name was Lee.) I have as much grace with chopsticks as a duck in pink satin ballet slippers. To me, they're not so much eating utensils as they are a way to lose weight. Nothing ends up in my mouth, plus I get a mini upper body workout.

Mental note: Write The Chopstick Diet *in spare time. Could be the biggest thing since Atkins.*

Thank God for the plastic fork in the crumpled brown paper bag marked Chicken Teriyaki—WELL DONE. I'm glad I mentioned my fear of contracting salmonella food poisoning from half-cooked poultry. You can't be too careful nowadays—and I'm not just talking about food.

According to Dr. Jade, contracting a computer virus has become more common than catching herpes or gonorrhea—and much more dangerous, though getting genital warts hardly sounds pleasant. To be honest, I'm more interested in the hockey game on TV than the techno-babble Jade's throwing my way. It's the NHL playoffs, for crying out loud—and it's almost intermission. I'm already drooling just thinking about having Cam Keon inside my loft. Just looking at him feels better than a full body massage.

"Many people are blindly leaving themselves wide open," she says. "They can't see what's hit them until it's too late."

Ain't that the truth, sister.

"That about does it," she continues. Your system is now 100 percent clean. No more Mr. Carrot or anyone else. Now what about your router; let's see if it's secure." She connects to it with her laptop. "Uh oh, you didn't change the default password! What do you want to use as your new password?"

"Oh. Well actually, Jade, I'd like to do the honours," I respond, gallantly reaching for my laptop with three minutes to go in the first period. I'm a new woman—my fearless fingertips approach the keyboard intending to change the default password like they're the Allied forces landing in Normandy. Only problem is, they are getting zero direction from my brain, immobilized out of fear of picking a numbskull password that every hacker in town will figure out.

Jade's eyes follow mine as I survey the room like a preschooler playing Eye Spy. But nothing jumps out at me other than slimytuna and yuckyfisheggs and they're not exactly the things I want to remember. Yikes, the pressure of picking a password lickety-split.

I look beyond the coffee table of Japanese foodstuff in politically incorrect Styrofoam containers. What about landfill? Hockeygame? Redbrickwall? Bo-ring. Wait, I've got it: If Valentino's my network, why shouldn't I make Boss my password?

"Make sure it's at least six digits long, mix letters and numbers, and be mindful of caps and punctuation," she suggests.

That's why. Okay, nix Boss. What about D3lar3nta? That's nine digits. Fourteen if I add Øscar.

"And stay away from anything predictable like your name, address, or network name," she continues, foiling my well-laid-out plan. "Pick something no one would think of."

Okay, clearly this is no time to play fashionista. Besides, if I'm a modern woman balancing her career, family, and love life, my new password should damned well reflect that. And then, as dreamy Cam Keon pops onto my TV screen, the perfect password hits me in the head like a can of V8 from those old commercials and sends my fingers afluttering: • • • • • • • • •

It's brilliant, without question. Fun. Memorable. Not the least bit predictable, nor pretentious. Very modern woman, indeed, I think, smiling on the inside, wishing I was home alone (though for very different reasons than Macaulay Culkin had in the movie). Fat chance of that happening. With half her sushi platter still to be devoured, I suspect Jade's going nowhere any time soon. I grab my Rockit to record my password (even a modern woman's memory can fail…) and turn away from Jade to protect the innocent.

v 1 b R 8 R g A 1

If snails ate sushi, I bet they'd finish before Jade. No offence to the sluggish critters but that's scary. I mean, it's not as if Jade's eating a veggie wrap or buttered bagel. We're talking about raw fish—strike one. The fact it hasn't been refrigerated for well over an hour—strike two. If she doesn't hurry, she could end up strike three in the local ER. Be that as it may, if she is incubating any nasty bacteria, she's certainly showing no sign of it. Jade is as happy as a raw clam (a huge geoduck clam to be exact), which as it turns out is one of the few remaining pieces on her platter. Anyhow, I'm not about to engage her in another conversation about contracting viruses. It was tedious enough the first time round.

We're into the third period of the game and Jade's picking up hockey more rapidly than I'd expect for a highbrow engineer whose favourite sport till now had been chess. As far as friends go, there's definitely potential because if she likes hockey, she's going to love baseball. And of course, it doesn't hurt that she's a technological genius—not that I need any more guidance; I'm just saying.

"Can I ask you something, Erica?"

"Anything," I reply, praying I won't need a PhD to translate the question.

"What are your thoughts on a roll-away OLED screen?"

Why me? I sit back, put my index finger on my chin, and reflect, trying to remember if Teddy ever talked about IKEA going into smartphones, but it's no use. I'm coming up blank. I'll have to fake it. "I think it's worth exploring."

"Agreed. Being able to roll up a large screen and tuck it away has its benefits. Customers currently trying to view a wide spreadsheet or watch a movie on their Rockit can attest to that. I know I can. But I wonder, do you see it as a value add or upgrade option?"

Right. Okay, now I can respond intelligently. "It would be nice to make it a standard Rockit feature. You know, give 'em more bang for their buck. But Brett and Teddy would have to work through the numbers. Good idea, Jade."

"I've got another."

"Like?"

"We could make the screen reflective so it can be used as a

mirror when in off mode."

"I love it."

"But I don't think it's as big a selling feature to our largely male customer base."

"Good point, but let's forget about them for a minute," I suggest, my mind suddenly working a mile a minute. "Let's pretend we're selling to women. Career women, yummy mommies, Goldie grannies (as in Hawn)—all of them. What else could we do—you know, realistically, without reconfiguring the Rockit chassis too much?"

"We could add a lipstick brush onto the stylus pen."

"Smart. Anything else?"

"We could carve out an area to house refillable palettes of lip gloss or eye shadow. It would take some planning but it's doable."

I start to imagine licensing Rockit "Beauty On-The-Go" inserts to cosmetic companies. CoverGirl, L'Oréal, MAC, Bobbi Brown, who knows? This could be bigger than Botox. "I think you're on to something, Jade, but let me do some research."

"I'm not finished," she says. "I have another idea worth exploring."

"Go on."

"Well, you know how the ringer can vibrate? It *can* be leveraged in other ways."

Well, I'll be… Seems I pegged little Ms. Engineer wrong. We may not be so different after all.

I'm not exactly sure how Jade envisions transforming the Rockit into a personal massage device (adding an attachment, I assume, for hygienic reasons) and personally, I think she may be going a bit overboard. But to be totally honest, in the twenty-four hours since she brought it up, I've gotten excited every time I've picked up my red-hot smartphone. I mean it. Phone, text, email—doesn't matter what I do, it's a huge turn-on—and in more ways than one. Professionally speaking, I can't think of a better way to extend the product and cater to a whole new demographic. I can't stop thinking about it. It's just so exciting. Did I mention that?

For the moment, however, I've got more imminent matters to attend to. I've invited Teddy and our moms over for dinner and I've got less than two hours to tidy up and cook.

"What are you serving?" my mom asked when I called to invite her.

"Is your acceptance contingent on the menu?"

"Of course not, honey. But since you're asking, you should know that I started seeing a dietician and have been cutting carbs. I know how much you and your Italian friend enjoy lasagna. Should I eat before I arrive?"

She's got gumption, I'll give her that, but making lasagna for Mrs. Francesco would be like showing Mick Jagger how to be a rock star. She's a pro. "Actually, I was thinking of trying to make chicken scaloppini."

"I see," she replies with a long pause. "No offence, dear, but would you tell Oprah how to host a talk show? You make a salad. I'll come early and make my chicken."

Omigod. I sound just like my mother. Don't panic, I tell myself. Not yet, anyway. The only chicken dish you really know how to serve is leftover Sweaty Duck wings—and let's be honest, your first dinner party is not the time to start winging it.

In all the years I've known Teddy, this is the first time I've met his mother. I study Mrs. Francesco's round face from across the dinner table: her strong chin, long nose, thin parched lips, and round soft brown eyes—all without a stitch of makeup and topped by salt-and-pepper, no-fuss short hair.

Teddy must have got his looks from his father because other than her olive skin, I can't see any resemblance. If anything, she looks like her lasagna. A female Chef Boyardee of sorts—without the mustache, natch. Better keep that to myself. I can see how an old-fashioned Italian woman might get her nose out of joint being compared to a man—especially one synonymous with canned ravioli.

"Wine, Mrs. Francesco?" I ask with a smile, displaying the green bottle of pinot grigio I picked up in her honour. "It's from Italy, 2006. The stock boy said it was an excellent vintage." *Christ, did I just use stock boy and vintage in the same sentence? Classy, Erica.*

Mental note: Sommeliers are trained to recommend wines; stock boys are trained to clean up broken bottles of wine.

I still have my stupid smile pasted on my face, waiting for Mrs. Francesco to accept but she just shakes her head and politely says, "No, thank you."

"Ma doesn't drink wine," Teddy whispers to me.

"What about San Pellegrino?" my mother asks. "I think it's Italian, too."

"I'm sorry. I don't have that kind," I say, afraid that the way drinks are going, we might never make it to the meal.

"What about Voss water then, dear?" Mom asks. "My dietician says it was once Madonna's favourite and she's Italian. Madonna that is. I have no idea where my dietician is from."

"I had Voss once," Teddy joins in. "Dani gave me one of the bottles she keeps in her office."

Of course she did, that two-faced, pretentious suck-up. As a matter of record, Ren and I downed Voss by the gallon on the golf greens.

"Tap water is great, too," Teddy quickly adds, catching the look on my face. "The fluoride's good for your teeth."

"It's my favourite," Mrs. Francesco says to my relief, nonchalantly waving her napkin in the air, signalling the start of dinner.

From that moment on, the evening went amazingly well. Mom's chicken scaloppini (an Italian delicacy, she pointed out...) was a hit—even Mrs. Francesco asked her for the recipe. I got to know the woman behind the lasagna and quickly found a kind soul with strong values and a solid work ethic.

I learned about Teddy's late father, Roberto Francesco, a handsome carpenter who worked three jobs so he could buy his young bride, Zola, a house; about how he had a heart attack on a job site when she was five months pregnant; and about how she worked as a housekeeper and raised little Teddy as a single mother.

In finding out about Zola and Roberto, I learned more about Teddy over dinner than I had in four years working with him. I was wrong when I said Teddy bore little resemblance to his mother. I simply didn't look deep enough.

Technically, if you're having a problem with cookies:

(a) you should work out for an extra thirty minutes to compensate for the extra calories

(b) you may want to try using less baking soda and more chocolate chips

(c) there's a reason you keep getting Internet pop-ups about your favourite stores' holiday sales

chapter
twelve

Is that Tobey Maguire in a red dress or are my eyes playing tricks on me again? It's the end of the workday and I'm the only one left in the posh mahogany-panelled reception area of Schiffer, Smythe & Prusky. Peering up from the copy of *Metropolitan Home* I picked up from the glass coffee table in front of me, I decide Spidey has gone undercover for a new office girl role and is doing a fine job looking the part.

He approaches me in a pair of red ballet flats. I size up the small frame, gentle facial features (lightly made up with a bit of foundation and mascara), round blue eyes, shiny brown hair grown just long enough for a ponytail, and decide he could pass for a Breck girl—no Cameron Diaz, mind you, but much prettier than fellow thespian cross-dresser Dustin Hoffman and his *Tootsie* alter ego. Yep, Tobey Maguire can indeed play a good woman. Add a long wavy black wig, larger silicon breast forms, a pair of magical bullet-proof arm cuffs and, boom, he could play Wonder Woman.

I mean, he's already got the superhero thing down.

"Erica? Tina Glazer. Nice to meet you," the Tobey look-alike says, extending her hand.

Mental note: Get appointment with eye doctor. May be suffering from male-sightedness. Eat more carrots, too.

"Pleasure," I say, stunned. Even close up, they could pass for siblings. "Your maiden name isn't Maguire, by any chance?" I ask as we walk down the corridor to her office.

"I was born a Glazer. Only thing I'm married to is my job." She gives half a giggle and turns into her office.

"Oh," I say as she motions for me to sit.

"I know what you're thinking," Tina says. Without giving me time to respond (thank God), she starts building her case. "You see me as young, naive, fresh out of law school. A driven workaholic without a clue as to what it's like to be in a relationship with anyone other than a client. You've been through hell and back and don't want to waste your time or money on a newbie attorney still learning the law. Is that about right?"

Hell, I just wanted to know if she was related to Tobey. But she does raise some valid points. How can she specialize in divorce if she herself never tied the knot? That's like Jack Nicholson getting a job as a marriage counsellor. What were Sloane and Wes thinking referring me to this Chatty Cathy?

"Now I'm going to tell you what you don't see: A woman whose world was shattered almost twenty years ago when her precious, narcissistic lawyer father took his bimbo secretary on a quote-unquote business trip to Paris and never came back, except to pick up his things. Do you know the resentment that can be harboured by a pubescent eleven-year-old and an alcoholic-in-training, falling-to-pieces mess of a mother? Do you know the shame and guilt that girl kept bottled up all through school? All the clever excuses she made up to avoid bringing friends home?" She pauses to catch her breath.

"Are you okay?" I'm hoping she doesn't need CPR.

"I'm fine...thanks to my therapist," she says, wiping her sweaty brow. "Listen, Erica, I may be young and single but I've survived divorce. I know what it's like to have your life squashed by a philanderer and I have no tolerance for it. For me, it's not just business—it's personal. So if you'd like to nail your soon-to-be ex-husband to the wall, I can help."

"So I guess that's why you went into divorce law?" I ask my sledgehammer of an attorney before we get into the nitty-gritty of my case.

"It played a significant role. Plus, my father's a divorce lawyer, as was his father. It's in my blood. But enough about me—what about you? Sloane didn't say much other than you have," she stops to look at her notepad, "a double-crossing loser of a husband—her words, not mine."

"Sloane never liked Lowell, but in this instance, her description is reasonably accurate," I say, then take Tina on a whirlwind tour of my marriage.

"A Botox bimbo, really? So, Erica, at the end of all this, what do you want?"

"A divorce."

"Oh, you'll get that and tons more," Tina insists. "It's the tons more that I want to focus on right now. Since no children are involved, it should be pretty painless."

"Good. I don't like hearing about ugly divorces."

"Then plug your ears. There's nothing pretty about divorce. It's an ugly beast. When I said it should be painless, I meant for you. You are my client. You are the victim. Lowell will feel the wrath of Tina."

For a woman who looks as sweet as Peter Parker in drag and talks in third person like Elmo, Tina is a legal eagle with one sharp beak. Sloane wasn't kidding when she said I was in good hands. This woman makes Allstate look amateurish.

"What do you want, Erica?"

"Truthfully?"

"There's no lie detector test. Just tell me what you want."

"I want a speedy divorce. I want what's rightfully mine: my car, half the house, half our savings, all of my dad's vintage baseball card collection—including the mint 1936 Joe DiMaggio rookie card. What I don't want is a divorce that drags on and on, or turns into Iraq. I want to move on with my life already."

"What about inflicting pain? I know people… Kidding. Divorce law humour."

"Tina, I just want it over."

"Then that's what you'll get. It's hard to believe you and Sloane are really *best* friends..."

"How did it go with Tina?" Sloane's perky voice asks over the phone that night.

"Can I call you back after dinner, Sloane?" I say, pulling leftover chicken scaloppini from the microwave.

"Okay, but did you hear she just negotiated a $4-million-dollar settlement for another client? Four mill! Wes says she's as good as gold. We're going to hit that loser where it hurts."

"Don't spend our settlement yet. Lowell doesn't have that kind of money."

"First of all, I'm sure he's worth more than you think. Second of all, I'm sure he's worth more than you think. I've always thought he was hiding something."

"Yeah, her name is Meryl. Sloanie, you're not hearing me. I

don't care about gads of money. I just want my fair share."

"Four million sounds fair to me."

I know she means well but I just haven't the energy or the inclination to argue. "Hey," I change the subject, "guess who I bumped into after my meeting with Tina?"

"Nick?"

"Wes tell you?"

"No, he left for Chicago this morning. I told Nick you'd be there. You know, I could talk to that man all day."

"Sloane, stop meddling."

"I do not meddle. I assist. Nick saw me at the office the other day and asked when you were coming in. He drew me into those hypnotic, dark eyes and I couldn't help but tell him. So, did he stake out Tina's office?"

"There was FBI surveillance equipment and everything."

"And?" Sloane tunes out my blatant sarcasm.

"We're going to the ballgame on Friday night. The Red Sox are in town and we both love baseball."

"I know," she replies confidently, as if she set up the date herself. (Hell, she probably got the tickets.) "What about Ren?" she asks.

"He's not invited."

"You're a regular Jon Stewart. Seriously, what's up with you and Ren? Still getting red roses?"

"Is there any other kind?" I reply, still on a roll.

"What about Seattle?"

"Check. Bill and Melinda called. They can't wait to meet me next month."

"Short-term plans?"

"We might pull a Brangelina and adopt from Ethiopia. Ren's going to pick up the baby on his way back from Europe. Meanwhile, we chat on the computer most nights."

"And?"

"And I'm hanging up so I can eat my dinner." I click End on my cordless and glance at the chicken and mushrooms on my plate. Once swimming in Mom's creamy scaloppini sauce, they are now encased in congealed cream cement. There goes my appetite.

Grabbing my laptop from my bag, I sit down and log on to check my email. There goes my phone again. That girl just won't quit.

"What now, Sloane?"

"Who is dis Sloane person?" says an unfamiliar voice. "Is Erica dere? Dis is Sanjay."

"Sorry, who?"

"Dis is Sanjay. Calling from Skype in India."

Oh right, Skype. I signed up for their cheap Internet long distance service a few months ago. Must be their call centre in Mumbai responding to the question I emailed them about phoning Thailand. "Ah, you work for Skype."

"No, I do not work dere. I use Skype. I got dis number from yir profile."

"I don't understand." Until Skype opens up on my screen and I see a headshot of this East Indian guy sporting a pencil-thin mustache and red polo shirt.

```
     hello       7:51:12 PM
 i am sanjay     7:51:23 PM
 i am calling u  7:51:25 PM
```

why r you calling me????? I staccato type at 7:51:39 PM.

"I want to talk with you," Sanjay says as I view my profile. There, to my horror, is my phone number for the whole world to see. I don't recall putting that info there but who the hell knows?

"But you don't know me," I say as I remove my number and last name from my profile.

"I like to know you."

"I'm sure you're very nice but I don't know you. We've got nothing to talk about."

```
why don't u        7:53:25 PM
wana talk with me  7:53:28 PM
i like to talk with u 7:53:56 PM
```

"Sanjay, I have to go now. It's not a good time."

"I call later?" Sanjay asks like a pesky telemarketer.

"I'd prefer not. Bye," I say, hanging up and closing Skype.

Not even thirty seconds pass before the phone rings again. "I told you, Sanjay, I am not interested!"

"Who's Sanjay and what aren't you interested in?" Sloane asks, her voice more lively than ever. "It's not because he's from India, is it?" she says after I tell her the story. "Because Liz Hurley did very well for herself marrying that Mumbai textile mill heir."

"Drop it, Sloane."

"I wouldn't want you moving so far away anyway. Listen, I just got the name of a fabulous forensic accountant," she says as if she's talking about a new decorator.

"I'm begging you. Please, no more blind dates."

"I'd never set you up with a ho-hum accountant, silly. This guy is like a magnet when it comes to locating hidden assets. We're going to hit the mother lode."

"Later, Sloane." I hang up and refocus my efforts on answering email.

```
eraca?   8:09:34 PM
eraca??  8:09:37 PM
eraca??? 8:09:42 PM
eraca???? 8:09:49 PM
```

Holy crap, I'm being cyber stalked. What the hell do I do?

"Block him on Skype and meet me for tea in an hour," Laurel instructs me on the phone.

Thank God. In the absence of a chocolate martini, I could also use a few biscotti.

From my favourite plush purple window-side chair, I've counted twenty-seven men and four women walk by talking on their Rock-its before Laurel walks in the java haven down the street from her store. "How was work?"

"Not great," Laurel says. "Oliver quit and joined the Army."

"So you're worried about sales?"

"Hardly. Sales will go up. Do you know how many customers Oliver annoys daily? He's not the most intuitive guy."

She's being kind. Oliver's invaded more space than Atari. Uncle Sam and the troops are in for a big treat. But I'm not about to add insult to injury. "So what's wrong?"

"My auntie May. To say she's a pacifist is an understatement. She is a granola-loving Birkenstock hippie from Berkeley who marched with Joan Baez in the sixties and still wears a button that says "Butterflies not Bombs." Oliver's her only child. She talked him out of enlisting six months ago. Why do you think I hired him?"

Enough said. "Tea's on me tonight," I say, hoping that will improve her spirits. "Want a chocolate-dipped biscotti, too?"

"Make it a double."

"I hear ya, sister." I nod and order two humongous lemon teas. Plus four biscotti for the price of what a case would run me at Costco.

"So tell me again, why did this Sanjay guy call *you*?"

"Lucky shot?"

"Your photo wasn't on Skype, was it?"

"Yeah, but only my friends can see it, I think."

"Similar thing happened to me on Facebook. I posted my photo on my page without adjusting the permission controls. Then before I know it my mug was on my friends' pages, too. Heck, I even ended up on iRene's page. It's crazy, you know? We live in an information-obsessed society. If we're not careful, privacy will be obsolete. I was talking about this very issue with one of our regular customers today."

"Tech bashing? Doesn't that violate the store's code of ethics?"

"Very funny. Actually, Perry's a very special customer. He's a successful computer consultant and book author. The fact that he's easy on the eyes doesn't hurt either."

Ah, now we're getting somewhere. Yikes—I sound like Sloane.

Laurel's got this funny look on her face—it *must* be love. "He's around forty, very intelligent, and a bit on the shy side but you can't look at that as a bad thing," she says, smiling. "He's never been married and, like I said, he's awfully handsome."

"He's perfect!" I exclaim, so pleased that Laurel's getting back in the dating game.

"So I can give him your number?" she says, sipping her tea.

"What?" I say, nearly choking on mine. "I meant perfect for *you.* I just told Sloane no more blind dates."

"I'm not ready to date but you seem to be a natural," Laurel says. "The least I can do is set you up with a truly nice guy who you can actually see more than twice a month if you want to. Come on, worst-case scenario: You'll learn a lot. He's brilliant!"

"You already gave him my number, didn't you?

What a day. I'm pooped. Just wanna get into my pajamas, slide into bed, and crash. First I better slide into Facebook and make sure my face isn't anywhere it's not supposed to be. I know I clicked on a lot of privacy controls when I set up my account, but I may have left some things to the default setting. Who the hell remembers? It was months ago.

Whew—everything seems fine on my page. Beyond my name and photo of a Rockit, my profile lists only a few scant details about me. Nothing too personal, just my high school, college, friends (both real friends and countless others I've known for about ten minutes and exchanged emails with), hobbies. Not too much info or too little. To quote Goldilocks, it's just right. Except for my marriage status. With a click I change it from "married" to "it's complicated." Christ, there's also a photo of Lowell in my friends area. I'll have to fix that. He may have to exist on Earth but not on my page. I'm curious though—do I still exist on his?

I click on his name and scroll down his page to his friends area. Shocker. There I am beside his other so-called friends. I scan their profile pics: his buddy Kent Dawson, me, and Meryl Wynter. (He never had the widest social circle.) Hmmm, that's bizarre. His photo album says it contains thirty-four photos. Call me crazy but for a man with only three friends—one of whom is suing him for divorce—that seems a bit much. I mean, who's going to see them?

Click. There are shots of Lowell and Meryl at a restaurant, in a garden, on a boat, in front of a stainless steel KitchenAid fridge. *Hold on. That's my goddamned honeymoon!*—I spot a Rockit magnet just over Meryl's bony osteoporosis-in-waiting shoulder. *Ouch. Sucker punch.* I could use a friend and a drink (not necessarily in that order) and tea's not going to do it this time.

        teffy, can u come to the dick?

I walk into the Sweaty Duck, a ghost town tonight except for Teddy who's already there, chatting it up with Phyllis near the bar.

"Chocolate martini?" he asks.

"Is there any other kind? Hey, Phyl, I'm cutting myself off at one tonight." I smile. "So can you make it extra chocolaty?"

"You got it. Want one, too, Teddy?" Phyllis asks.

"Not for me. I feel like something Italian," he cracks.

"Very funny," I say.

Phyllis has no clue Teddy's doing a smartass imitation of my mom. I think she has a secret crush on him. "We don't have much I'm afraid, sweetie. Some red wine and Brio, I think."

"Brio it is," he says, rapping the table with his knuckles, signalling Phyllis's exit. "So what's up?"

Like a tipped glass of milk, I spill, telling him about my go-for-the-jugular attorney, Mumbai-based cyber stalker, and the Facebook photos of Lowell and his geriatric lover. Everything just pours out of me, leaving me remarkably calm yet severely dehydrated. Where *is* that drink?

"Why didn't you call me?"

"I've caused enough trouble for you. But not to worry, Laurel and Sloane have been helping me through it."

"That's exactly what I'm worried about. Didn't Sloane introduce you to that lawyer with the soap opera name and alleged connection to Bill Gates?"

"Not exactly. The lawyer is Nick. It's Reynolds Ault who's friends with Bill. He's an investment executive." *Ah, here comes Phyllis with my drink.*

"Which one are you dating?"

"Both, technically, though it's physically impossible to date someone who is always halfway around the world. And I don't really count my first date with Nick as a real date, since I thought he was my attorney, remember?"

"You're dating two men?"

"Three, if you count this guy Laurel is setting me up with.

Name's Perry Birken or something."

"Perry Bergen, the author?"

"That's the one. How'd you know?" I ask, sipping my alcoholic chocolate mousse.

"He's a pretty well-known geek. Some might even say he's famous. Hey, Phyl, I'll have that martini, after all, hold the chocolate," he calls out. "Erica, do you know what you're getting into?"

"Aye, aye, mate. A man in every computer port." I laugh out loud, raising my now-empty glass and feeling the vodka bypassing my empty stomach and going straight to my head (the chocolate, I suspect, is going straight to my ass). "I'm the new-and-improved Erica. I don't need 500 photos of me and Lowell on Facebook. I don't need to be tied down to anyone. I'm a mover and shaker. I've got big plans."

"Oh?"

"That's right. Me and Jade, Jade and me, we're tight and we're going to revolutionize the Rockit for modern women like us. Me and Jade, that is. Know what I mean, jellybean? Whaddaya think about Dead Sea scroll screens and mirrors and eye shadow and vibrators and good stuff like that? Whaddaya have to say about that, huh?"

"You think I'm a jellybean? Really. What flavour?" he says updating the classic "If you were a tree what kind would you be?" job interview stumper.

He catches me off guard. "Uh, lasagna? But don't try to change the subject. I'm serious."

"I could tell."

If you can't get enough of SMS, you:

(a) need more than basic S&M can provide

(b) probably love getting PMS too

(c) even text-message your friends on the toilet

chapter thirteen

It's official. I've got the alcohol tolerance level *and* bladder of a goldfish. It could be worse: my breasts could be the size of guppies and then where would I be? (Sloane's words, not mine, after I share my inebriated-on-a-single-martini story with her on the phone just before lunch.)

"Phyllis must have put in a double shot of vodka," I say in my defence, staring at my sorry reflection in my desk lamp.

"I'm sure that's it," Sloane says almost too sympathetically, the words rolling off her tongue like she's said them a thousand times before. *I'm sure that's it, Mother* (when a low pressure system brings out Mrs. Walden's uncontrollable spending tendencies at Neiman Marcus the way it does migraines for others). *I'm sure that's it, Wes* (when a big case at work prevents him from getting it up in the bedroom). "But look on the bright side. You didn't pass out this time."

Is she trying to make me feel better? Believe me, I am well aware that my memory didn't fail me this time round. I remember every second—hence my current case of embarrassment. Telling Teddy I had a man in every port? That I was promiscuous? Who the hell did I think I was—Nelly Furtado?

That's a laugh. I can't even tease my hair.

"I wouldn't worry. None of that affects him," Sloane rationalizes.

"Oh crap!"

"Watch the language, Er. You're not one of the boys anymore; you're trying to catch one of them."

"Holy Christ!" I go on shaking my head. "I mentioned the new product ideas—what was I thinking?"

"Language," she sighs. "Now explain this to me: as a product manager, wouldn't he be interested in new product ideas?"

"Not if they involve cosmetics and vibrators."

"I see your predicament. Well, I can't speak for Teddy," Sloane continues, "but I'm all ears. Sounds like a fabulous idea!"

That's what I'm counting on. Deep down, I know this product will appeal to women. But I need hard numbers to get Teddy and Brett to take it seriously. "Actually, I'd love to pick your brain but I've got to dash for a phone meeting with my market research firm."

"Wait! Did you see my email about the forensic accountant?" she asks. I check my inbox.

From: Mrs. S. Schiffer
Subject: Taking Loser Lowell to the cleaners

Why won't she leave well enough alone? I'm starting to suspect that getting me to date Nick White isn't the only way Sloane's living vicariously through me. She's hijacking my divorce. "I didn't get it," I say, instinctively crossing my fingers while I delete her email (everyone knows it makes telling a white lie permissible.). "Our email server must be down."

"I'm sure that's it," she says.

Oh crap. I'm in trouble now.

~~~~~

Excellent. My market research experts are on the case. We're going to connect with today's modern women on the web, on the phone, and in a series of focus groups. We're going to find out what makes them tick and what type of functionality they'd like to see in a smartphone.

I click on my calendar and try to contain my excitement. Oh joy, oh bliss. Five minutes till my first PR status meeting since Dani tried to screw me over. If that's not bad enough, I forgot to bring lunch again so I rummage through my desk drawers. No Mentos. Nothing but pens, paperclips, and paper. I survey my office for leftover snacks and swear I saw the red roses on my credenza tremble in trepidation. *Fear not, innocent creatures*, I assure them telepathically. *I learned my lesson. Hey, I bet Tory has snacks at her desk.*

I'm just about to buzz her when my phone rings. It's Dani. "Hi, Erica?" she says in a scratchy, hoarse voice. "I think I may be coming down with something, so can we meet over the phone? Wouldn't want you to catch anything."

"That's thoughtful, thanks," I reply, rolling my eyes. She's been avoiding me even more since I foiled her coup d'état. Whatever. I've got more things on my plate than work hours in the day. "Sure. Let's keep it brief. I need you to review all the customer case studies we've done in the past eighteen months and pull any that profile women. Please email them to me by first thing tomorrow."

"Anything I should know about?" she says with a sad attempt at a cough.

"Not really. You just feel better, okay?" I say before hanging up and lunging toward the door, hungry as all hell. I'm not even halfway down the hall when I see Teddy walking out of Brett's office. He wouldn't have told Brett about the new product ideas, would he have? Of course not. Two straight men talking about makeup and vibrators. Very uncool. Besides, my secrets are always safe with Teddy. He's a human vault.

"Hi," he says, walking up to me. "Up for some lasagna? Ma sent enough for two."

"You must have an invisible halo," I tell him as I link my arm through his and head toward the company lunchroom. It's a shoebox of a kitchen with a flurry of activity inside. People retrieving lunch bags from the fridge, grabbing cups of coffee, putting dishes in the dishwasher, but they just come and go.

"Good to get you out of your office for once. Ever dined here before?" he says as he hands me my plate, covered in bubbling mozzarella.

I cut my cheesy lasagna into about a dozen good-sized pieces and shake my head for emphasis. He knows I rarely leave my desk at lunch—everyone knows. The only time I'm out at lunch is if I have a meeting or industry luncheon, which coincidentally has always fallen on a Wednesday.

Ah yes, Lunch Sex on Wednesdays: I remember it well. Great concept, liar of a lover—in the end, a fatal combination. These days, I don't have sex (plastic partners don't count—they can't vote) on Wednesday or any other day. The bright side is that I can eat as much lasagna as I want. I mean, who cares what you look like naked when you're lying next to a quivering cactus? "Tell your mom I say thanks."

"Tell her yourself. She's coming over for dinner on Friday. You could join us."

"No, I couldn't."

"You wouldn't be intruding, honest. Ma really likes you."

"I really like her, too. But I can't. Not this Friday."

"Big date with soap-opera-name rich guy?"

"No, still overseas. But I told Nick I'd go to the ballgame with him. The Red Sox are in town."

"Lucky duck. Hey, how about you and Ma have dinner and I go out with Nick?"

"That's a good one."

"Seriously. I haven't been to a game in over a year. Besides, Nick's not exactly your type."

"Whaddaya mean, not my type?"

"He's the opposite of Lowell."

"That automatically makes him my type," I respond matter-of-factly.

"Funny. But I still think I should go in your place."

I'm just about to ask Teddy if he went to Fenway Park to see the Sox play last time he was in Boston when I hear a brouhaha heading our way.

"He's taking you to Dove Supper Club tonight?" a woman's voice shrieks. "What are you going to wear?"

"You and Carlton?!" exclaims another, their voices getting nearer and nearer. "Omigod, Dani!"

"Girls, let's not get too excited." It's the duchess addressing her royal attendants, Paige from HR and Ruth from Accounting, without a single scratch in her voice. "It's just a first date," she coos, oblivious to the fact that anyone might be listening in—oblivious to the possibility that *I* could be listening in—until her designer heels click-clack onto the grey tile floor in the lunchroom and her eyes meet mine.

"Thank heavens you're feeling better," I say as sweet as cotton candy (I wish Sloane could hear me) and stand up from my chair. "We wouldn't want Carlton to catch anything, would we, girls? As for what to wear, Valentino has worked well for me. And I recommend the pistachio-crusted rack of lamb at Dove—though I have to admit the Tasmanian ocean trout also looked quite nice. Oh, and do give Henri my regards. He'll remember me from the VIP Room with Reynolds Ault. Now if you'll excuse me," I say, picking up my plate, "I'm going back to my cave."

"Too pretentious?" I ask Teddy once we're clear of the still, silent lunchroom.

"Too funny is more like it." He smiles as we enter my office. "I've never seen Dani speechless."

My Rockit rings. I glance at an unfamiliar number on my LCD display. Wrong number. I'll let it go to voice mail and finish my meal in peace. "You didn't tell anyone about those product development ideas from last night per chance, did you?"

"Sorry," he says his dark eyebrows arching high over his glasses. "I couldn't really make out your words. You were kind of mumbling. We can talk now, if you want."

"Not yet. I'm still fleshing out some concepts," I reply, relieved as all hell, as my phone rings again. Same unfamiliar number. Could be Mom calling from one of her friends' places. "Hello?"

"Hi, Erica? Erica Swift?" Instead of my mom, I'm greeted by a monotone male voice that screams telemarketer. Wonder what they're selling now?

"Yes, this is Erica, Erica Swift. Please take me off your list. I'm not interested in anything you have to sell. I am interested, however, in getting your phone number so I can harass you while you're trying to enjoy lunch." I smile at Teddy and raise my left arm, making a fist and flexing my muscle. I'm not taking crap from anyone today!

"But um—" He pauses. "Laurel Jenkins gave me your number. My name is, um, Perry Bergen."

Quickly I straighten my arm and reposition it graciously on my desk. "Oh, Perry. Sorry, I thought you were a telemarketer."

Teddy looks at me, eyes popped out and mouthing Perry's name.

"Okay, um, I know it's short notice and, um, you probably have plans so I understand if you can't but, um, I thought it might be nice to, well, um, okay…" Long pause. "Would you like to go, um, for dinner tonight?"

Wow. It takes this guy eight years to get a sentence out but once he does, he moves fast. Dinner's only six hours away. At this rate, we'll be married with two kids by next week.

"I'd love to, Perry," I respond, making funny faces to Teddy as he shakes his head, smirking.

"Um, that's wonderful. I was, um, thinking we could go to my friend's new restaurant."

"Sure."

"Okay, then. So, um, can I pick you up at seven?"

"Can we make it 7:30? I have to change," I say, deciding on my new jeans and sleeveless black silk mock turtleneck.

"Oh right, um, I almost forgot. The restaurant has, um, a dress code."

I throw the thought of wearing my new jeans out the window. Better find out where we're going.

"Dove Supper Club," Perry says. "It's, um, supposed to be quite good."

I look in the mirror, thinking about Nick. Wishing my date with him was tonight, not on Friday. Wondering what he'd do if he saw me right now. Everything's working in my favour: my undersized La Perla push-up bra (borrowed), Pink Tartan brown ruffle wrap dress (ditto) exposing mega cleavage (all mine), strappy Gucci high-heel sandals (also borrowed), hair ironed pin-straight (mine except for a few overpriced highlights here and there), a bit of eye makeup, bonbon lip stain, and a few dabs of Marc Jacobs Perfume. I have to admit, I'm quite the dish. I just wish dinner was with Nick.

Oh well, Friday will be here before I know it. In the meantime, I must say I'm getting rather proficient at dressing for a date. I'm ready to go and it's only 7:15. I study my face in the mirror, examining the cinnamon-colored eye shadow in my lid creases. Oh crap. The right side extends an eighth of an inch lower than the left. If I were Sloane, I'd fix it in a second. But I'm me so I decide it best to leave well enough alone. The last time I attempted to even out my eye shadow was for our high school prom and it was a disaster. Just when I thought I fixed the bad eye, the good one needed help. Imagine playing ping-pong on your face, bouncing back and forth with a foam paddle covered in blue shadow. If not for Sloane, a nearby ladies room, and my full bosom, I would have been confused with Todd Garvey, our school's class clown. Anyhow, the experience was enough to swear me off eye shadow until just recently, and to remind me how fortunate I am not to be a guy—I'd have no sideburns left.

No, just leave the creases alone, I decide, raising my stare to the brow bone area. I applied the frosted fawn eye shadow brilliantly. If only I had plucked my brows before shadowing. Oh well, I'm not about to inflict pain on myself minutes before my date arrives and then have to redo my makeup. Besides, it's not as if me or my eyes are going to be under a microscope. Guys never notice stuff like that.

I eye my laptop lying comfortably on my bed, waiting for me to return home and continue working on my top-secret Rockit research (codenamed Operation Ovary or O^2 for short). Working from bed sure beats slaving away at a desk, though I have to say it would be even better if I had a lap desk. I mean, my legs aren't so level and to be honest, I'm paranoid the heat could cause leg cancer some day.

A minute later I open my door to a bouquet of lavender roses and an extremely good-looking guy reminiscent of Robert Redford's Hubbell in *The Way We Were*. Short blond hair with a side part. Starry blue eyes. Fair skin. Strong jaw line. Short, even sideburns (I wonder if he does them himself?). Light grey pinstriped suit. Too bad he's not wearing a white naval suit. I love a man in uniform—navy or baseball, it's a turn-on.

"Perry?" I say, shaking his hand firmly, trying to stay strong despite the fact that my knees are weak and my thighs are calling out "Hubbell!"

"Um, hello. These are for you," my golden boy says stiffly. "It's, um, a real pleasure to finally, um, meet you. Laurel has, um, said wonderful things about you. Um, I hear you're a marketing whiz and a genuinely, um, nice person."

Hold your horses, Hubbell. You had me at um, hello.

Mental note: Loosen him up with a few drinks but no more.
Don't want him to pull a Hubbell and pass out after making love.

"They're beautiful. Thank you," I say, wondering what the hell lavender means—hoping it's closer to red than white on the passion scale.

Downstairs, a black stretch limousine awaits us. Déjà vu. If I didn't know any better, I'd swear I was going to my high school prom. To be sure, I retrieve the compact mirror from my brown beaded evening bag and double-check my eye shadow. Perry has pulled out all the stops. Inside the limo there's champagne, foie gras, and classical music playing. Man, this guy goes all out, I think, sipping bubbly and smiling at Perry. He's not touching his champagne and he needs it more than me.

"A toast," I say, raising my glass. "To a memorable night."

We enter the restaurant through the elegant, frosted glass double doors. Within seconds, Henri escorts us immediately back to the VIP Room, fawning over Perry—telling him what an honour it is to finally meet the lifelong best friend of his boss, the proprietor of Dove Supper Club. I decide not to outwardly acknowledge Henri and give a simple nod. Thankfully, he doesn't make out like we've met before. He's trained to be discreet, though I'm not sure I appreciated the big wink he gave me. I mean, it's not as if I work for an escort service or something.

Henri brings us to the same table Ren and I had for our first date. Coincidence? Either that or this table is reserved for VIPs on first dates. (I admit it's unlikely but it probably happens more often than one might think.) In any case, it's a romantic, candle-lit, window-side table overlooking a quaint cobblestone courtyard and garden and it's just as nice the second time round.

Perry has buried himself in his menu so I do the same, using mine as a shield as I scour the room looking for Dani. She's nowhere to be seen but coming our way is another somewhat familiar face.

"Hi there," I say, putting down my menu, observing a taut, even more plastic-like Kendra than normal. "Good to see you. How's Marc?"

"He lost twenty pounds," she says, the skin beyond her lips barely moving. "Training for a marathon." She stops and focuses keenly on Perry.

"Oh, I'm sorry," I say. "Perry Bergen, this is Kendra Canard. Kendra is a good friend of a friend and my landlord. Likewise, Perry is a good friend of another friend of mine, not to mention a successful book author." Kendra must also see the Hubbell resemblance because she's still looking at him quite attentively. "Would you like to join us?" I ask to be polite.

"Heavens, no," she says in her posh country-club voice. "I have to run along. Marc's waiting for me. Ta-ta!"

"She seemed, um, nice," Perry says earnestly.

"She did, didn't she?" (I wonder what's up with that?) Changing the subject I ask what he's in the mood for, secretly hoping he says sex. I'm ready to bolt for the limo.

"The, um, pistachio-crusted rack of lamb looks good."

"Oh, it's excellent," I reply without thinking. "That's what one of my colleagues told me, anyway. I think I'll have that, too. So, Perry, tell me about your book. I hear it's a best-seller."

Ten long minutes and five glasses of water later, both my head and bladder are about to explode. Perry may be easy to look at but listening to him is torture. Let's just say he makes Lowell's stories about the software challenges facing hospitals sound like John Grisham thrillers. I'm sure his computer books are excellent. He's just not great at communicating, um, verbally.

Luckily, I know how to handle matters like these like a pro. I've been zoning out since I was ten and pitching Little League. I'd focus on the batter and pretend I was in one of those soundproof TV game show chambers. I couldn't hear the hecklers in the stands trying to prevent me from throwing strikes. I had no idea if the other teams were cheering for their batters or trying to rattle me— and I didn't care. I was untouchable.

Next to learning how to throw a killer curveball, zoning out was the best thing Dad taught me on the ball field. In hindsight, though, zoning out has proven far more useful—I practised the technique with Lowell for years and tonight, Perry gets to gab as much as he wants to a seemingly captive, smiling audience. It's a win-win for everyone. I focus on Perry's mouth, thinking he would have made a great actor during the silent film era. Alas, it looks like he's about to wrap up the story (I've developed a great sense of timing over the years)—I better tune in to this regularly scheduled program.

"And it's, um, even become part of the curriculum at some, um, technical colleges."

"Good for you. Educating our young people is no easy task," I reply as our sommelier pours a dark red wine into Perry's glass and waits for him to pull a Frederick.

"I'm sure it's, um, fine," he says, dismissing him without the expected swish, sniff, and swig. Bravo! I knew there was more to this guy than his pretty-boy looks, though I have to be honest: getting it on with a Hubbell-double is enough for me at this point in my life.

As much as I'd still love to bolt to the limo, the only place I can even think about bolting to right now is the ladies' room.

From: Mrs. S. Schiffer
Subject: Eyebrows—URGENT!

I make the mistake of checking my email in the powder room—not because I am expecting any great Hemingway of an email but simply out of habit. It's become a sickness, like alcoholism. I have become a multitasking junkie—I can't help myself. I check email in between (and often during) meetings. In the car. On the toilet. If I could check my email in the shower I would. The funny thing is, I don't think I'm alone.

Mental note: Talk to Jade about a waterproof Rockit.

Sad, isn't it? I've got a gorgeous hunk of a Hubbell waiting to dote on me and all I can think about is reading an email from my best friend on the john.

You know better than to go on a date with a Bert-caliber unibrow. Who is Perry and why haven't I been debriefed? P.S. I know you are getting this email.

Kendra—that spying little piece of plastic! I'll get back at her one day (translation: when my lease is up) though it probably serves me right for being too connected too often. I hold my breath, close my eyes (peeking only once), and—for the first time in two years, no, for the first time ever—turn off my smartphone. Feeling liberated knowing no one can reach me, I strut my sexy stuff back to Perry, suddenly exhilarated.

If you know about scalability, you:

(a) know the score at Weight Watchers

(b) could have written Beethoven's *Fifth*

(c) know the rate at which a fish swims has nothing to do with its scales

(d) know when a salesman is trying to scam you into buying a new computer instead of just adding memory

chapter fourteen

There's nothing like a horse-drawn carriage for eliminating any chance of having Limo Sex. I'm sure Perry had the noblest of intentions when he hired Ricardo and PrettyGirl Bess to take us on a romantic ride home. It's a lovely open white buggy with cushy red velvet bench seating, but to be frank I had a completely different type of ride in mind (and the only animals it involved were me and Perry).

For what I had in mind, even my dad's beloved 1979 blue wood-panelled Pontiac LeMans station wagon would have been better. It's a rusty eyesore of a jalopy to be sure (it still sits in the garage; Dad could never part with it, and now that he's gone neither can Mom), but it has tons of room to sprawl out in back.

As kids, Jack and I would always end up lying there during the long drives to Aunt Ida's (who wore seatbelts back then?), waving and making peace signs to cars behind us. Three decades later I can tell you our beloved old LeMans may have guzzled gas, but it never passed it like PrettyGirl. Whoa, Bessie!

Neither Perry nor I have said a word so far the whole smelly ride. My libido has all but disappeared. Actually, I'm feeling a bit queasy (I've never witnessed a horse poop so much in my life; PrettyGirl didn't even stop to catch her breath) so I sit back on the bolstered red bench and for the first time all day, truly relax. It's a radiant night. The sky is so clear I can actually see stars overhead. The soft breeze grazes my face as we trot along the cobblestone streets in the old part of town and slowly I start to feel better.

As if on cue, Ricardo clears his throat and starts serenading "Moon River" while Perry wraps his arm around me with a serious, protective look on his face. I don't know why I didn't see it earlier. He looks more like George Peppard than Robert Redford, which is very apropos. To make matters even more fantastic, I feel young and carefree like Holly Golightly—without the dark hair, rhinestone tiara, and misleadingly glamorous cigarette holder, of course. Almost everything is perfect. Perry hasn't yet presented me with a sterling silver telephone dialer (the fact that Tiffany's doesn't make them anymore is not the point; I'm being nostalgic) but apparently he did arrange for a photographer to take our picture as we passed by City Hall. What an original idea for a memento!

We pull up to my building, a one-time glass factory built around 1915, and Perry helps me out of the carriage. "I had a nice time tonight. Thank you," I say, leaning into his cheek. Mmm. His soft, freshly shaved skin smells nice. Too nice to let him leave. "Can I get you a nightcap?" (I've always fantasized about saying that line; it's so 1960s Rat Pack.)

"Um, okay." Perry shrugs and waves Ricardo free to go. I take his hand and lead him up the marble steps in front of the ornate neo-Gothic building. This is a good sign, my brain says, arousing my dormant libido with a gentle surge and putting First Date Sex back on the menu. He holds the door open (another good sign; Lowell always gave me such grief over that) and we walk toward the steel freight elevator.

Laurel was right. Perry is a perfect gentleman, just like Dad. Mom would approve—so would Sloane, I bet—that is, had Perry been her find. I think about all the care Perry put into the date: the roses, limo, Dove VIP Room, horse-drawn carriage ride, romantic serenade, and photo—and he only had six hours to pull it all together. (In all the years I was with Lowell, he never did any of that, not even once. What did I see in him again?)

"I can't wait to see the photo," I say, beaming as we gain altitude in the elevator. "Arranging for that photographer by City Hall that was so thoughtful. Thank you."

"That, um, who?" Perry responds with so much humility I could press the emergency stop button and kiss him all over. (Elevator Sex seems a fair trade for missing out on the limo.)

"The photographer at City Hall, silly," I say flirtatiously, twirling my hair with my finger.

"I didn't, um, hire him. I thought he was, um, a horse photographer. PrettyGirl Bess and Ricardo are, um, pretty famous."

I guess it's possible, I think as we enter my apartment and I move my attention to more pressing matters—namely me pressing up against Perry. "Want the fifty-cent tour?" I ask, reclaiming his hand without waiting for an answer.

"This is the living slash dining room slash kitchen. Very urban professional," I say, making a speedy beeline down the hall. "Bathroom's on the left if you need it. And our final destination—the bedroom." I glance around the room, relieved to see I didn't leave any bras or panties crumpled on the floor. "Perry," I say, pulling him onto my bed. "I'm really glad you're here."

"So am I," he says, excitedly reaching across the bed. "Is this your laptop? You should really upgrade it. Can I check a few things for you?"

"What?" I say, exasperated, giving my apparently archaic laptop the evil eye. I could kick myself for leaving it out but how was I supposed to know it would be my rival in the bedroom? All I can say is, it figures. One way or another, modern technology's going to be the death of me.

As Perry fiddles with my system (take your mind out of the gutter; he is literally fiddling with my laptop settings), I stretch out on the bed and stare into the cloud-white ceiling. My mind keeps going back to that horse photographer. I don't get it: some *National Geographic* photographer coincidentally happens upon the one and only horse prancing through the city late on a Wednesday night? What are the odds? It doesn't add up, the Sherlock Holmes in me says. If he was a horse photographer, why was he focusing on us and not PrettyGirl?

Then it dawns on me: Sloane. Of course! Sadly, it makes perfect sense. First Kendra gives Perry the once-over. Next comes the email from Sloane. And now the photo. The girl's absolutely out of control.

"You should go LTE, I dunno," Perry says.

"LT-what?"

"Long story. It's a next-generation broadband wireless. It's faster and has a greater range than your existing wireless network—miles, not feet. And you can still connect all kinds of devices to it—gaming systems, digital cameras, security cameras, you name it," he explains without a single, solitary "um."

Security cameras? "Is it easy to install?"

"For someone like, um, you? I bet you, um, could do it with your, um, eyes closed."

~~~~~

That's the last time I go out on a school night. I'm wiped and have no plans to get dressed till at least noon. "Hey, Tory," I say into my phone receiver. "I'm working from home today if anyone's looking for me."

"Only Dani so far," she says. "She's cornered me three times since I got here."

What the hell does she want now? It's not even 8:30. "Sorry, Tor. I'll call her and get her off your back. Anyone else—tell them to text or email me—I'll be online all day."

I hang up and give my laptop yet another dirty look. I'm still sore about last night. Perry was supposed to be all over me, not my crappy laptop. Maybe if I wrap myself in wires and glue a keyboard to my chest next time, he'll try to cop a feel. All I got was a good-night kiss on the cheek. That, and a complimentary technical audit of my wireless network. Some girls have all the luck. Speaking of which, of the sixty-nine emails I've received this morning, five are from Dani.

> From: Danielle Carou
> Subject: Burying the hatchet
> I feel horrible about what happened. How about lunch?

Shocked, I look behind me as if she's asking someone else in the room.

> From: Danielle Carou
> Subject: Lunch
> How about the Blue Ruby at noon? My treat! Call me!

Hmm, I do recall liking the taro-root chips but something's not kosher here and I don't mean the chips.

```
From: Danielle Carou
Subject: Lunch
Saw you at the Dove looking fab! Was that
Reynolds Ault? I heard he was older.
```

Well whaddaya know? Dani was at the Dove after all. It must be killing her that I seem to have a more fabulous social life than her.

```
From: Danielle Carou
Subject: Lunch
I'll make reservations—you don't have to
worry about a thing!
```

She's as transparent as her Voss bottled water.

```
From: Danielle Carou
Subject: Lunch, etc.
Best time for you?
```

God help me. She's either finally afraid for her job or she wants to be my friend now that she finally sees me for the fabulous person I seem to be. Either way, I'm not going for lunch. I'm not going for fabulous. I'm not going anywhere.

```
Thanks but no can do. Not in today.
```

A couple hours and a couple hundred incoming emails later (everyone except the Pope wants a piece of my marketing budget), I get a call from Laurel.

"So? How did you like Perry?"

"He's good looking all right. But I think he's just not into me."

"Why would you say that?"

"Whaddaya call a man who spends ninety minutes in your bed all over your laptop but doesn't give you so much as a handshake?"

"Old fashioned? Shy?"

"Come on."

"Did you come on to him or do anything overly suggestive?"

"What are you suggesting?"

"I'm only asking. Perry only looks like a Casanova. In reality, he has a lot more experience with computers than he does with women. When he's out of his comfort zone, he trips over his words and says 'um' a lot."

Does he ever.

"But he said you guys had a great conversation over dinner. Anyhow, I have a feeling he'll ask you out again. When he does, as horribly sexist as this sounds, do yourself a favour. Let him be the man."

That was my ultimate goal, I think, but I decide to keep it to myself.

"I've got to run," Laurel continues. "I'm meeting Aunt May for lunch, but keep me posted!"

"Good luck," I say and look at my watch. It's just past noon, I'm still in my pajamas and I'm feeling a bit grungy and parched. A quick shower should fix both my problems nicely. I'll just drink from the shower to save time.

I've barely got one foot out of my car the next day when I hear the dreaded voice call my name from across the parking lot. "So are we on for lunch?"

I turn into the rising sun. "Sorry, Dani, I've got to pull an all-luncher at my desk. Another time perhaps." *When ducks learn to water ski*, my inner voice says, as I carry my gear up to my office three steps ahead of Dani and the click-clack of her Jimmy Choos.

~~~~~

I've just spent all afternoon with my nose in a half-inch-thick stack of customer case studies analyzing how women are using their Rockits.

Jackie from Montreal says: "I couldn't juggle work and home without my Rockit. I pick up the kids from school, do the grocery shopping online, coordinate our social plans, and still manage to meet my article deadlines!"

Rose from Cincinnati says, "Thanks to my Rockit, I can temporarily relocate my consulting practice anywhere—even my son's baseball field. Who says you can't have it all?"

Maris the travelling massage therapist from Houston says, "Getting a Rockit was the best business decision I made all year. I can email my clients between appointments. I also love the GPS voice-guided tours—they save me time and haven't steered me wrong yet!"

All the studies confirm my suspicions: most women see smartphones differently than men. Hey, I'm not pretending to be Gloria Steinem. I'm the first to admit technology is gender-neutral (except for maybe a voice-activated toilet seat); it's how we use the technology that differs.

Most of the men I know have to have the latest tech toys on the market. Most women could care less, unless the product speaks to them. It seems that when it comes to technology, we're not only the fairer sex, we're also the more practical and prudent (all bets are off when it comes to shoes, bags, and cosmetics, however). That's my theory, anyway. Pretty soon, I'll have the market research findings to either back it up or tear it to shreds.

I race home at 6 p.m., wash up and quickly change into my rhinestone-studded tank top and new jeans, and throw my hair into a pony moments before I hear the buzzer.

"Hey, beautiful," Nick says through the intercom system as I buzz him up.

I dab on some last-minute lip stain and study myself in the hall mirror. Damn, I keep forgetting to pluck. No worries, I'll just throw on a baseball cap and keep my not-ready-for-prime-time brows under wraps.

A minute later Nick's at my door wearing jeans and his Red Sox jersey, handing me a bouquet of peanut and Cracker Jack bags, whistling "Take Me Out to the Ballgame." I can't help but laugh.

"For you, gorgeous," he says, pulling me close and choreographing his lips under the brim of my cap so well they could have apprenticed under Bob Fosse. He's a great kisser. Not that I'm a bit surprised—a man like Nick comes with mucho experience. The bouquet drops to the floor and I start lifting his jersey over his head.

"Slow down, hon," he says, smiling. "We've got all night. If we don't get going, we'll miss first pitch. Game's gonna start soon." *Who cares about the first pitch*, I think as Nick pulls away from me and walks to the door. *I'm ready to hit a homer right here.*

"You're gonna love our seats!" he shouts in his uncovered Jeep as we race to the stadium. "Second row—right at third base!"

"Yeah, whatever," I mutter, still hot and bothered despite the fierce cool wind that just swept my favourite ball cap off my head into the busy traffic behind us.

If you're reading about external media:

(a) you know just how invasive the paparazzi can be

(b) you specialize in advertising on billboards, blimps, and bus placards

(c) your computer just told you it has no more room to save the digital photos you took at the nude beach

chapter
fifteen

Nick White undoubtedly deserved to have beer dumped over him at one point or another during his long and illustrious dating career. Tonight wasn't one of those times.

We got to the ballpark with enough time to grab a couple hot dogs and beers (why Nick assumed I liked beer I don't know; I can't stomach the smell) and get to our second-row seats for first pitch. Nick was right—our seats were fantastic. Not even thirty feet from third base, we had a clear view of almost everything: the attempted steals and associated tag-outs at second, the right fielder diving into the stands to catch a stray foul ball, the finicky pitcher shaking off signs from the catcher, even the third baseman spitting onto the artificial grass and adjusting his jock—I was in heaven. We cheered. We did the wave. We talked baseball like the bubble-gum-blowing, dirty-fingernailed Little Leaguers we once were. It reminded me of the times Dad brought Jack and me to games.

"Favourite baseball movie?" I quizzed him.

"*The Natural.*"

"Over *Bull Durham* or *Pride of the Yankees*?" I threw back, more than a bit surprised. I mean, I like Robert Redford as much as the next guy (maybe more, given my Hubbell fixation) but puh-lease. *The Natural* didn't even make me cry. Watching the Lou Gehrig story made me bawl more than chopping onions without swim goggles. Next question: "Favourite slugger?"

"Johnny Damon. Red Sox 2004 World Series homerun hero. You?"

"Reggie 'Mr. October' Jackson—Hel-lo? Ten World Series homers—four of them consecutive at bats. Johnny D. can't touch that. Hey, I have another one for you." I turned to Nick as the ump called the third out in the bottom of the first inning. "If you could induct anyone into the Hall of Fame, who would it be?"

"Anyone?"

"Sky's the limit," I proclaimed. "You can even vote in dead people."

"No-brainer then. Joe Jackson."

"*Shoeless Joe,*" I blurted out. "But he's ineligible."

"You said sky's the limit. Besides no one ever proved he was in on the 1919 World Series fix."

"Seriously?"

"He didn't deserve to be banned from the majors for life. A few of his buddies might have been crooked but not Joe. Not the way he loved the game. He said he was innocent till the day he died. You know, I'm not a big literary guy but I think W.P. Kinsella got it right in his book. Maybe it's time to right the wrong and induct the guy. Hell, it happened almost a century ago. We didn't have televisions or traffic lights back then. We didn't have insulin or microwave ovens. And we certainly didn't have computers and smartphones. Joe's been dead and gone for over fifty years. He has nothing to gain by being inducted to Cooperstown. We do. Inducting Joe could be one of baseball's most redeeming moments."

On cue, Nick and I stood and threw our arms up and down to maintain the momentum of the wave currently rolling through the stadium. As I sat down and watched the wave move on to our left, I deliberated over Nick's closing arguments to the jury.

I remember running to the college bookstore to order Kinsella's novel after seeing Kevin Costner in *Field of Dreams*. The more information I dug up in the library on disgraced Joseph Jefferson Jackson of Greenville, South Carolina, the more I felt for the guy. How could you not? He was an uneducated, simple man (he apparently couldn't even read) who was born with a golden glove. Baseball was all he knew.

His statistics during that infamous series were better than most players: twelve hits, the only home run of the series and no errors in the field. Curiously, however, some said he wasn't playing at the top of his game. Chicago paid him peanuts and his White Sox contract prevented him from signing with another team for more money—which apparently established motive. And then there was the $5,000 in dirty money he tried to give back (rumour has it he was threatened into accepting the loot). In 1921, a jury found him not guilty but the damage was done. In the eyes of the league and the court of public opinion, he cheated baseball. He cheated the fans. He cheated himself.

An image of Shoeless Joe in full vintage White Sox uniform flashed through my head. Only it wasn't Joe at all. It was Lowell. Looking down at the dirt beneath his tattered old cleats. Figures, even in my head, he couldn't look me in the face. "He cheated," I mumbled. "I can't forgive him for cheating."

"What's that, hon?" Nick said, turning to me. "You okay?"

"I need to use the ladies' room," I lied. For one of the first times in my life, there actually wasn't a toilet calling my name—no doubt because I hadn't touched my stinky beer—but my head was starting to pound and I was feeling like a sardine in those stands. I attempted to squeeze through the sliver of air between Nick's knees and the seat in front and hand him my untouched cup of beer, oblivious to the wave making its faithful return to our section. Oblivious to the man in front of us waiting to throw back his arms so exuberantly. Oblivious to the chain of events that was about to take place.

"How'd you get in?" I say, peering at Sloane from under my covers. The pounding in my head has subsided to a dull but constant pitter-patter over my eyes. I've been in bed for the past twenty-four hours, sleeping for most of them, though it hasn't been easy given that both my landline and Rockit have been ringing off the hook. "I guess you heard about Nick," I say, clueing in to the cause of Sloane's apparent anger.

"Heard about Nick? That's a good one, Erica. I heard and I saw—just like everyone else who picked up the morning newspaper." She's waving a folded piece of newsprint barely slow enough for me to catch a fuzzy glimpse of a picture of me and Nick at the baseball game.

"Holy Christ," I say, wiping the crusty crystals out of the corners of my eyes, readjusting my focus on the front-page photo. "I mean, holy cow."

"No, I believe you had it right the first time," Sloane begins to rant, throwing the paper on my bed. "Holy mother of Jesus! After all our hard work! What were you thinking?"

I wasn't thinking Nick and I were front-page news, that's for sure. (Catherine Zeta-Jones and Michael Douglas didn't even get this much attention when they were spotted in town last year.) But there I am, in living colour under the paper's masthead, pouring beer over Nick. Or so it looks. There's no trace of the man with the flying arms. No cutline explaining it was the accidental by-product of a wave gone wrong. Just a large, bold headline: Red Sox Get Dumped 8–3.

"Whoops," I say with a nervous laugh, praying my already-sore head doesn't get bopped by Sloane's enormous Kate Spade satchel. It's quite a cute caption, actually. I can see why the news desk went with it.

"I hardly see the humour. But since both you and Nick seem to find it entertaining and the paper won't make it to Ren in Europe, I suppose no harm has been done. But seriously, Er, are you okay? Nick said you were acting odd."

"I don't know. I think this whole divorce is starting to get to me."

"Don't worry. I promise everything will work out, okay?" Sloane sits on the bed beside me and tucks my hair behind my ears as if I'm Molli or Maddi and I just got a needle at the pediatrician's.

I give her a little nod from my flattened down pillow. "All we need to do now," she says, reaching for her shiny red patent bag to retrieve matching red enamel tweezers, "is frame your eyes as well as the Mona Lisa."

As she plucks each horribly offensive hair from my on-again throbbing brow, I flinch and remind her about my headache. "Oh puh-lease," she says, "this is nothing next to childbirth." (Talk about taking a browbeating.) Having no experience in that department, I assume she's right and decide to just take it like a man.

After Sloane leaves, it occurs to me that she never said how she got into the loft (I presume she got a key from Undercover Agent Kendra). It also occurs to me that I should probably apologize to Nick again—especially once I hear all the messages he left. Thankfully he doesn't answer his phone so I leave a gracious message, complete with contact information for my drycleaner. De-beering his beloved Sox jersey is the least I can do.

I listen to all my other messages and hang-up clicks on my voice mail. Aside from Sloane, Mom called to say the photographer got my better side (she waits till now to tell me I have a bad side?) and that Dad would be proud to know I still share his love of the game.

There's a message from Teddy, joking about how Nick would have been better off taking him to the game—and a second more serious message asking if everything is okay. I listen to a message from Laurel inviting me to tea—her treat. Not to be excluded, Dani called to offer her "sisterly support" and lambaste "the disturbingly good-looking creep who crossed you at the game." Finally there's an innocuous message from Perry that mentions nothing about the game or the paper. Just an invitation to brunch. Lord, he really must not get out much, which, right about now, makes him the only person on earth I want to call back.

I can't remember when I've had a more productive Sunday afternoon. After Perry and I went out for brunch, he helped me install my wireless security cameras and test out access from my laptop. He even shared his gazpacho recipe, after I told him that as inexperienced as I was in technology, that paled in comparison to my failings as a cook. An afternoon with Perry and it turns out I'm not a half bad cook after all. I didn't even need my swim goggles.

Mental note: Remember that cutting onions under cold water prevents the bulbs' sulfuric compounds from reaching your eyes.

The more time I spend with him, the more I realize he's a great guy. Just not for me. The attraction is gone. Feeling mighty accomplished, I get up from the table and inspect the cameras I've installed by the front door and in the living room.

"So I can see if anyone's in the loft when I'm at work?" I ask Perry.

"You can do better than that," he says. "You can connect the system to your Rockit and have remote access to the system. You can monitor the loft wherever you are."

"And if someone breaks in?"

"The motion detector will sound off the alarm and trigger the cameras to record."

"You're the best, Perry. What else can we install today?"

Later that night I get an instant message from Jack.

```
left thai jungle 2 train 4 UN
emerg telecom response unit in italy
meet me there when im done? miss ya
```

He may be my little brother, but I look up to Jack. Always have. He never lets anything or anybody come in his way of doing what he wants and—with the exception of letting his high school buddies in our house for a panty raid—he's always done the right thing.

```
love to croc
can we go 2 gleaning tower of pita?
```

Coincidentally, we both ended up working in the telecom industry—me in marketing, Jack in engineering. But unlike me, he didn't pursue a cushy job close to home. He said he needed to spread his wings. To see the world and help make it better. If there's a disaster (natural or not) happening somewhere in the world, chances are Jack will be called in to help implement or restore the communications infrastructure. Darfur. Phuket. Bosnia. The Congo. There's nowhere he won't go. As much as I worry about him, I also wish I could be more like him.

Tory brings my latest delivery of red roses into my office the next morning and places the vase on my credenza. "Does Reynolds have a brother?" she asks. "I could get used to roses every Monday. Trade you for a snow globe?"

"Thanks, Tor," I reply with a chuckle. "I'll keep that in mind. Any luck booking a meeting with Brett and Teddy?"

"Yeah, just got confirmation from Joyce. You're good for four this aft."

I wheel my chair over to my so-called blooms of passion (I've gotten more action from vitamin E hand cream than I have from Ren so far...) and reach for the card.

```
Erica, Absence indeed makes the heart grow
fonder. Returning home Friday. Love to spend
the evening with you. Dinner at the Dove at 8?
                Yours, Ren
```

What exactly does that mean: spend the evening with you? Are we talking dinner and a kiss on the hand like the last time or does he intend to come up to my loft for a pajama party? And what's with "Yours"? Does Ren use that on everyone or is he really all mine? Asking Sloane would be asking for trouble so I decide to Google another expert on etiquette.

```
"Emily Post" and "Letter Etiquette"
```

Here we are: Chapter XXVII, Notes and Shorter Letters from Emily Post's *Etiquette*, copyright 1922. Let's see:

```
The Complimentary Close
Close of Personal Notes and Letter
Appropriate for a Man
The Intimate Closing
Not Good Form
Other Endings
```

Cutting to the chase, I scroll down to Appropriate for a Man:

```
"Faithfully" or "Faithfully yours" is a
very good signature for a man in writing to
a woman, or in any uncommercial correspon-
dence, such as a letter to the President of
the United States, a member of the Cabinet,
an Ambassador, a clergyman, etc.
```

Christ, I can't remember the last time I wrote the president, the clergy, *or anyone* something other than an email or text message. Not to say I've ever emailed the president; I'm just making a point. I scroll further down to The Intimate Closing:

```
"Affectionately yours," "Always affection-
ately," "Affectionately," "Devotedly,"
"Lovingly," "Your loving" are in increasing
scale of intimacy. "Lovingly" is much more
intimate than "Affectionately" and so is
"Devotedly." "Sincerely" in formal notes
and "Affectionately" in intimate notes are
the two adverbs most used in the present
```

day, and between these two there is a
blank; in English we have no expression to
fit sentiment more friendly than the first
nor one less intimate than the second.

I feel like I'm being given a lecture by Professor Henry Higgins. (Wake me up when we get to Eliza Doolittle singing "The Rain in Spain Stays Mainly in the Plain.") Nick was right about times having changed since Shoeless Joe's day. These etiquette rules appear to have been written by a stodgy society dinosaur—and she wrote them three years *after* Shoeless went down, poor guy.

Mental note: Sign online petition to get Shoeless Joe inducted into Cooperstown.

I read on:

Other Endings
"Gratefully" is used only when a benefit
has been received, as to a lawyer who has
skillfully handled a case; to a surgeon who
has saved a life dear to you; to a friend
who has been put to unusual trouble to do
you a favour. In an ordinary letter of
thanks, the signature is "Sincerely,"
"Affectionately," "Devotedly"—as the case
may be. The phrases that a man might devise
to close a letter to his betrothed or his
wife are bound only by the limit of his
imagination and do not belong in this, or
any, book.

Hmm, let me think about this for a second. *The phrases that a man might devise to close a letter to his betrothed or his wife are bound only by the limit of his imagination and do not belong in this, or any, book.* "Yours" definitely falls into this category (though to be honest it's not so imaginative). *Well that settles it. Ren and I must be betrothed—or be on our way to becoming betrothed*, I think and chuckle. Sloane will be ecstatic—that is, if and when I eventually decide to share our semi-conclusive happy news.

After a lasagna lunch with Teddy discussing everything outside work from global warming to my loft-warming (nothing too ambitious and no gifts, just a few friends for brunch this Sunday), I return to my office to review the presentation I've prepared for my four o'clock powwow with him, Brett, and Jade. Methodically, I point to third-party analyst projections showing the smartphone category continuing to grow over the next three to five years. I put into context the qualitative findings obtained from our recent market research focus groups, explaining that most women find technology boring, complicated, and intimidating. Next slide: Most women view smartphones more as personal lifestyle accessories than business tools.

I quietly tell my reflection in my shiny desk lamp (as good a rehearsal audience as any) why I am recommending we reallocate 20 percent of my marketing budget to specifically target women. I elaborate on how it will serve as the lead-up to the eventual birth (I'll use a more manly word during our meeting) of a new O^2 Rockit smartphone that connects with women as easily and magically as Oprah. I sit back in my chair and take a deep breath. I'm as ready as I'll ever be. I just hope the boys are as ready for what I'm about to pitch their way.

"Knock knock—herbal tea break!" Dani chirps as she walks into my office carrying a white paper bag and pair of shiny red

Rockit mugs. "I also picked up some yummy blueberry scones as a little treat for us." She smiles, shaking the bag in my direction.

Us? I didn't realize we had become an "us." I quickly sit up and minimize my PowerPoint presentation before the duchess has a chance to snoop and end up being more of a royal pain in the ass than she usually is.

"Since when do you drink tea? I thought you preferred coffee," I say.

"The old Dani loved java," she says. "The new Dani is in detox. I started seeing a naturopathic doctor who has me off caffeine, nicotine, alcohol, and sugar and eating more antioxidants like blueberries. Here have a scone. They're fabulous."

Graciously I shake my head and try not to grin as I think about the deliciously toxic sugar granules militantly counteracting the effect of the wholesome blueberries. "Couldn't possibly. Big lunch," I explain. "But I'll take the tea. I'm late for a meeting and don't have time to make a cup myself. Thanks." Holding my laptop in one arm and my tea in the other, I scoot out of my office and leave Dani behind in my trail of fragrant citrus steam.

If you've hit a dead spot, you:

(a) have stumbled upon a nightclub filled with fifty-year-old computer programmers who still live with their mothers

(b) are likely cursing your cellular provider

(c) are probably using a wooden baseball bat with a hairline crack

(d) should try tilting your pelvis. If that doesn't work, fake it.

chapter
sixteen

I feel like Christopher Columbus without the *Nina*, the *Pinta*, or the *Santa Maria*, let alone a crummy compass. Jade, my O² ally, isn't back from her offsite lunch, Dani just weaseled her way in to sit in on the meeting, and I am totally lost. I have no idea where my presentation is going or how to read these guys. (Dani, I can read perfectly. She's up to something, I just don't know what.)

Normally Brett's head bobs up and down in total harmony with each point I make. Sometimes he even taps his pen on the table to the same beat (who says white men have no rhythm?). But today, I'm coming up empty. There's no bobbing. No pen patter. Nothing. If not for the fact that a few of Brett's stray hairs have caught the draft of the air-conditioning vent overhead, I'd swear he was part of Madame Tussaud's wax collection.

Teddy's not much better. I can usually count on him to throw in an impressive statistic or two to back me up every now and then.

But his mouth hasn't moved a muscle. There he sits silently across the boardroom table, his head tilted slightly to one side as if he's a golden retriever sitting obediently in a college biochemistry class trying to make sense of molecular genetics. It could be worse, I guess. At least he hasn't mistaken the red lectern for a fire hydrant.

I take a step back from the lectern as a precautionary measure (you never know…) and smile at Brett and Teddy as if everything is normal. But my gut's a wreck. Am I boring them to death? Did I miss a slide? Magically grow a third breast? No, perhaps I'm just being overly sensitive and imagining things.

I take a quick glance down at my chest to confirm that I haven't gone circus freak and continue. "To recap, this is a long-term strategy designed to connect with the average woman and significantly grow our market share within this demographic. While creating a new smartphone chassis will involve additional R&D and a product development cycle of up to eighteen months, we can start taking ownership of this emerging category as early as this spring. I am proposing that we initiate a niche marketing campaign to generate hype for the Rockit brand and encourage mainstream women to use our existing smartphones. We call it 'Techs and the City,'" I say with another forced smile, putting aside my cup of tea and wiping my brow.

No reaction. Even Dani is blank. I better spell it out.

"It's a take on *Sex and the City*. The movie, the TV series, the whole sexy shebang, get it?"

Apparently not. Not one of Brett's stray hairs is even moving now. The air conditioning has stopped blowing, which may also explain why it has suddenly got so stuffy in here. If it was solely Brett who didn't get it, I wouldn't be sweating bullets. I mean, he signs my paycheques and all but he's basically a big kid and a flighty one at that.

Case in point: Brett is a Richard Branson wannabe, who, among other things, occasionally fakes a British accent to woo women and wants to extend the Rockit brand into the space tourism industry just like Branson is doing with Virgin Galactic. Rockit SpaceLine attendants in tight red flame-retardant space suits and helmets with Swarovski crystal bling: I can picture it now. No really, I can—I've seen the artist's rendering. Hey, I'm not saying it's not a good idea, it's just a bit future-forward for me. Then again, I swore off space travel many moons ago after a computer-simulated flight to Mars took my stomach on a ride I won't soon forget. Long story short: I won't be taking advantage of any Rockit space travel staff discounts. That is, if I still have a job after today.

Like the captain of a sinking ship, I'm going down alone. Dani hasn't looked my way since she sat down and started scribbling pages of notes. Jade still hasn't returned and Teddy hasn't come to my rescue, leaving me little choice but to take charge of my own rescue mission.

"By leveraging the almost cult-like popularity of Carrie Bradshaw and friends," I continue, "we will position Rockit smartphones as sexy lifestyle accessories and show how four very different types of women use Rockits to enhance their lives."

"So you're proposing," Brett says, "that we go into the beauty biz?" Dani looks up and raises a brow.

Not the question I was expecting, but okay. Maybe I should slow down. Waaay down. "Not at all," I say, modelling my speech after my first-grade teacher, Mrs. Seaver. "Rockit Wireless is. And will continue to be. A cutting-edge. Wireless technology innovator. I am proposing. That we investigate a long-term strategy. Whereby Rockit partners. With a health and beauty leader. To create a smartphone. That puts everything the modern woman wants. In the palm of her hand."

"Like a mirror?" Teddy asks, to my amazement.

"Don't forget the eye shadow and lip-thing brush," Brett adds, smiling at Dani.

"You mean lipstick," Teddy says. "A lipstick brush."

"That's what I said," Brett argues, catching a smile back from Dani.

"You said lip-thing," replies Teddy.

"Lipstick, lip-thing, same thing, isn't it?" Brett is bickering with Teddy as if I'm not even in the room. As if *Vanity Fair* is interviewing him on the beauty biz. As if he is goddamned Max Factor or someone.

"Gentlemen," I interrupt, trying to stay focused and calm as Jade, thank God, slips into the room and takes a seat between the boys. I can almost hear Mrs. Seaver talking to Teddy and Brett, her words pouring out slower than bottled ketchup. "Our first phase. Is to get women. To use the new smartphones. We are introducing this spring. To show them. How they can make their lives easier. Better. More efficient. If the numbers. Are as good as I project—" I smile "—we will look. For cool ways. To extend Rockit smartphones. And make them. *Even more* meaningful. Relevant. And indispensable to women."

"I see," Brett says, staring me in the eye like a linebacker protecting his manly turf before swivelling his red leather chair to his right. "Dani, would you buy a Rockit if it had an integrated mirror and lip-stuff brush?"

"I'm not sure, Brett. I love my Rockit the way it is," she replies as well as any kiss-ass could. *Not sure?* She'd be all over this phone as fast as it takes rain to fall.

He turns to his left. "Jade, you?"

"Personally no," Jade says.

"But—" I quickly interject.

"I don't wear makeup," Jade finishes my sentence.

"I see," Brett repeats.

"I might, however, be interested in the other accessories, such as the travel toothbrush or vibrator attachments."

What the hell did she just say? We didn't commit to travel

toothbrushes and vibrators. They were points for future consideration. And modern woman or not, I'm not quite prepared to discuss menstrual cramps, tampons, pap smears, yeast infections, and/or sexual preferences, including vibrators, with my boss.

"Come again?" Brett asks to Dani's amusement, not realizing his poor choice of words. "A vibrator?"

"Brett," I jump in. "This is all still very conceptual. We've got a ton of ideas—all of which are very rough and will be put through market research evaluation and product testing once we get to that stage of the game. Right now, we're focused on Phase One."

"Yes. Phase One: Techs and the City," Jade continues, sporting a blush that matches the bright red Rockit paraphernalia around the room.

"Indeed." I nod and give her a sympathetic smile, hoping she doesn't retreat back into her quiet, shy shell. "To generate added excitement and make a splash, we'd like to build Techs and the City around a no-purchase-necessary contest to win one of four all-expenses-paid trips to New York. Prizing will also include new wardrobes, shoes, and our new smartphones, of course—customized and preprogrammed to help the winners enjoy all Manhattan has to offer. To enter, participants simply go to a special Rockit microsite and complete the following sentence: If I had a Rockit smartphone I could...."

Referring back to the screen, I point to Chart A. "Our advertising budget will be divided between select national and regional dailies' Lifestyle sections and a handful of leading women's websites. The best part, Brett, is that it's 100 percent measurable. We'll monitor which publications and sites are pulling the best results. Plus, we can start building a database of prospective new female customers."

"It's a very interesting idea. Very clever, really. A total departure from our typical approach."

"Thank you, Brett," I say, thinking that perhaps this ship isn't going down after all.

"But honestly, I think it might be too out-of-the-box for us. It's risky."

"But it's not, not really," I say optimistically. "As I mentioned earlier, we would still move forward with the Fortune 500 and Small Business campaigns you already approved. Techs and the City is a supplementary campaign. Set in a totally different market."

"Still. It's a risk."

"What about the risk in not connecting with women?"

"We're the market leader by a long shot."

I take a seat across from Brett. "Sure—today. We've got a great install base of business customers who continually upgrade their smartphones. But we've almost saturated the business market. The women's market is emerging. It's going to be huge. If we want Rockit to grow, we need to tap into it before the competition does."

"I'm not saying no," Brett says.

But he is. My ship's about to hit rock bottom and there's nothing I can do.

"I'd just like to give the strategy some more thought. Bounce it around a bit. In the meantime, if you come up with a Plan B, let me know," Brett says dismissively with a tap of his pen before closing his red leather folio.

Plan B? I have no Plan B—and why should I? Plan A is bloody brilliant. How can they not see that? I look at the others around the table. Dani's whispering something to Brett. Jade shrugs and gives me an "oh well, we gave it our best shot" look. To her left, Teddy sits pensively jotting down some notes as if everything is as right as a ninety-degree angle.

What the hell am I doing here? I've given everything but my right arm to this company. And now I've got nothing left—no marriage, no baby Riley, nothing—but Plan B? I'll give Brett a Plan B all right.

Walking back to the lectern I quickly create a new PowerPoint slide on my laptop and walk out of the boardroom without so much as a word or glance back.

```
Plan B:
Hire new marketing director.
I quit.
```

"Pass me another." I motion to Laurel from my plush purple throne. In the forty minutes since we met at Starbucks for an emergency tea therapy session, I've cut off all communication with the rest of the world and had who-knows-how-many butt-plumping chocolate-covered biscotti. But guess what? I don't give a fat rat's ass. I'm steaming more than my fresh mug of lemon tea—which, ouch, just burned the damned skin off the roof of my mouth.

"No can do."

"Screw tough love, Laurel. I *need* another cookie. I think they might be laced with nicotine."

"Then you *need* a smoker's patch or another Starbucks because you've cleaned this one out."

"Come for the ride?" I give my car keys a jingle.

"Very funny." Laurel smiles back, only I'm not joking.

"I'd drive to Tijuana for more. You know if they have Starbucks there?"

"Doesn't everywhere worth going to?" she says sarcastically in a pretentious little voice that could easily pass for Dani's.

It occurs to me that Starbucks is the new McDonalds. The brand du jour—or should I say du generation? Growing up, whenever we took a family vacation, we couldn't stay anywhere that didn't have a McDonalds. It was Dad's benchmark, but it had nothing to do with the food.

McDonalds, he reasoned, did their homework. They wouldn't put their name just anywhere. "Who needs a travel agent when you have Ronald and Grimace working for you?" he would say every time our station wagon rolled off the highway toward some motel that had the good fortune of being situated on the same road as the golden arches. It didn't matter if the motel wasn't as nice as the Holiday Inn we had passed at the last exit—you don't break from tradition.

I wonder if Dad ever compared Starbucks to McDonalds, or what he would think about me reinventing his travel rule. "Hey, I could embark on a Starbucks world tour," I exclaim to Laurel.

I wait for her reaction. She just sips and shakes her head.

"I've got nowhere to be tomorrow morning. No one to check in with. No plans. I could finally see the world—like Jack," I say, mentally diverting my flight path from third-world countries where lattes aren't yet sold on every street corner.

"What about your loft-warming on Sunday?" Laurel says.

"I'll call it a bon voyage party and leave on Monday."

"And your trip to Seattle?"

"The perfect place to start. I'll meet with Head Office and propose that they sponsor me as a travelling goodwill ambassador. Like the guy from Subway."

"You're kidding."

"Well, I doubt I'll lose any weight with all the free biscotti but, hey, why not? After Ren and I leave Bill and Melinda's, I'll ask him to drop me off in Italy. I'll meet Jack and see if biscotti taste any different there. Who knows? I could become a minor celebrity—scooting off to new store openings at a moment's notice and posting the latest coffee talk on YouTube and my biscotti blog."

"Go on. This is fascinating."

"And if I run out of cash, I'll get a paying job as a barista. Or maybe I'll go to Australia and work at a sheep station. I could always lead tours at the Baseball Hall of Fame." In my spare time, I'd lobby to get Shoeless Joe inducted, of course. "For all I know, I could end up working as a toll-booth attendant on the Florida Turnpike."

"You could always work at Best Buy," Laurel says.

"I could shave my head and take Ollie's spot." My mother would be horrified—my Sinéad O'Connor phase all over again.

"You're hired!" she laughs.

"You'll have to hold the job for me until I return from the Outback. I'm gonna be like Rachel Ward in *The Thorn Birds.*"

"Having a forbidden affair with a priest?"

"Only if he looks like Richard Chamberlain." I wink and we burst into laughter.

"Seriously, Erica. What in the world are you going to do?"

"Seriously, Laurel, I have absolutely no idea."

Back at the loft, I change into my stretchy black Lululemon yoga pants and matching top, which very kindly accommodate my bloated belly, and turn on the news. How wonderful is this? Lying on the sofa, I munch on more biscotti (I raided the other location on my drive home) and catch up on my current events.

Truth is, I haven't watched the news in eons. I mean, not the old-fashioned way—who has time? Getting the news off the web is so much more efficient. I get only the news content I want (business news, technology news, entertainment news, and sports news—not necessarily in that order) and I get it up to the minute with the click of my mouse. We've come a long way from the days of Walter Cronkite's "And that's the way it is."

I focus on the Barbie and Ken news anchors on the boob tube. "A fourteen-year-old student died in a school shooting today in the city's east end," Ken says. "With more on the tragedy, Alicia Madden-

Graham reports from the scene." That's the way it is, indeed. No wonder I never watch TV anymore. I turn down the volume and start making a mental list of people I need to tell I've left Rockit.

Mom
Jack
Sloane
Ren
Perry
Nick
Tina
Kendra
My real estate agent

As for Lowell, the less he knows about my life the better. He and his lawyers can deal with Tina. Speaking of which, she said she'd send me an update this week. Better check my email before the company disconnects my phone. I dig my Rockit out from the bottom of my bag and review the emails and text messages missed since setting the phone on vibrate in the coffee shop.

From: Nick White	Subject: Another try?
From: T. Francesco	Subject: Call me
From: Brett Lawrence	Subject: Let's talk
From: RealtorLand	Subject: Open House
From: R.C. Ault	Subject: FWD: Seattle itinerary
From: LabRats.tv	Subject: LTE demystified
From: Haiku, J	Subject: So sorry
From: LoveBurst	Subject: Half-price massage oils

From: T. Francesco	Subject: 911 — Dani
From: Perry Bergen	Subject: Spinach quiche recipe
From: eBay	Subject: eBay Watched Item Ending Soon: Vintage Dior Gown
From: eBay	Subject: eBay Watched Item Ending Soon: NWT Red Sox Jersey
From: T. Francesco	Subject: Where r u?
From: Lowell	Subject: Lunch

The turd's inviting me to lunch now? In all our time together, Lowell never once asked me out for lunch. Quite frankly, it never bothered me before, because I was too busy to leave the office anyway. But now, it bothers me big time. Our marriage is down the toilet and now he wants to wine and dine me? No way. The fact that I am no longer tied to my job and have all the time in the world to go for lunch is totally beside the point. I tried to salvage our marriage. I coordinated—and catered—Lunch Sex on Wednesdays. He did absolutely nothing (other than satisfy his own adulterated sex drive). No lunch dates. No dinner dates. Nothing. Why now? He must want to discuss the divorce in public so I don't make a scene. Evidently he has no idea who he's dealing with. Not only won't I make a scene, I won't meet him for lunch. *Oops!* I smile as I delete his email from my inbox.

Same goes for Brett. Delete. Delete. Delete. *Oops.* As an ex-employee, I owe him no response. Teddy's a different story, only I don't know what to say to him right now. I'm still upset. Besides, I've got a party to plan and there's a story about Kevin Costner on the news.

If you have a FireWire drive, you:

(a) have more speeding tickets than you can count

(b) have a stronger sex drive than a john cruising Hollywood Boulevard

(c) won't freak if your laptop runs out of space without warning

chapter seventeen

Other than blonde hair and a husband who left me, I have little in common with Martha Stewart. Normally, not a big deal. Normally, I wouldn't even make the comparison, but as fate would have it, I find myself in unfamiliar territory, sizing up the splatter of reddish-pink tomato vodka sauce across my exposed cement kitchen ceiling. Normally, the only vodka that can be found within three yards of me is in a chocolate martini.

But there is nothing normal about me planning a house party. I mean, I can throw a fabulous business luncheon or cocktail party for up to 500 people with my eyes closed, as long as it involves co-ordinating a team of maître'd's, chefs, waiters, bartenders, and audio-visual people who actually do the grunt work. But doing the cooking and serving myself? That's just never been part of my professional or matrimonial job description.

I am a culinary virgin. Dining out. Ordering in. Calling a caterer. They all come naturally to me, so don't think my saucy little fingertips aren't dying to pick up the phone. They're on speed-dial standby—under strict instructions not to call the caterer (or my mom or Perry) unless I slip and fall and hit my head on the polished grey concrete counter, at which point they should probably forget the food altogether and dial 9-1-1.

There will be no caterer. I need to be practical and take responsibility for this myself. All of it. I have no income and nothing else to do for the rest of the week other than meet with Tina and go to dinner with Ren on Friday. All in all, that should take maybe six hours, seven if Dove has biscotti on its dessert menu. I've got five whole days till my guests arrive—loads of time to take control of my domestic destiny. Piece of cake. After all, I mastered making gazpacho (a jar of which still sits in my fridge) pretty easily. How tricky could a little brunch be?

More difficult than Martha makes it look, I am quickly discovering (and she doesn't even use store-bought tomato sauce), as I stare up in wonder at the vibrant ribbon of sauce above me. I turn forty-five degrees to my right and, like a puffy cloud on a sunny day, the ribbon turns into a flaming red dragon in a Chinese New Year parade. It's quite beautiful, actually, with a Roma tomato chunk perfectly positioned as an eye.

Another forty-five-degrees-of-a-turn later and the dragon has transformed into a rather disturbing pool of blood on a cement city sidewalk. The only thing that's missing is the chalky white outline of a dead body. If I was an artist, I'd call it "Waste," an upside-down, post-modern interpretation of the effect that gun violence has on our young people. I can't help but lose myself in the sadness of my latest subconscious art installation—I blame the doom-and-gloom TV news.

Then something hits me. No, not another epiphany: a big, fat glob of vodka sauce drops right into my left eye, stinging like a hive of angry bees. To be honest, I've never technically been stung by a bumblebee, honey bee, killer bee (duh), wasp, hornet, yellow jacket, fire ant, or any insect other than mosquitoes. The point I'm making is that my goddamned eye is on fire.

Using the back of my hand, my sleeves, the curve of my shoulders, even my kneecaps, I wipe the evil, burning tomato paste from my eye as if I'm playing a sick game of Twister. Did I mention the sauce was spicy?

"Goddamned stupid sauce!" I reach into the flatware drawer for my trusty swim goggles (they're there for when I chop onions) and prepare for battle. From my post beside the fridge, I look up at the ceiling again.

I can see other globs forming, but now they're blue and look like UN humanitarian food packages ready to drop. Then I remember my goggle lenses are turquoise. Thank goodness. I hate moldy food almost as much as spicy tomato sauce in my eye. I've got to act quickly or things could get ugly—and I'm not talking about the fact that from an aesthetic perspective, tomato sauce droppings will do nothing for the white high-gloss cabinetry. I mean, if I don't get all traces of the sauce off the ceiling (and wherever else it may wind up), Kendra and Marc will kill me.

But how the hell am I going to get the sauce off from down here? Open-mouthed, I gaze up almost nine feet to the ceiling and it hits me again. Right in the kisser. Surprisingly the sauce isn't half bad. A little zesty but not the inferno I expected. I see another glob about to fall and move over to make the catch. Yummy. I'm just about to catch another glob when my buzzer rings.

"Hey, beautiful."

Oh crap. I totally forgot about our truce date: Monday Night Baseball on ESPN. Nick insisted on picking up wings. I said I'd handle the drinks. "No beer," I assured him with a laugh over the phone.

"Sorry I'm late," he says at the door, before kissing me on the lips. "Mmmm, spicy."

"I'm cooking."

"Of course you are," he says, clearly entertained by my underwater eyewear.

Casually, I remove the goggles as if they're regular reading glasses and show him to the sofa. "The game should be starting soon so make yourself comfortable. I'll get plates and drinks," I say, excusing myself to the kitchen.

"I'll help," he offers, following me. Three steps later and I slip on the floor, grabbing onto Nick on the way down.

Kitchen Sex on Monday. Or maybe I should call it ESPN Pre-Game Sex. For all intents and purposes, it could also be called Slippery Floor Sex. Whatever it's called, I'm just thrilled to be having it—and even more thrilled another human being is involved, especially someone with Nick's experience. Without going into detail, I will say that if Nick is half as good in the courtroom as he is in the kitchen, I bet he gets his clients off every time.

"I've considered committing a crime to have him represent me," Sloane whispers on the phone later that night after I tell her my drought has ended.

"What are you talking about?" I say, shocked.

"Shoplifting a mink from Saks. Don't worry. Nothing taboo."

"What about Wes and the kids? And wait—don't you support PETA?"

"I'd turn myself in to Nick," she continues, "wearing the coat and nothing else. We'd do it in his swivel leather desk chair before heading down to police headquarters. We'd swivel for hours," she sighs.

Omigod. I knew she thought Nick was good-looking but one of her fantasies? I don't want to hear any more so I change the subject. "I quit Rockit."

"I don't believe you. You love that place."

"Well, I did. I walked out. Left them high and dry and I have to tell you it was empowering."

"Good for you. Congratulations! I've been waiting for you to leave that silly tech place."

Silly tech place. Loser Lowell. For the record, Sloane's been encouraging me to leave both for a while.

"Now we can allocate more time to our plan."

"About the plan, Sloanie. I think I might quit that, too."

"But we're so close to pulling an Elizabeth Taylor!"

"I know and I'm so grateful for everything you've done for me. I just don't know what I want anymore."

There's nothing but silence coming from the other end of the phone. I can't tell if she's pouting or sleeping. In high school, she used to call me at midnight claiming insomnia. I, of course, would be on the verge of nodding off and would have to pry my eyes and ears open to listen to her rant about the "atrocious fashion crimes" committed by our fellow classmates.

Privately, I wondered if she really liked my baggy sweats or simply overlooked my lack of style—not that her disapproval would have changed my jockette ways. I was curious, though not curious enough (translation: not confident enough) to ask her directly.

Truth is, I couldn't have cared less what I or any other girl wore to class, but listening to Sloane was always so much fun. I didn't see what was so horrific about wearing argyle with polka dots but I laughed my sleepy head off just the same—usually under my pillow so as not to wake the rest of the household.

When Sloane eventually finished her spiel, I'd reciprocate with a hysterical play-by-play of my baseball practice, track meet, or whatever other sporting event I'd participated in that day. Nine times out of ten, I was a human sedative. Never did I actually hear Sloane yawn or snore but I quickly realized that she had simply talked herself to sleep and that the silence at the other end of the phone was my cue to hang up and count sheep.

"Sloanie?"

"I'm here."

"So am I. Always will be, you know. No matter what I decide to do. You can't get rid of me that easily."

My loft has turned into a pigpen. My mom would call it that, anyway, if she popped by unexpectedly. All I can say is I'm lucky she's not one of those mothers whose chief role is minding (translation: controlling) her children—even when they're full grown.

She'd surely frown at me for not cleaning up my "culinary disaster zone," or something like that, and say she raised me better than to live in a sty. The words she would have for me and my kitchen would be cold, but the bucket of bleach and water would be warm and the perfect antidote for the tomato pigment staining the white cabinets.

I would, of course, remain speechless, praying she didn't see the smeared handprints for what they really were: a graphic postmodern portrayal of a soon-to-be-single white female learning how to cook in ways she had never imagined.

Beaming with pride, my attention turns to the ceiling, now almost back to its raw, naked cement self. Without a ladder or very good eyesight, the faint salmon-coloured mark on the ceiling is virtually undetectable. Thank goodness for small miracles.

I dunk my head under the large waterfall showerhead for the second time in twelve hours, examining the reddish sludge under my fingernails. I can feel the hot steam creeping up on my skin only to be blocked from the pores by what can best be described as a tomato plaster of Paris.

As the water begins to dissolve the plaster into a buttery paste, I rub it into my skin like massage oil (Nick came up with the idea last night). Not only is it relaxing but I figure if eating tomato sauce helps reduce the risk of cancer, diabetes, and heart disease, it'll do wonders for my skin, too. Who knows, we could have stumbled onto a new phenomenon. Swift's Roma Tomato Body Lotion could be the best thing for skin since moisturizer with SPF 30.

Mental note: Research benefits of tomato sauce on skin. Start writing business plan.

I can't remember the last time I took a long hot shower. I didn't even know my showerhead had a massage option till a few minutes ago. I close my eyes in the thick fog and feel each pulsating water jet on my back, sore from all the floor action last night.

If I wasn't so environmentally conscious I could stay in here forever. I feel like royalty, disregarding the fact that I just spent forty-five minutes scrubbing the kitchen like Cinderella. Indeed, this has to be the best Tuesday morning I've had in ages. No stress. No meetings. No management. No Dani.

My skin feels soft and supple. I smile at the attractive woman staring at me from the cloudy mirror as we wash our face. She—I mean, *we*—have come a long way: no longer "Unfulfilled, Dependent Wife of Lowell" but a new self-sufficient, modern woman with a healthy new outlook and glow. Actually, I can't quite remember having such a sexy glow as this since, well since ever. All I can say is, it's about time.

I quickly dry off, throw on a pair of army fatigues and a khaki green tee and realize I haven't eaten anything since yesterday afternoon. Not really. There isn't a heck of a lot of sustenance in vodka sauce and Nick and I never got to the wings.

I grab a cold drumstick and water bottle from the fridge and hear the door buzz.

"Hey, beautiful."

Oh no. So Nick's one of those guys who look super cool but are actually really clingy. Either that or I have more sex appeal than I thought possible. "Aren't you supposed to be in court?" I ask as I open the door a minute later.

"Can't something something," I hear him say. His lips have quickly found their way down to my cleavage and his words are getting muffled. Resisting every urge I have to throw him down on the welcome mat outside my front door and take our relationship to kinky new heights, I pull him inside and ask him what's going on.

"I had to request a continuance. Or risk being held in contempt for distracting the jury. Speaking of distractions..." He smiles and looks into my eyes.

Nick's a charmer but I can see how anyone might be distracted by him—I mean, more than usual. He's glowing.

"Darlin', I can't go anywhere besides a Blue Man Group concert," he says, pawing me. "But I love how you're taking things in stride with this camouflage look!"

It's only after I barely escape his grasp and run frantically back to the bathroom mirror that my fears are confirmed: I don't have a sexy glow. I have a goddamned tomato tan just like Nick. Our faces—and entire bodies—have been dyed red with spicy vodka sauce.

Mental note: Scrap Swift's Roma Tomato Body Lotion.
Call sauce manufacturer about adding health warning to label.

"First beer, then tomato sauce. Jell-O wrestling should definitely be next," Nick says devilishly. "Yellow might even neutralize our skin—I'm up for trying if you are."

"Be serious, Nick. We're orange."

"I never joke about Jell-O," he replies, dumping a whole bunch of little white boxes marked Lemon from his brown leather briefcase.

Exasperated, I grab my phone from the coffee table and Google `tomato dye skin removal`.

`Toothpaste can be used to remove hair-colour stains from the skin. Its abrasive qualities safely remove stains without harming the skin.`

Sounds like a great idea for an all-natural exfoliation product but someone else will have to pilot that project. I'm through with the health and beauty biz.

"Toothpaste? No kidding. Well, I'm all for it," Nick says with a cheeky wink. "Mint turns me on."

Shocker. This guy doesn't have an off switch.

No wonder Estée Lauder has never introduced an Eau de Aquafresh fragrance line. I smell like an after-dinner breath mint. The good news is, Nick and I no longer have tomato tans and life can get back to normal, whatever that means.

"Hungry?" Nick asks me as we watch last night's game re-broadcast.

"Starving." Tomato Sauce Sex at least filled our tummies a bit. The only thing we got from Toothpaste Sex on Tuesday was fresh breath and well, you know. "How about leftover wings?" I ask, walking toward the kitchen in my pink terry bathrobe. "For dessert, I'll make Jell-O."

Nick just left. Finally. Don't get me wrong. He's incredible. He's compassionate, intelligent, athletic, and super easy on the eyes.

Lucky for me he's also very accomplished in the bedroom (and the kitchen for that matter) and has given me good reason to change my wireless network password. But he's not my only hobby (okay, so he kind of is—unless you count Cooking 101) and I've got my own life to lead.

Truth is, since Lowell, I've gotten used to spending my spare time on my own, doing what I want (translation: absolutely nothing) when I want to do it. That may sound a little selfish but I'm okay with that.

Now that I'm a lady of leisure, I should probably do my nails or pluck my brows (Sloane would be aghast if she saw my new growth) but decide against it on the grounds that beauty is boring and grab my Rockit instead. I must have a million emails to answer, half of which I will expeditiously redirect to my former employer.

This can't be right: four measly emails? Is everyone on holiday or something? I haven't even been gone a day for Pete's sake. Oh well, more alone time. I scan my inbox again. Not even a single email from Dani. Not that I expected otherwise. She's probably busy positioning herself as next in line to the so-called marketing throne—you know, since the Prada phone folks haven't yet come calling.

From:	Subject:
From: T. Francesco	Subject: CALL ME
From: Joyce Rodriguez	Subject: Meet w/Brett
From: Mikki Swift	Subject: Test 123— Erica, are you there? Can you believe I know how to do email?!!!
From: T. Francesco	Subject: Stella Casey

Huh? Mom is "doing" email? She doesn't even know how to boot up a computer. And what's with Teddy and my neighbour Mrs. Casey? I barely know the woman and she lives next door.

```
        need 2 chat about yr job
  stopped by 2 drop off yr laptop but no answer
     stella casey offered to hold on to it
               till you got home
   reminded me of granny from tweety toons so
            figured safe with her
            r u ok? call me asap  T
```

"Oh hello, dearie," my little-old-lady neighbour says through the crack of the door, opened as far as the multiple stainless steel chains will allow to reveal a slice of her grey bun, wire-rimmed glasses, and a blue old-fashioned schoolteacher's dress. Teddy's right, the only thing she's missing is an umbrella. "You must be wanting your case. Come in, won't you?" As she shuts the door, I wait patiently for her to unhook the chains and wonder how her antiques and mothballs will look in a modern loft. "I'm so glad you stopped by. I'm making a pot of tea," she says, opening the door. "I have freshly baked biscotti, too."

With my twisted arm and dropped jaw, I follow her into the living area, amazed at her taste in modern design. Except for an eighteenth-century marble-topped French commode, Mrs. Casey is the oldest thing in the loft. I slide into one of the two tubular steel and white leather Wassily chairs behind a Noguchi glass coffee table with a stack of knitting magazines and a plaster bust of some guy who looks like Winston Churchill.

I recognize the sleek black leather and walnut sofa across the room as classic Eames—not that I've studied interior design. I grew up lounging on this stuff after school at Sloane's parents' house. Mrs. Walden may not have been a designer but that didn't stop her from referring to furniture by designer. She wouldn't ask you to use a coaster on the chrome and glass side table but on Eileen Gray. You wouldn't be asked to get your shoes off the chaise lounge but the Le Corbusier. Pretentious for sure but who knew I was getting an education?

"That's a fine young man you have calling on you," she says, carrying a large black enamel tray. "Handsome and polite."

I couldn't possibly tell her these qualities, while desirable, were just the tip of Nick's iceberg. I mean, she could be my grandmother. "He's pretty wonderful," I say instead, getting up to help her carry the tray to the table—or, in Waldenese, the Isamu Noguchi.

"Well, he seems very fond of you, too, dearie. Reminds me of my Herman," she says, motioning toward the piece of plaster on the glass table. "It was the way he blushed when he said your name."

"Really?"

I know Nick likes me but I wouldn't say it's more than physical attraction. Mrs. Casey must have been fooled by his tomato tan.

"Oh yes. I know love when I see it," she says, passing me a glass cup and saucer. "Besides, why else would he wait for you in the lobby for almost two hours?"

If you received a false negative:

(a) don't bother trying to sue the manufacturer. Home pregnancy tests are never 100 percent accurate. Save your strength for the baby.

(b) contrary to your email inbox, you didn't win that UK lottery windfall. Make sure someone shows you the money before maxing out your credit cards.

(c) you may have been *Punk'd*. That questionable photo of you and your best friend's husband was doctored and is a total fake.

chapter eighteen

I can't get over it. Tina looks more like a Peter Parker drag queen than ever. Of course, the fact that she cut her hair several inches shorter and is dressed in a mod blue-white-and-red tunic with red tights and go-go boots doesn't help. As I follow her past the labyrinth of hushed cubicles at Schiffer, Smythe & Prusky, it feels like we're on parade. Admittedly, Tina's outfit is as brassy as a tuba and not the least bit lawyerly, but as my glance catches that of a nosy junior law clerk, I can't help but feel a bit protective of my divorce attorney. I mean, she may be a little eccentric, but she didn't have the easiest childhood. And anyone can see the dress has a nice shape and flow to it once you get past the fact that it looks like the Union Jack.

"Everyone's been waiting to meet you since the beer dumping," Tina says, closing the door with her British behind. "Who can blame them? Nick's our most eligible bachelor. The fact that you're Sloane's best friend only adds to your notoriety."

"Me?"

"Nothing to be alarmed about, I assure you. As your attorney, I have divulged nothing. But I have to say, I feel a little like Gloria Allred. Not that I see myself going on CNN. Not really. But the possibility is rather exhilarating, don't you think?"

Notoriety? Gloria Allred? CNN? Is she off her rocker?

"Tina, about my case... Why would Lowell invite me to lunch?"

"Strategy. He's trying to butter you up. On the advice of his callous and conniving attorney, no doubt."

"He can try all he wants. He's not getting the baseball cards."

"Forget about the cards for one sec," Tina says, leaning over her desk and grabbing my hands. "He's worth millions."

"Huh?"

"He's no Warren Buffett but he's done pretty well since that little hospital software company went public last year. We're talking 25,000 vested options that cost him only a buck a share but are now worth somewhere in the neighbourhood of $100. Not too shabby. Add to that the fact that hubby dearest was appointed executive vice president before you split and I'd say we've got quite a case," she says and gives me a double thumbs up.

Executive VP—did I know that? Lowell definitely never mentioned options, investment or otherwise. I do remember him saying we couldn't afford both an engagement ring *and* a house. We couldn't get the honeymoon *and* the stainless steel appliances. Who had options? I went along with whatever he said, casting aside my plans for St. Kitts and ignoring my yen for a diamond that, for the first time in my life, had nothing to do with baseball. I didn't do it for me—I did it for us. I did what Dad used to tell us to do when we went to his company's boring family barbecues and smiled like we were having the time of our lives. I took one "for the team" and I ended up getting taken.

"I just want to be sure," Tina says, "that he was the only party who had sex outside your marriage."

"Before I moved out?"

"Yes. Nick doesn't count."

"That's awfully presumptuous."

"Not when it comes to Nick. Erica, I know this may seem awkward but let's not sweat the small stuff. I want to focus all our efforts on nailing Loaded Loser Lowell and getting what's legally yours. I've already initiated contact with his no-good, immoral troll of an attorney and can tell you you're in good hands. He's afraid of me."

"Oh?"

"Lowell hired my dad."

Outside her office, I trace my steps back to the dark-panelled lobby, glancing down as if I'm Gretel looking for a trail of breadcrumbs, trying hard not to make eye contact with any of the legal busybodies. I make it all the way to the elevator until I look up and see Wes stepping out with Nick.

"Hey there," Wes greets me with a friendly hug and kiss on the cheek. "Sloane tells me the Tina-rator is taking good care of you."

"The Tina-rator—how cute...and yet so appropriate. Hi, Nick," I say, assuming Sloane hasn't been quite as forthcoming about what she thinks of him and his swivel chair. "Nice to see you both, but I've got to run."

"I'll catch up with you soon," I hear Nick say as I press the G and Close Doors buttons. "Whoa," he says, sticking his shiny brown oxford lace-up near the electronic sensor. "Wait up, beautiful." He smiles as the doors reopen and he presses up against me. "The ceiling is mirrored in here. How about some Elevator Sex on Wednesday?" He presses Stop, bringing everything to a standstill except his raging testosterone.

"You think it's funny? The way I categorize sex?"

"I think it's categorically creative," he whispers, fumbling at the button on my trousers. "And kinky."

"What about everyone in your office?"

"Categorically boring."

"Stop!" I pull away from him. "They were all gawking. Like I was a hooker or something. I even saw a jar of tomato sauce at someone's desk."

"You're better than a hooker." He winks. "Pretty Woman has nothing on you."

"Is that supposed to make me feel better?"

"I'm comparing you to Julia Roberts."

"Yeah, picking up johns on Hollywood Boulevard."

A few feet away from me in the small walnut-panelled box, Nick puts his hands on his forehead, covering his furrowed brow. "Of course they were staring, hon. They recognized you from the newspaper. If you must know, they laughed their asses off and teased me for days. Someone even parked a toy dump truck on my desk. But that's as far as it went."

"What about the tomato sauce?"

"Must have been Antonella's Paul Newman shrine. Did you see her Butch Cassidy Bowler hat?" he says, inching his way toward me and trying to unbutton my blouse with his teeth.

"Well, even if you're right, I think we should cool things off for a while. My divorce is getting complicated," I say, sliding out from under him and my half-truth. Things with Nick are moving too fast. I'm in way over my head.

"The only cool thing I need is a shower. But okay, do what you have to do."

"What do you think about sixty being the new forty, dear?"

"I don't." I'm watching Diane Keaton and Jack Nicholson stroll along the beach. Jack bends down to pick up a stone. All of a sudden he freezes as if he's doing some new kind of yoga posture.

"Don't pause it," I whine, turning to my mother sitting beside me in her pink-and-taupe striped flannel pajamas with the all-powerful DVD remote in hand. Needless to say we're having another one of our movie nights and we could pass for inmates of a women's minimum-security prison in Alaska.

"You've seen it a thousand times. How often do we get a chance to talk?"

"You're right, sorry." I almost forgot why I suggested the sleepover. I still have to tell her I quit. "What's up?"

"Do you think I need work?"

"We all need work, Mom. We're human."

"But what about me, dear?"

"You can get a little bossy sometimes, sure, but no one's perfect."

One of her brows arches up, making her eye suddenly look evil. "My face, Erica. Does it need work?"

Oh. I decide to choose my next words more carefully. I study her face though I know it almost as well as I know my own. The faded circular scars by her hairline, droopy eyelids, and matching jowls. She inherited them from me and Jack. Funny how most people think it's the other way around. Everyone's always told me I have my mother's big green eyes, fair skin, and small nose with a slight slope. Similarly, my short forehead and high cheekbones have always been attributed to my dad. But somehow in an ironic twist in the human lifecycle, the tides change. Our parents might give us the face we're born with, but we're the ones who give them the face they live with.

I remember Mom giving us oatmeal baths and head-to-toe chalky pink douses of calamine lotion when we were little, though it never occurred to me that in doing so she basically declared open season on her defenseless thirty-something-year-old flawless skin. She was around the same age I am now and just getting chicken pox. I've never seen anyone covered like a quilt with so many red scabbing blisters. It's amazing she ended up with only a few permanent pockmarks.

Does her face need work? It is a work. A work of art. A work in progress. A living, breathing tribute to everything she is, was, and will be.

"Carla, from my widows' group, got a facelift after her husband died. She swears by her surgeon. He's a regular on the *Today Show* and says sixty is the new forty."

"Yeah, I've heard that, too."

It's a great line but I'm not convinced it's such a great sentiment. What was wrong with the old forty? Or the old sixty, for that matter?

"I think you're beautiful as you are, Mom, but it doesn't matter what I think." I lean into her, kissing one of the pockmark scars on her forehead. "If a nip here, lift there, or tuck wherever is going to make you feel better, you should do it. Not because your friends are doing it, but because it'll make you happy."

Mental flashback: Throwing myself into my work after Dad died.
After all my friends got married. Hardly ever saw Sloane anymore.
I was all alone. Checking my email at a cyber café.
Accidentally elbowing the cute guy at the computer next to me.
We both worked in tech and were engaged within the year.
I got married. Just like my friends.
Everything was beautiful. Until it wasn't.

"You know what else I think?" I say, not so angry at the world as I am at myself. "I never should have got married."

"Speaking of which, how's the divorce, dear?"

As upset as I was to learn of Lowell's buried treasure, it offends Mom even more when I tell her. Not that I expected otherwise. She considered him her second son. He promised her he'd be good to me. He called her Mom. And apparently, I just learned, he also borrowed some money from her, the crook. I tell her everything Tina told me. It's enough to drive me to drink. Instead, I head to the kitchen for a tub of chocolate frozen yogurt and two spoons.

Mom resumes the movie and we begin reciting along: Mom as Diane, Amanda Peet, and Frances McDormand's characters; me as Jack and Keanu's, leaving the two-bit supporting roles for the actual actors. We put on a great show, only occasionally messing up our lines, but always delivering them with conviction. After the credits finish rolling, we take our bows. Neither of us tired, we sit in the kitchen with some tea.

Like two peas in matching pink-and-taupe fuzzy pods, we sip and talk for what seems to be all night. Mom tells me about the computer course she's taking at our city college. About how she is finally cleaning out the garage and giving Dad's things—even the station wagon—to the local men's shelter. About how she is nervous about getting back into a dating scene that has changed dramatically in forty years. She asks me about how it feels to date so many different men at once and how I keep the relationships straight in my mind. She asks about Nick. If he was my "rebound" or "boy-toy" or someone with whom I considered building a future. She asks about Ren. If he is as serious about me as Sloane was about him for me. She asks about Perry. If he is as good-looking in person as he is on the back cover of his book (she had to buy it for school). She asks if I acted too hastily in quitting my job. If I could really see myself working anywhere else. And then just when I think we've said as much in the span of three hours as a pair of auctioneers at Sotheby's, Mom asks if I've seen Teddy since he stopped by her house the other day looking like a lost puppy, wondering where I was. It's one of the best talks we've ever had.

"You're a tough woman to track down, Erica. How are you doing?" Brett asks.

"Much better, thanks," I say, balancing my Rockit between my ear and shoulder as I pour boiling water into a mug in the lunchroom. It feels good to be back at work.

"Better enough to come back?"

I walk out of the staff room with my lemon tea and march into Brett's executive office. "A hundred percent better," I reply as he looks up surprised and fumbles the phone. "By the way, I officially retract my resignation."

"I never officially accepted it." Brett smiles. "I know you've been dealing with a lot of stress and figured you needed some down time. I knew you'd be back eventually. You're a Rockiteer through and through."

"Well then," I say, pulling at my vest. "I should get back to work. By the way, have you seen Teddy? He's usually here by now."

"He's at the Taiwan plant. Back in on Monday."

Monday? But I wanted to see him *today.* Who knows what could happen by Monday? I could be hit by a bus or worse, lose my nerve and not apologize. How could I doubt him? He wasn't abandoning me during my presentation; I see that now. He just didn't get it. I feel horrible. I need to apologize now.

```
teddy, pls 4give my recent behaviour
back @ work n wings on me when u return
safe trip home
```

"What are *you* doing in *my* office?" I ask Dani, typing away at my desk like she belongs there. I can't believe I was stupid enough to let this happen. I haven't even been gone two full workdays and she is trying to take over.

Engaging in a silent staring match, I notice something vaguely different about her—though what it is I just can't say. Her hair appears to come from the same bottle. Teeth still as white and shiny as a double strand of South Sea pearls. Boobs still as pushed up as a pig's nose, maybe a bit more, but no, that's not it. I dunno, maybe these few days away have distanced me—kind of like when you come home from a holiday and the house looks different than you left it even though absolutely nothing has changed except the dust level.

Across the width of the room, I see Dani's reflection next to mine in the window and the difference becomes as plain as day. Instead of wearing her trademark Burberry beige, Dani's clad in black trousers and vest, a white T-shirt and black oxford lace ups. That's my look. Granted her shoes are Gucci but still.

"I'm the acting marketing director," she says.

"You can stop acting," I say, closing my door while resisting the urge to slam it shut. "I *am* the marketing director."

"Brett asked me to step in after you stormed out."

"How convenient for you. You're trying to steal my job. And we both know this isn't the first time."

"Steal your job? Save it is more like it. I'm the one who helped Brett present Techs and the City to the executive board yesterday. I'm the one who helped pitch it. That's what *I* did while you were giving the frontal lobe of your brain a breather the last couple of days."

"You little opportunist! 'I love my Rockit the way it is, Brettipoo.'" I imitate her in my best baby suck-up voice. "Get out of *my* office and stay out of my way."

Fuming, I dial Brett's extension.

"I take it you saw Dani."

"Brett?"

"Erica."

"I was barely out the door."

"I had to put someone in place. I didn't know how long you'd be gone and launch is around the corner. I told her she could be assistant marketing director when you came back."

"You didn't."

As upset as I am with Brett, it's nothing compared to how mad I am at myself. I let this happen. I knew Dani was after my job and I pretty much handed it to her on a silver platter when I walked out that door. *Urrrgh!*

Mental note: Look forward, not back.
There's no use agonizing over what's already happened.

On the positive side, I never knew I could be so productive by bottling up this much anger. I mean, I could give a Coca-Cola plant a run for its money. In the last twenty minutes alone, I've scheduled meetings with our advertising, event planning, and market research agencies and booked a full-body massage, courtesy of Brett and the spa gift certificate he just emailed me. (Who's sucking up now?)

"Erica, I hope we can put our differences behind us. I am sooo thrilled to be co-chairing this campaign with you," Dani says later, back in my office.

Co-chairing? Assisting is not the same thing as co-chairing.

"No disrespect to the Fortune 500 but been there, done that," she goes on. "We can finally reach out to these other people."

If she's not careful I'm going to reach out and choke her. "You mean average women," I interject hastily.

"Not just the average ones. The ones who know the difference between chartreuse and chardonnay and get invited to the Prada sample sale. We mustn't forget anyone."

"Our challenge, or rather one of them," I say, clearing my throat, "is that we have little to no mindshare in the women's market and we need to start building it fast."

"What about hiring the *Sex and the City* girls as spokeswomen?"

"No budget."

"Let's just get Charlotte then," Dani says.

"Most of our money's committed to advertising and contest prizing. We need to cost-effectively create headlines about women and smartphones."

"Stanford?"

"We can't even afford Samantha's horny dog, Gidget."

"Is there anyone we can budget on?"

"Maybe a viewer," I utter despairingly. "Wait! That's it! Our market research pulled some great findings from women—some of the questions even touched on *Sex*."

"I guess. It's a shame about Gidget though. Women love dogs."

Whatever. "I'll have Tory email you the data. Let's regroup tomorrow."

"Sounds good. By the way, you have an apple seed in your teeth."

Praying I haven't again declared war on an ant colony, I seal my lips and roll my tongue across my upper bridge, stopping at a sharp and pointy apple seed sitting comfortably in between my two front teeth. I play with it for a few seconds and gently jimmy it out with my tongue as I watch Dani sashay out of my office. Good riddance.

If you expect a token ring, you:

(a) don't need the ceremony, just a sparkly symbolic gesture

(b) expect a courtesy call when he's going to be late

(c) know a lot of elves and hobbits

(d) might as well be working in Bedrock

chapter nineteen

"Of course you're going out to dinner with Ren," Sloane says as she reaches into my closet for the vintage 1960s Christian Dior black lace cocktail dress I won on eBay. "We're so close to pulling an Elizabeth Taylor your eyes are starting to look violet. I have a feeling something big is going to happen tonight!"

"Who said I want to remarry? I'm in the middle of a divorce that's getting uglier by the minute."

"About that," she says, holding the sleeveless bodice to her chest and looking into the mirror. "I knew he was hiding more than that mother of a lover of his."

"You just wanted more reasons to hate him."

"That's only partly true. I can smell wealth. It's a gift. By the way, how much did this cost? The scalloped hemline is absolutely darling."

"Three hundred. Oh, and that gift of yours? I wouldn't brag about it."

"You got a steal. Original vintage Dior couture can go for thousands. Reese Witherspoon wore one to the Oscars a few years ago.

And why shouldn't I brag? I'm still a lawyer. I'm still a member of the bar."

"She did? You are?" I had no idea Sloane still wanted to practise law. "I thought you were done working," I say, slipping the dress over my head.

"I'm waiting till the twins get a bit older, but then I'm going back. No disrespect to my fellow stay-at-home comrades but I need more. I miss working at the firm. Not fourteen-hour workdays, mind you. I'll have to arrange for a lighter case load that takes into consideration the collective needs of Wes's clients, Wes's children, and Wes's wife—not necessarily in that order," she says, taking the words right out of my mouth.

I'm thrilled to learn Sloane isn't the Stepford wife I pegged her for. How could I not know that?

"You're divine in Dior," she purrs, fastening the silk-covered buttons and fluffing out the skirt. "Only thing missing is a pair of heels and a smile."

"I don't deserve you or Dior. I figured you for a trophy wife. Aren't you even a little miffed?"

"Not enough to think twice about it. You forget Mother has been grooming me to be a trophy wife since the day I was born," she laughs. "It kills her that I'm going to go back to work because I need balance in my life. Now, onto an item on my agenda," she says in a more serious tone. "You have to end things with Nick now that Ren's back."

"Okay," I sigh. I forgot to tell her I already ended things—or put them on permanent hold, depending on how you look at it. The fact that my reasons had nothing to do with Ren's homecoming doesn't matter. As far as Sloane is concerned, I graduated from the minors and am ready to play ball with the pros (her words, not mine).

She passes me her tweezers. "Now tell me more about that Jezebel at work. Does she realize whom she's messing with?"

"No," I declare as I gaze confidently into the mirror. I'm Katherine Hepburn meets Grace Kelly. "She has no clue."

"Speaking of clueless rogues, are we anywhere nearer to creaming Loser Lowell?"

I go through the motions and tell her the latest developments of my case, even though we both know she knows more than she's letting on. I mean, I certainly didn't sign off on hiring a private investigator or forensic accountant.

"Can I ask you a favour?" She stares me in the eye as I beat my brows into shape under her watch.

I know exactly where this is going. She's been jockeying her way into my divorce since the beginning. "You want to be co-counsel? Ouch!"

"I thought you'd never ask! Keep plucking, Erica. Ren will be here any minute."

Henri just escorted me and Ren to the same VIP window table we had on our first date; the same table he brought me and Perry to on our first date. I've already decided to reorder the white truffle risotto, organic greens, and pistachio-crusted rack of lamb (third time's a charm).

As Ren browses through the menu, I turn my attention to the quaint courtyard view through the leaded-glass window and see PrettyGirl Bess pull Ricardo and the white carriage past the restaurant into the sunset. I feel like I'm in a dream sequence. I could have sworn I heard Kendra's snooty voice ordering someone around. Quickly I scan the room for her, Perry, Kevin Costner—any trace of the past catching up with the present. Nothing. *Phew.* Then Ren looks up. Not as Ren but as Rod Serling and he tells me, "You're travelling through another dimension, a dimension not only with your sugar-daddy boyfriend but your boy-toy legal lover and a couple of geeky brother-type figures. A journey propelled by that fraud of a husband and prima donna best friend."

Through the window, I see all the men in my life. Ren, Nick, Perry, and Teddy's heads fly by. Followed closely by Sloane swinging a baseball bat at Lowell's skull. "You're on a one-way ticket through your imagination. Next stop, the Twilight Zone."

Breathe, I tell myself as Ren returns to being Ren reading his menu. *Relax. Focus.* I put on my Anthony Robbins hat and repeat one of my pep talks: *You are not losing your mind. You are an intelligent modern woman with a lot on your plate.* I look down at the white bone china plate mocking me. It's bare except for the chic *DSC* in gold up at 12 o'clock. I could use a drink or two, right about now.

"Champagne?" asks a young waiter with a French accent and impeccable timing.

"Two please," I blurt out and catch a curious look from the waiter. "I mean, *do* please bring a bottle. Ren?"

"*Mais oui,*" he says, putting down his menu. "*Bollinger Blanc de Noirs Vieilles Vignes Francaises, s'il vous plaît,*" he croons in fluent French. "So," he continues as soon as we're alone again, "to what shall we toast?"

Good question. *To calming my nerves* isn't exactly romantic. "To your safe return home," I propose.

"I'll drink to that. I've been looking forward to tonight for so long," he says, giving my hand his trademark royal kiss. "I missed you."

I wish I could say the same in return. So I fake it and say I missed him, too. How can I not? I mean, he's staring at me with these blue puppy-dog eyes and it's not my fault I've been too busy with work, the divorce, and dating men I had no desire to date in the first place. Besides, there's something about Ren that makes me feel safe, comfortable, content, nice. I know I would have missed him had I had the opportunity.

"See any Kevin Costner movies while I was gone?" he teases me.

"No, but I tuned in to Katie Couric a few times," I reply, batting my well-coated dark eyelashes.

The conversation continues along the same flirtatious vein until dessert, when Ren pulls out a little white box wrapped up in ribbon. "This may seem sudden, but technically we've been dating for months."

Technically I've been dating the whole world for months. "Ren, I don't know what to say." If only he knew why, he'd take the box and run. I'm a fraud.

"When we first started dating, I was going through some very difficult life changes. I had to resolve things before I could fully commit to you."

Omigod. Sloane was right.

"I'm a new man now and I'm ready to take our relationship to the next level. Erica, I'm yours if you'll have me." He opens my clenched fists, placing the ominous box on my shaky palms. The purple ribbon slides off without any help from my trembling fingers. I'm destined to hurt this nice man's feelings by confessing that not only am I not ready or legally able to remarry but that I am a hussy unworthy of his affections.

"It's beautiful," I say as I stare, stunned, at the pavé diamond and amethyst broach inside. No one has ever given me anything this special before. Overcome with emotion, my eyes well up with tears. It's as nice as any engagement ring I've ever seen.

"I saw it in a store window in London and instantly thought of you. I know how much you like Elizabeth Taylor," he says, and I nearly choke on my tea. "I remember you and Sloane going on and on about her at the club."

"I love it. Thank you, Ren." I smile and wipe my eyes. Then I lean over the table to give him a proper kiss on the cheek. But before I know it, he turns the table (not literally) and kisses me first. Not on my cheek. Not on my hand. Not even on my mouth. His tongue is so far down my throat he could get a job as a human chimney sweeper. *Chim chiminey, chim chiminey, chim chim cheree.* If not for my *Mary Poppins* distraction, I'd choke or bite his tongue off—either way, not the fairy-tale ending you hope for on any date, let alone one with your billionaire boyfriend.

I think back to being ten, watching Mary and Bert on the Technicolor rooftops and carousel horses. I wanted so badly for them to get married, adopt Michael and Jane and fly far, far away. For a young romantic, it would have been the perfect ending. But of course it was not meant to be. She just packed up her carpetbag and drifted up into the clouds solo with her umbrella on autopilot. *Chim chiminey, chim chiminey, chim chim cher-ee. When you're with a sweep you're in glad company.*

"Shall we go?" he says with a confident twinkle in his eye. I have to admit, cannonball kiss aside, he is rather dashing. We walk arm-in-arm to the front of the restaurant, passing Henri, who gives me his customary wink on the way out.

"I had a wonderful evening," he says in the limo. "You're pretty amazing."

"I wouldn't say that," I reply self-consciously, tucking a strand of hair behind my ear.

"I would." Ren leans into me. I can sense his tongue about to spring into action so I turn my face to the left. I have no idea what happened in Europe, and in all fairness, it's none of my business. What happens in Europe stays in Europe (it's like Vegas, right?). Be that as it may, as patient as Ren has been since we met, patience is a virtue that has clearly been lost on his lips.

I secretly enroll him in my Kissing 101 class. I start kissing his neck, working my way up to his lips. He moans and thrusts out his oral missile. Deftly, I dodge his tongue and shake my head no. I kiss his nose, his chin, and his lips slowly, tenderly, amorously.

"I took the liberty of instructing my driver to bring us here," he whispers in my ear. "I hope that wasn't too presumptuous."

We're at the waterfront, a mile or so away from my loft. "I live over there," he says, pointing to a familiar-looking low-rise stone building that looks more like a castle than a condo. It has a series of enchanting copper dome-shaped roofs, which have turned green over time, and matching urns overflowing with ivy and dainty red geraniums stationed on either side of the cobblestone walkway leading up to the mahogany Tudor double doors.

I've been here before. Jogging by a few weeks ago, I wondered if it was a historic building or a new structure made to look old. I think I even slowed down my pace, admiring the grounds as much as any recreational runner could without affecting his or her heart rate. I remember that the building struck me as an architectural oddity amidst the plethora of modern glass-front condos down the street, but then I picked up the pace, jogged onward, and put it out of my mind. Till now.

"It's beautiful," I say, stepping out of the limo. "Which floor are you on?"

"I live on the fourth floor, work on the first. Haven't yet decided what to do with the floors in between."

I have no idea how to respond because a) I'm not an interior designer and have no training in spatial planning and b) I'm afraid to open my mouth out of a very real fear I might drool all over the sidewalk. He owns the whole building?

"Come, I'll give you the royal tour," he says as he takes me by the hand.

I can't decide which is more stunning: Ren's castle interior or the waterfront view that spans the entire rear of the house. He hands me a glass of white wine and leads me from one room in his penthouse to the next, each more outstanding than the one before. I feel like a teeny-tiny Polly Pocket walking through the larger-than-life pages of *Architectural Digest*.

The spacious common rooms are done in warm earth tones and are awash in handsome antiques, which no doubt could tell secrets of centuries gone by if only they could talk. I walk by the three-sided glass fireplace in the living room and lose myself in the dancing flames. The kitchen is a masterpiece with hand-carved walnut cabinetry, marble countertops, heated stone floor, and vaulted cathedral ceiling. And remember the stainless steel appliances Lowell made such a big deal about? Ren doesn't even have appliances—not at first glance anyway. Other than the chef's gas cooktop, they're all hidden under the cabinetry.

In his study, we gaze through the window at the waves rippling in the moonlight. Ren has his arm around me now and my head is resting on his shoulder. I notice there's no watercraft outside. I don't even see a dock. It may sound presumptuous—pretentious, even—but I would think that if you have a limo, a private jet, and a castle on the water, you'd also have a boat (a yacht, actually, if we're being totally honest here). I mean, if the shoe fits…

"The water, well she and I have a love-hate relationship," Ren says, quietly stroking my arm. "I fell into a lake when I was four and never totally recovered. Since then, I've loved her from afar."

Okay, so the way he talks about the water like it's his ex-wife—that's a bit weird, but hey, we all have baggage. I pull out my Rockit once Ren has excused himself and left the room. My beaded bag has been vibrating all night. Aha! I've missed three calls and five text messages from Sloane in a span of three hours.

I turn off the phone and find myself drawn to an oil painting across the room. I lose myself in the pastel hues of the seaside town built on a hill, in the town's reflection in the calm waters below as a small boat approaches. Or it is leaving? I look to the brushstrokes for clues but what do I know? I didn't take art past eighth grade.

"It's called 'Vétheuil at Sundown.'" I hear Ren's French accent approaching from behind. "Claude Monet painted it in 1881. It's every bit as captivating today, don't you think?" He doesn't wait for my answer. "If you think this is something, come with me." He leads me into the next room. A black hole, completely dark except in the corner where a gilded picture light is perched above another oil painting, this one much more arresting than the Monet.

I tilt my head in a few different directions to make sure I get the best perspective of the work but it doesn't matter which way I approach it. All I see is a reddish blue part-man, part-fish with a big pointy nose and phallic looking white fedora.

"It's so daring," Ren says.

More like *scaring* if you ask me.

"Does it speak to you?" he asks, still enamoured by its concealed beauty.

"Oh yes," I say, biting the inside of my cheek. It speaks to me all right. It tells me to run the hell away. What would Katherine or Grace do?

"I still can't believe it's mine. Picassos aren't as easy to find as they used to be."

An original? Now I get it. I mean, if I spent a bloody fortune on a painting, I'd also learn to love it.

Mental note: No need to mention the last time you bought art you were at IKEA.

I can't look at the cubist fish-man anymore. I turn around and Ren is so close I can feel his heartbeat. Or is that mine? *Ker-thump. Ker-thump. Ker-thump.* He carries me to the centre of the dark room and eases me onto a low platform that turns out to be his bed.

"I don't want to hurt your feelings, but I can't do this," I say, sitting up.

"What's wrong? Is it the age difference?"

"It's that Picasso of yours. It won't stop staring and it's creeping me out."

"Shhh," he says. He gives me a kiss before hopping out of bed and hauling the painting off the wall and into the closet as if he bought it at IKEA. "My eyes are the only ones on you tonight."

And just like that, we take our relationship to the next level: Better Than Picasso Sex.

I stand corrected. I should have called it Better Than Picasso, Monet, and Matisse Sex.

"I expected something big, but not this. With Wes, I only get Picasso and that's on a good night," Sloane says the next morning on the phone. "You'll have to give me some tips."

"It's not me—it's him! As if he was banned from the Louvre and is making up for lost time."

"Omigod. That's it. This says erectile dysfunction all over it."

"Huh? How would you know?"

"Between you and me, I was getting a massage at the club a few years ago and accidentally overhead Mother talking in the next room. You'd think the walls would be thicker based on our membership dues. Anyhow, I was shocked that Daddy couldn't get it up anymore."

Of course you were. You still think he has a full head of hair. First time I met Sloane's father, at her Sweet 16 birthday bash, I observed that his hair was a shade darker and thicker on top than on the surrounding fringe. That and it looked like a dead rodent. I was 98.7 percent sure he was a bald eagle but when I quietly asked Sloane, she quickly changed the subject to her black-and-white taffeta strapless gown—which ironically reminded me of a panda, another endangered species.

Believe it or not, she's never seen her very own father's head *au natural*. Ne-ver. When she was a kid, he was away on business more than he was home. And when he was in town, he even wore the muskrat to sleep. Fast forward almost twenty years and he's still pulling the wool (or should I say horsehair?) over her eyes.

"You're sure it was your mother?"

"I know her voice. Plus she said Bertoia caused her sore back. Who else refers to their furniture by name?"

"Right," I reply, picturing that steel grid chair. Trying to understand why the Waldens—why anyone—would pay thousands of dollars to sit on something so uncomfortable looking.

"Anyway, she said Dad rarely kissed her anymore and resisted her advances. Naturally, she thought he was having an affair. But when she confronted him, what did he say? 'I should only be so lucky'—and then he broke down and cried in her lap."

"She told all this to a massage therapist?"

"Not just any therapist. Ryan."

"Oh. Is he one of those hybrid psycho/massage therapists I read about online?"

"Hardly. Mother was ending their affair. She told Ryan she needed to channel her sexual energy back to Daddy. I was relieved and horrified at the same time—I left my massage with more knots than I started with. My point, Erica, is that you experienced the same symptoms. You are the closest thing to a wife Ren has. I mean, just look at that broach. It's no Taylor-Burton Diamond but I bet it's worth more than the average engagement ring. It won't be long now till you are the queen of his castle."

"What are you saying?"

"I'm saying keep being supportive."

"Any more supportive and I won't be able to walk."

"You should be happy. It wasn't that long ago you were dying to have sex."

"I used to dream of taking the Concorde to Paris, too. But not six times in two days."

"Can't be that bad."

"He's like Barry Bonds on sexual steroids," I whisper. "I gotta go. He's coming out of the shower."

"You're still there?" she squeals. "Hello, Degas!"

Sunday morning I'm running around the loft (albeit more slowly than normal) looking for a vase for the stalks of white gladiolas my mother brought, but all I can find is a bud vase capable of only committing to a single flower. I open the shiny white cupboard door under the kitchen sink and settle on a large, empty tomato juice can I use to water plants. I'll just say it's from some sort of Warhol pop-art vase collection if anyone (translation: Sloane) asks.

"They're beautiful, Mom. You didn't have to bring anything." I give her a hug and go to the kitchen to cut the knee-high stalks under cold running water. "I'm just happy you came early to help."

"Looks like you've got everything under control, dear. Everything smells great," she says, looking through the glass oven door and poking her head inside the fridge, doing a Gladys Kravitz.

I have to admit, she's right. After I got back from Ren's yesterday, I cooked up a storm. Only the easiest recipes, mind you—nothing has more than five ingredients:

Baked brie with slivered almonds and brown sugar
Tzatziki with pita
Thai vegetarian cold rolls in rice wrappers
Israeli couscous with spinach and sun-dried tomatoes
Green salad in lime vinaigrette
Onion soufflé
Fettuccini Alfredo

And for dessert:

Fresh berries & melon
Chocolate biscotti (natch!)

Playing food stylist, I garnish the food with fresh parsley and throw a few extra stems on the couscous for fun. Mom's filling in as greeter as my guests arrive, making chit-chat, and pointing them to the makeshift bar in the living room. She and Sloane are hugging each other like long-lost girlfriends, leaving Wes to fend for himself at the bar.

Quickly, I flutter through the room for a quick hello, introducing Laurel and Perry to Wes, Jade, and Mrs. Casey. Then it's back to my kitchen duties. I put the food out on the table: an eclectic smorgasbord symbolic of world peace. There's French, Greek, Thai, Israeli, Italian, and whatever ethnicity is best known for green salad and fruit (Malibu-ite, maybe?). The best part is, I did not call a caterer and only ran out to the store to buy tzatziki, pita, and biscotti. I mean, really, who bakes their own biscotti anyway?

I invite everyone to the buffet and alternate between serving the soufflé and pasta. "You have another guest," Mom says. "I'll serve."

Standing by the front door is Teddy. He looks so jetlagged and yet amazing at the same time, wearing fitted jeans and a dark, striped button-down. I almost jump out of my skin and rush to give him a hug. I haven't seen him since the day I quit. "Sorry for ignoring you. I just needed time to think."

"Don't worry about me. I saw Dani moving in on your job and was trying to warn you. How's it going, by the way, having an assistant director?"

"You mean an assistant director and shared custody of Tory?

"Oh boy. Well, if anyone can make it work, it's you. You're a survivor."

"You're my friend—" I smile "—you have to lie. Enough about me. Look at you! Like the new threads! Turn around?" I check out the embroidered Rs on his butt. "Rock & Republic. Great choice."

"Yeah, well, someone once told me that you've got to dress for the role you want."

"Great advice. Maybe I should start dressing like Napoleon Bonaparte. Hey," I say, "are you hungry? There's lots of food."

As we walk toward the dining table, Sloane pulls me aside. "Have you seen Ren? I'm worried about him."

"Don't be," I whisper back. "I didn't invite him." Her perfectly shadowed eyes slowly shift downward and to the side. "Sloane, you didn't, did you?"

"I only mentioned at the driving range this morning that we would see him later. It was all very innocent and he jumped at the chance to see you again. Why didn't you invite him, anyway?"

"I thought he'd be in Europe. Then when he came home, I was afraid I'd offend him with a last-minute invitation."

"Well, aren't you worried he's not here yet? He's almost thirty minutes late."

"He's a big boy."

"Not funny," she snaps, her mind clearly in the gutter.

I decide against trying to explain that I was merely suggesting that Ren is a fifty-something-year-old billionaire with a limo and driver, not to mention the ability to get to and from Europe on his own. Right now, I have more pressing matters to attend to.

In through my front door like Yin and Yang have walked Nick and Lowell. Confidence and magnetic energy is oozing out of Mr. GQ; the only thing exuding from Mr. IT is mediocrity. As for me, I simply freeze. I haven't seen Lowell since the night I walked out. I don't know what it is, his hair maybe, but he seems different. Or maybe it's me.

"Why in good heavens is he here?" Sloane asks.

"Which one?"

"Loser Lowell, of course, but I see your point. Ren could walk in anytime. Quick, you take Loser and I'll take Nick." She calls out our game plan as assertively as any of her former quarterback college boyfriends. "Let's get them out of here."

Sloane whispers something in Wes's ear and proceeds over to Nick, still chatting unwittingly with my ex. Then, like something out of a sitcom, she taps Lowell's outside shoulder. Predictably, he looks away from Nick and she steers Nick out of the loft, elbowing Lowell in the gut as she brushes by.

Following Sloane's lead, I approach Lowell, forgoing the jab in his side (though the thought does cross my mind). "What are you doing here?"

"We need to talk," he says—as if he has any authority.

"No, *you* need to leave. *I* need to get back to my guests."

"I've been trying to reach you for days. Hear me out and I'll leave. I promise."

As if his promises mean anything, vow-breaker.

"Three minutes. That's all I'm asking for."

"Not here." I quickly text Teddy, apprising him of the situation, and ask him to hold down the fort. "If I knew you were coming, I'd have served turkey sandwiches," I say as we walk down the cement stairway to the second-floor pool area. "Okay, so what's so important?" I demand, looking at his reflection in the indoor pool.

"You. I want you back."

Is this his idea of a joke?

"I screwed up."

"That's an understatement, Lowell."

"I know, I know." I watch his mirror image pace from the shallow to deep end and back again. "It seemed like we were drifting. You were never home and when you were, all we did was fight."

"It was debating, Lowell," I insist. "You know I love a good debate. Don't I always watch *Meet the Press*?"

"I felt like we were over. So I buried myself in my work. I

worked closer and closer with Meryl and we just seemed to connect. I didn't know what to do so I did nothing."

"You call Lunch Sex On Wednesdays nothing? You were a pretty active participant."

"I was weak. I was torn. I didn't know what to do. And then you found the email and I didn't have to do anything. You made the decision for me."

Major cop-out.

"But then my attorney showed me the photos of you with those men," he says. "I haven't been able to get you out of my head."

"What are you talking about?"

"At the baseball game. On the horse ride. At the pub. My attorney said your attorney was a real ball buster and my case needed all the help it could get. I didn't know he was going to leak the private investigator's photos to the press. Honest," he says, stepping in my direction.

"Get away from me," I shout, raising my gaze from the water's edge to his beady little eyes.

"I swear I didn't know."

"Even if you are telling the truth, what about the stock options? What about all the money you've been hiding? You aren't just a cheat, you're a crook, too."

"Is that you, Erica?" I hear Teddy's voice coming up from behind. "You okay?"

I give Lowell one last sorry look before swinging around—and accidentally knocking him into the shallow end.

"Everything's going to be just fine. I think his three minutes are up. Shall we?" I loop my arm through Teddy's, leaving Lowell once and for all—to drown in his own stupidity.

If you have BHO, you:

(a) are a dyslexic couch potato and meant HBO

(b) have a rare type of BO called Body Hair Odour. Try a vanilla sponge bath twice a day to curb smell and dirty looks.

(c) do cool things on the web thanks to the Browser Helper Object mini-program you installed in your web browser

(d) have Bacterial Hepatitis Oxidation and should go to the ER pronto

chapter
twenty

"Over 40 percent of respondents associated going wireless with wearing a bra without underwire. Fifty-five percent thought good bandwidth referred to wedding rings. A third knew a dead spot had something to do with cellular technology though another third thought it had a sexual connotation," Dani, back in her native beige Burberry, reports during our meeting.

"And the third third?"

"They didn't care," she says flippantly, not to mention a tad too quickly for my liking.

"What about smartphones?"

"Just over 25 percent owned one—mostly female execs, entrepreneurs, and society moms—but *almost* everyone agreed they would love to have one to keep their lives organized."

"Everyone except?"

"Apparently a few grannies sneaked into the mix. I guess smartphone focus groups pay better than dentures and incontinence pads."

"I guess. Any good data related to the show?"

"I found a few juicy nuggets," she says, almost humming. "About 7 percent of respondents have, at one point in time, downloaded a *Sex and the City* screensaver."

"What else?" I ask in my best Lou Grant. I want more than a tartlet of a screensaver fact. I want meat and potatoes, hard-core tech. I've got a product launch crawling up my ass—and I don't care what anyone says, I'll take the fall if it fails, not the new assistant marketing director.

"Eighteen percent bought a Mac laptop largely because Carrie Bradshaw uses one. About 50 percent identified with her uneasiness with technology in the movie. Eleven percent said that the show could have put Berger to shame more had he broken up with Carrie via email instead of a Post-it note. Something about viral mud-slinging?"

"Better. Anything related to smartphones or cell phones?"

"Twenty-seven percent considered downloading a *Sex* ring tone; of those half actually did. And of the 60 percent who called themselves 'huge fans' of the show and movie," Dani says making air quotes with her fingers, "almost 80 percent agreed that Big telling Carrie she was 'the one' was the second all-time most satisfying moment on both the series and movie."

I stand up to stretch and admire the fresh bouquet of scarlet roses from Ren on my credenza. How lucky am I? I mean, sure white's still my favourite, but he's sent me almost enough red ones to make a Rose Bowl parade float. And really, I should be the one sending him flowers, especially since I backed out of our Seattle trip. I didn't want to cancel and give up the opportunity to become lifelong friends with Bill, Melinda, and Warren, but since returning to Rockit I have lived at the office and have had to work every weekend. The fact that I was secretly uneasy about jumping back into bed with a man with a thirty-six-hour erection had nothing to do with my decision.

Anyhow Ren was a perfect gentleman, saying he understood and that we could reschedule with our Seattle friends after the launch. Sloane, on the other hand, wasn't quite as sympathetic. Travel was the next step in our relationship. It can even induce a marriage proposal, she said, citing how Elizabeth Taylor remarried Richard Burton in 1975 after bumping into him at a charity celebrity tennis tournament in Johannesburg. How can I argue with logic like that? I smell the fragrant blooms and turn back to Dani.

"Finding out Big's real name on her cell phone was number one, wasn't it?" Sloane and I shrieked so loud in the final moments of the TV series' finale her matronly Swedish housekeeper, Effa, came running downstairs sporting nothing but a green facial mask and swinging an aluminum baseball bat. Needless to say, we all had a little scare that night. "I think we've got enough to go on."

"I'll get to work on a press release after lunch. I'm going to that new Ethiopian fusion restaurant around the corner."

Whatever, I think, typing feverishly on my laptop, silently wondering when Ethiopian food become so cosmopolitan (whatever happened to eating stew and flatbread with your hands?) as Dani sees herself out of my office. My lunch date should be here any minute, though I should probably have cancelled.

We're two weeks away from the new product launch and I've still got a million loose ends to tie up—despite the fact that, like Jade, I've been practically sleeping at the office. The good news is I've made a point of getting to know her better—and not because I need anything, but because we've become friends.

We've been ordering in every night at eight—Thai, Greek, Italian, Chinese (anything but sushi, I pleaded with her)—and cutting up the worst tech gadgets we've seen (which is more stupid: a portable voice-recorded shopping list printer or a wheelchair with army tank wheels?) and getting our minds off the stresses of work, and in my case, divorce.

A few days after Lowell crashed my loft warming, he threatened to sue me for assault and emotional distress, claiming I intentionally pushed him into the swimming pool. Tina and Sloane have both assured me it's nothing to worry about because I have a witness who can testify that it was an accident and it's likely another desperate move on Tina's father's part to use scare tactics to gain legal ground. Be that as it may, I can't help but think that the divorce I was aiming to make quick and easy is getting slower and more complicated by the day.

"Lasagna Express at your service," Teddy says, rolling two big squares of mozzarella heaven into my office on a mail cart draped in white linen. As the cart draws closer, I notice that there's also green salad (tossed in Italian dressing, no doubt) and a bottle of San Pellegrino.

"Wow," I say, peering out from behind my laptop. "What's the occasion?"

"It's Monday."

"This is the first Monday lunch that's ever felt like room service at the Waldorf." There's even a set of silver salt and pepper shakers on the cart.

"I thought it would be fun to try something new. Wouldn't want you to get tired of same-old, same-old lasagna."

"Not possible. My butt and I live for it. But eating some roughage wouldn't hurt, I guess. *Grazie*." I smile and close my laptop. I may as well be sitting in an Italian restaurant next to a floral shop. It smells amazing in here.

Teddy pulls out a couple of squat water glasses from the bottom tier of the trolley and does the honours. Bubbles swim to the top, sparkling like diamonds in the light. It's almost a shame to disrupt such beauty—even in the name of personal hydration—but who am I kidding? A diamond may be forever but a carbonated bubble doesn't even live as long as a fruit fly.

"So, you ready for launch?" Teddy asks, his eyes meeting mine through my glass as if we're both inspecting for fingerprints.

"Depends how you define ready. Everything related to our main launch is basically ready to go: collateral, point-of-sale material, press tour, product demos, dealer training modules. We've been ahead of schedule on that for a while. It's the Techs and the City campaign that I'm worried about."

"But the teaser ads look great. I saw one on marthastewart.com last week."

"You were on Martha?"

"Searching for a recipe," he says, passing me a plate, "to make for Ma. Ever try Black Pepper Tagliatelle with Parsnips and Pancetta?"

Try it? I can't even say it. Chances are it has more than five ingredients, so safe to say no. That said, I would be just as impressed had he grilled bologna sandwiches instead of whipping up the black pepper whatever. The way I see it, any guy who cooks for his mother is a gem. Zola is lucky to have him. So am I—I couldn't ask for a better friend.

"Anyhow, I liked how you evolved the Rockit look. Feminine but not frilly."

"We modern women don't wear petticoats anymore you know. Mmm, this is delish." Between bites, I grab an oversized board with an ad layout from beside my desk. We both look at Rockit Robin, our campaign mascot, using the GPS on her smartphone while shielding herself from an oncoming New York City Transit bus tsunami with an umbrella. "So far, response's been good. Clickthrough rates to Robin's MySpace and Facebook pages are above target."

"So what's the problem?"

"I can't get new content on her blogs fast enough. We're getting ten times more repeat traffic than we expected. It's great except it means I've got to review and approve a whole new mountain of material every few days."

"You could delegate to your assistant marketing director."

I stop eating. "I'd rather keep working every night. She's a pro at PR but I still don't trust her. What if the Techs campaign falls apart? We go full throttle next week in New York."

"One: it won't. Two: it won't," Teddy says, cutting into his lasagna.

"Three: I'll get fired. Not her."

"Four: you'll quit. Been there, done that, no big deal. You know you could get another job in a heartbeat," he says. "What's really wrong? Is it your love life?"

"What love life?"

These days my stash of men is not what it used to be, I confide. Nick is on hold indefinitely. Ren (or "Mr. Soap Opera Name" as Teddy still calls him) is on hold until after launch. And Perry and I decided to just be friends, so he moved on. "You won't believe who he's moved on to," I tell Teddy. "I'm still in shock. I found out from my security system."

I watched surveillance footage of my loft warming, I continued telling Teddy. I was merely testing the security system but, to be honest, I felt like I was watching a movie. I even made popcorn. The camera angles weren't the best and there wasn't any zoom or other special effects but that aside it was quite entertaining, especially when Sloane jabbed Lowell in the ribs. I must have replayed that part a hundred times.

I watched myself huff out with Lowell and Teddy step in as host—inviting my guests to the buffet while making sure their glasses were refilled. Everyone seemed to be having a good time. Laurel chatting with Mrs. Casey on the sofa. Wes speaking to Tina by the window. Mom and someone kissing in the kitchen. *Wait, what the hell?* Rewind.

I watched the footage again and again, pressing Pause every few seconds trying to identify the kisser in question. Damn it! If I had installed another camera I'd be able to make out his face. I couldn't believe this was happening. I didn't know she was seeing anyone. How come she didn't say anything? I was furious. I shared so much about my love life with her. Why wouldn't she at least mention she was dating?

Determined to get to the bottom of things, I zoomed in on my laptop as much as I could, but the image only got grainier. I needed to know who Mr. MotherLips was. Desperately.

"Turn around!" I screamed at my laptop as if they could hear me. Secretly, I was hoping I would see Dad's face on the screen when their embrace ended a few seconds later. I certainly didn't expect to see Perry's. *Oh. My. God.*

"What did you do?" Teddy asks, his forkful of lasagna suspended in mid-air.

"Just sat there in shock. Then I got all misty eyed. I felt so betrayed."

"But you said you and Perry were just friends. Eat your lasagna. It's gonna get cold."

I nod and take a bite. "Not by him. By her. It was like I was fifteen years old and I had caught my mother cheating on my father with my biology lab partner, Fred," I say realizing how immature I must sound. I've often told Teddy how much I'd like Mom to date and find someone special. I just never realized how much it would hurt to actually see her with someone else.

"Your dad wouldn't want her to be alone," he says, his big brown eyes staring me down. He knows me too well.

"I know."

"And Fred's not fifteen anymore," Teddy laughs.

"My mother's not forty anymore either."

"Have you talked with her?"

"And say what? 'My spy cam caught you making out with my friend and it made me cry and miss Daddy'?"

"I'd go with something less direct."

"You think?"

"What's wrong with a woman dating a younger man anyway?"

"Nothing, I guess. Just don't tell Ren or he could leave me for Mary Tyler Moore. Oh no, wait. She already married one."

For Immediate Release

WIRELESS MAKES "BIG" IMPRESSION WITH WOMEN

Rockit launches Techs and the City contest on heels of findings revealing Sex and the City viewers' all-time most satisfying moments

Manhattan, NY—When it comes to satisfying *Sex and the City* fans, there's something even better than Smith Jerrod and Manolo Blahniks. According to independent research commissioned by Rockit Wireless, most *SATC* fans say that finding out Big's real name (John) on Carrie's cell phone outside Bergdorf's was their all-time most satisfying moment through the six-season, ninety-four-episode hit TV series and follow-up blockbuster movie.*

"Wireless technology plays such a big role in our daily lives," says Rockit marketing director, Erica Swift. To that end, Rockit announced a contest to show women how Rockit's new smartphones (also launched today in a separate news release) can help organize and simplify their lives.

Women can have and do it all with Rockit
With large touch-screen displays, QWERTY keyboards, and robust, faster wireless broadband connectivity, every Rockit smartphone combines a phone and digital organizer with email, text messaging, Internet, and rich media capabilities, such as high-resolution photo and video capture/view/edit, streaming audio/video, MP3 player, and GPS navigation.

Rockit smartphones, as a result, are increasingly becoming wireless lifestyle accessories that can do everything from scheduling a pedicure and plotting out the fastest route to a new client meeting to watching footage of your child's first hit in Little League—all while cooking dinner.

To pay homage to the hit TV series and movie, Rockit is sponsoring an exciting new contest called Techs and the City. Entrants can win one of four all-expenses-paid trips to The City (Manhattan), where they will each receive their own Rockit smartphone and a $10,000 shopping spree.

– more –

Entering is as easy as navigating through any of the four fictitious Techs and the City persona pages on MySpace and Facebook social networking sites and completing the following sentence: "If I had a Rockit smartphone I could...."

What if Berger didn't use a Post-it note?
The contest's fun technological emphasis poses some new questions for *SATC* fans, such as:

- If Carrie had had a Rockit smartphone with large touch-screen interface, viewers could have found out more than just Big's first name in the series finale.
- In the movie, Carrie could have received his love letters via phone and ended her heartache earlier.
- Had Berger broken up with Carrie via text message or email (vs. Post-it note), she could have efficiently revealed his cowardice by forwarding it on and dedicating the rest of Episode 81 to meeting someone new rather than sulking.

The study also found that only 25 percent of research participants owned smartphones, though industry forecasts show that figure starting to rise.

Ms. Swift explains that even though male executives have largely led the way in adopting smartphone technology, smartphones make just as much, if not more, sense for women.

"More than any demographic, women have a lot on their plate," she says. "Working or not, they are usually the ones juggling meetings, carpools, doctors' appointments, family dinners, and other social engagements—it's amazing they get to bed at night."

* #2 was Big telling Carrie she was "the one"

Rockit is a trademark of Rockit Wireless, Inc., registered in the U.S. and/or other countries. All other trademarks are the property of their respective owners.

– 30 –

For interviews, images, and/or more information contact:
Danielle Carou
Assistant Marketing Director
Rockit Wireless

If you are a Black Hat, you are:

(a) an artsy-fartsy Bohemian type with a penchant for ebony berets

(b) a sneaky devil who prefers the term to hacker or cracker

(c) a Hasidic Jew

chapter
twenty-one

"Special delivery," Tory says, knocking on my door like she has been doing every Monday morning since my second date with Ren. Only today things are different. Dani and I are reviewing our New York press tour schedule before we depart a few days ahead of the rest of our group. Tory hands me a single long-stem red rose wrapped in cellophane with a glistening organza bow and a card.

By the blasé expression on Dani's face, I know what she's thinking: that a single red bud may be a highly romantic gesture from a love-struck, pimply sixteen-year-old boy, but when you go from getting one dozen roses after another to a single stem, from a billionaire no less, the writing's on the wall. I, however, happen to disagree. Ren knows I'm leaving town; sending a dozen could be considered wasteful and environmentally unfriendly. On the other hand, sending nothing could be considered forgetful. Sending one is the perfect solution. Especially when it's accompanied by a card like this.

> Erica, Good luck and have
> fun in New York. Miss you.
> Yours, Ren

I smile, taking note of the enclosed Saks Fifth Avenue gift card, and decide I'm going to get Tory more than another snow globe— something expensive, something she wouldn't dare buy for herself. Ditto that for Mom and Laurel. A robe for Ren might be nice (God knows he needs to cover up). If there's anything left on the gift card, I'll go for broke and buy a lap desk or my very first Valentino (borrowing from Sloane doesn't count)—maybe both, depending on my mood and degree of Ren's overwhelming generosity. Dani of course will get nothing. Nada. Zip. Zilch.

"The photo op with the girls is scheduled for Thursday morning on Fifth Avenue followed by interviews back at the hotel," Dani says, handing me a glossy red folio. "Here's a sample hard-copy press kit. We have electronic kits on USB flash drives, too. The airport limo picks us up in an hour."

As she skips out, I flip through the flurry of finalized contest press releases and head straight to the biographies to re-familiarize myself with the winners.

Marlo Velez
Student Entrepreneur
Ithaca, New York

If I had a Rockit smartphone… I could stay in touch with my dog walkers and track them down with mobile GPS, no matter what forest or creek they find themselves in searching for a runaway dog.

Marlo (22) is enrolled at Cornell University's College of Veterinary Medicine in upstate New

York. An animal lover since childhood, Marlo is paying her way through college by running a dog-walking business. She has a staff of six and runs the business out of the apartment she shares with her two Yorkshire terriers, Mary-Kate and Ashley.

Yvette Lajoie
Teacher
New Orleans, Louisiana

If I had a Rockit smartphone... I could digitally store students' photos for security. In the event of a missing student on a field trip, I could show his/her photo around and immediately email it to authorities.

Yvette (28) teaches fourth grade at a New Orleans public school and volunteers on weekends with Habitat for Humanity to help rebuild public housing in the city. She spends her summers working at a special-needs children's camp in Martha's Vineyard. Her hobbies include sewing, sketching, and playing Guitar Hero.

Christy Lowenstein
Dental Hygienist
Vancouver, British Columbia

If I had a Rockit smartphone... I could connect it to my nanny-cam and see what's going on at home in between teeth cleanings.

Christy (37) and her husband, Mathew, a dentist, run a successful dental clinic in the city's trendy Kitsilano area. When she's not working or running after her toddler son, Christy enjoys sailing, skiing, and training for marathons.

Caitlyn Kirby-Smythe
Entrepreneur
Boca Raton, Florida

If I had a Rockit smartphone... I could turn my car into a mini office and save time by ordering supplies online while waiting to pick up the kids from school.

Caitlyn (42) is president of BocaBaskets, designers of custom gift baskets for all occasions. A former "domestic engineer," Caitlyn works at night and when her two children are in school. Her hobbies include floral arranging, shopping, and debating. She is divorced.

"Hungry?" I look up and see Teddy at my door, holding a plate of lasagna.

"Are you crazy? It's nine in the morning."

"There's bran in the noodles," he teases. "C'mon, you can't leave before having lasagna. It's Monday and I bet you didn't even eat breakfast."

"Wrong. I had an orange Mentos in the car."

"Good to see you're getting your daily dose of vitamin C but that won't do. You need your strength this week."

"Right. Dani 24/7."

"Seriously, you're going to be burning the candle at both ends. Between finalizing all the details, then entertaining the contest winners and courting the press, you're going to be a zombie. Here, have some." He feeds me a forkful.

This stuff is even more addictive on a 99 percent empty stomach. "One day, you're going to make some girl really happy—and fat." I grin, helping myself to another bite, then another and another and praying he wasn't serious about it being made with bran. I have enough of a problem flying with my goldfish bladder.

"Don't you love New York in the spring?" Dani says the next afternoon, taking a deep breath and lowering her window in the backseat of our limo en route from our final meeting with our events marketing agency. Far as I can smell, the only indigenous thing growing in this neck of the woods is bumper-to-bumper yellow urban groundcover.

Mental note: Remember to take early morning jog in Central Park; also ask hotel concierge about nearby oxygen bars.

"The pink roses on that brownstone we passed on the Upper West Side this morning were stunning," I reply without the slightest bit of sarcasm. Seriously, they were. There were hundreds of them climbing up trellises, covering the lower half of the building like crocheted leg warmers. As if it housed the Joffrey Ballet School or something.

"Oh? I must have missed that," she says and takes a sip of her bottled water. "Listen, I was thinking that after our dinner site inspection at Buddakan, we could see a show and then go clubbing. Julie can get us in anywhere."

"Who?"

"Julie. You know, our events producer. Actually she's the assistant to the assistant events producer but she's *very* well connected around here. If we asked, she could get us into George and Ira Gershwin's graves."

"I think I'm going back to my room after dinner. There's a Yankees game on tonight."

"Yawn and snore. We only have one night left to have some fun before the others arrive. Promise me you'll think about it. Have you seen the men on Madison Avenue?" she asks, almost drooling out the window. "I've never seen so much Hugo Boss, Giorgio Armani, and Ermenegildo Zegna per square block. Your days of getting roses by the dozen could resume sooner than you think."

Almost twenty-four hours later and I'm no closer to landing a "Madison Avenue Man" (or MAM) than I was yesterday, and I couldn't feel better. I slept a full eight hours and went for a 6 a.m. jog through Central Park, which from the nineteenth floor of The Plaza looks tiny. I spent the rest of the morning replying to email and working on my laptop in the stunning luxury suite we're using for our Winner's Welcome Lunch, press interviews, and VIP soirees.

"Our winners have arrived," a hyper-caffeinated Dani announces.

She looks as fabulous as always except for her droopy eyes. It's no wonder. I ran into her this morning at sunrise, chugging a coffee on 59th Street, arm in arm with some model-turned-MAM named Jesse she met at a hot new club in the city's meatpacking district. Meatpacking? Don't even get me started.

"Julie and co. checked them in to their rooms over an hour ago," she chirps on. "They'll be here in a few minutes."

"We're here! Let the festivities begin." Brett walks into the living room in his tailored dark navy suit two paces ahead of Teddy, all Greenwich Village in a hip Ben Sherman polo and fitted jeans. "Nice place but tell me again, ladies—why aren't we at the W?"

"The Plaza is *soooo Sex and the City*," Dani answers, thankfully. I'm so not in the mood to justify the choices we've made. Not at this late stage in the game anyway. "I heard Sarah Jessica Parker even celebrated her fortieth birthday here. Have you seen the bathrooms? I'm typically more of a silver girl but there's something to be said for twenty-four-karat-gold-plated faucets!"

"The Plaza is a pretty major New York landmark, Brett," Teddy pipes up, shooting me a quick wink. "Erica, where do you want the Rockits?" he asks as he unloads four shiny red boxes. "They're all souped up with everything you asked for."

I can't wait to see our winners' faces when they get their phones—custom-configured for an unforgettable time in New York. Pleased as punch, I set the boxes on the coffee table and excuse myself to the ladies' room.

When I return to the living room, Dani and the boys are mingling with four women: our contest winners. At last! As I approach them, I realize the sample press kit didn't have any headshot photos. No problemo, I will identify them using deductive reasoning.

- Christy I could spot anywhere. She's the athlete; the Sporty Spice of our group. I smile at the petite woman with brown eyes and freckles, wearing a pair of chinos, a lavender blouse, and her blond hair in a pony. The moment she smiles back, though, I know she's not Christy. Her teeth are as crooked as a politician. There's no way any dentist would let his spouse out in public like that. So who the hell is she?
- Playing the odds, I decide the tall, grey-haired woman in the conservative black suit and heels is Caitlyn. She's the oldest of the group and runs her own business. Besides, she has three children. Aren't kids supposed to make your hair go grey?
- Opposite our grey-haired maven stands a slim brunette with a black beret over her short pixie haircut. She has no makeup and is wearing jeans and a vintage-looking black Felix the Cat shirt. If she didn't have boobs, she could pass for a guy. Must be Marlo the dog-walker. I mean, if that feline shirt's not enough of a clue,

consider this: it's not as if vets have to dress up for their patients.

- I look at the one remaining unidentified Rockit girl with strawberry-blond pageboy hair wearing a geometric print dress in brown and robin's-egg blue. By process of elimination, she has to be either Yvette or Christy. I look down at her thick gams and I decide on Yvette. I'm no expert but that looks more like water retention than muscle. There's no way anyone could run a marathon on those babies.

"Erica, I'd like to introduce you to our contest winners," Dani says, and then proceeds to confirm that I make a much better marketing professional than I would a police officer, detective, or coroner. My deductive reasoning and investigative skills suck. Christy, it turns out, is Marlo. Caitlyn is Yvette. Marlo is Christy and Yvette is Caitlyn. Not only am I batting zero, I'm confused. Let me get this straight:

- Marlo Velez is a cute twenty-two-year-old blonde dog-walker and future veterinarian from Ithaca, New York, with a good figure and bad teeth;
- Yvette Lajoie is a tall, reserved twenty-seven-year-old teacher from New Orleans who went grey prematurely (maybe from teaching kids?) and is committed to making the world a better place;
- Christy Lowenstein is a thirty-seven-year-old dental hygienist from Vancouver who looks a little like Audrey Hepburn in *Sabrina* but with bigger boobs, no makeup, and a rocker's wardrobe. She is also very athletic and suspicious of nannies; and
- Caitlyn Kirby-Smythe is a forty-two-year-old Boca Raton–based mother of three with a preppy pageboy and great taste in clothes. She owns a gift basket company and exceptionally large calves (maybe from having three kids?).

"Pleasure to meet you all," I say sincerely to their wall of ear-to-ear smiles, trying not to stare at Marlo's nightmare of a mouthful. Everyone seems so nice and thankful. I feel horrible for being so catty and superficial.

Mental note: Work on improving self at DrPhil.com

"We're thrilled to show you New York like you've never seen it before. On that note, please have a seat by your very own state-of-the-art Rockit smartphone. Each Rockit is loaded with all the cool tools a modern woman could want in The City: contact info, bookmarked websites, and GPS maps of everything from Barney's, Bergdorf, Bloomingdale's, and other department stores and couture boutiques to hot clubs and restaurants.

"There's a special button just for real-life *SATC* hotspots and video clips from the movie and show. Plus the official *SATC* ring tone. I'd like to formally introduce you to Rockit's senior product manager, Teddy Francesco. Teddy's going to walk you through the product and answer any questions."

I step back and watch Teddy start his product demo.

"What do you think?" Brett whispers.

"I think at the photo op, Marlo should smile close-lipped and Caitlyn should wear pants. Other than that, they're perfect!" At least they will be once our wardrobe consultants and makeup artists get to work.

"Sorry I asked," he says, and takes a seat.

"When do we *actually* get to go shoe shopping?" Caitlyn interrupts Teddy, effectively hijacking his presentation. "I've been dying for a pair of Manolo ankle boots. Boca stores are perpetually out of stock."

Christy exclaims, "I'd like to pick up a diamond TAG diving watch at Bloomingdale's!"

"I wouldn't mind going to Bloomingdale's, too. They have a doggie Juicy Couture line," Marlo barks. "I want to get Mary-Kate and Ashley reversible bone-print parkas."

Everyone looks at her. "That's pretty cruel," Christy sneers. "They may be little gazillionaires, but they have feelings."

"What are you talking about? They're Yorkshire terriers and they freeze their heinies off every winter."

I look at Teddy who's clearly out of his league now. He's speechless, watching the women banter back and forth. He looks as if he's at Wimbledon, waiting for someone to get match point and end this sordid rally. I'm about to jump in and get things back on track but see Dani has beat me to it. Only she's not putting out any fires, she's adding more fuel.

"Bloomingdale's is great," she says, "but if I were you I'd go straight to one of Juicy's own boutiques. They'll have more selection."

"What about men?" Yvette asks Dani. "Where can we go to meet good-looking rich men like Big? Besides Brad Pitt, I haven't met that many good-looking rich guys in New Orleans."

"You've met Brad?" Christy sighs. "What's he like in real life?" All eyes turn to Yvette for a response.

"Ladies, we're in New York," Dani interjects. "I found a hot new club last night crawling with Madison Avenue Men."

As she rambles on, I text Teddy and Brett across the room.

need 2 cre8 dvrsion qwik

"Ladies," Brett interrupts, laying on the charm extra thick. "Why talk about meeting men when you've got two eligible bachelors right here who'd love to take you to lunch?" He looks at me and shrugs. I realize he's right—these ladies want to see and be seen in a trendy restaurant, not hide away in a hotel room with cucumber sandwiches.

"Do you *own* Rockit Wireless?" Caitlyn asks as they all stroll out of the suite. By the way she's playing with her hair, you can tell she's on the prowl and looking for someone to support her in the manner to which she became accustomed before making gift baskets.

"Didn't I see your picture in *Fortune*?" Christy asks, nudging in between them and taking Brett by the arm. "You were holding an astronaut's helmet, I think."

For Christ's sake, these women are as bad as the contestants on *The Bachelor*. And what's with Christy anyway? She's married to a dentist. Is she looking to trade up? Or is she just one of those competitive women who need to win everything?

"Brett's one of the brightest minds in the business world," Dani says, smiling at our fearless leader. I roll my eyes and see Teddy looking back at me like a chocolate Lab trying to swim up a waterfall (I'm surprised Marlo hasn't tried to collar him). I shoot him a reassuring look and a quick text back as he walks out the door.

"Lunch is served," Jeeves announces, a few minutes later, to me and the furniture.

"Hope you're hungry," I say, looking at picture-perfect sandwiches, salads, pastries, and fruit on the dining-room table. I grab my things and a couple of party sandwiches to satisfy my rumbling belly and request that he taxi over whatever food he doesn't eat to a food bank and charge it to our tab.

Back in my room a few hours later, my Rockit awakens me from what has to be the first afternoon nap I've taken in thirty years. I'm not sure what happened. One minute I'm reading some market research, the next I'm lying on a Mexican beach sipping a chocolate margarita and listening to Elton John's "Rocket Man." I open my eyes and reach for my phone on the bedside table, putting an end to my dreamy siesta. It's Teddy. He's talking a mile a minute.

"Slow down, Teddy. I can't make out your words."

"We're at the hospital."

I sit up and wipe my eyes. "What's wrong? Are you okay?"

"It's Dani and the winners. They have food poisoning. Brett and I are fine. We didn't order the duck."

"Oh God, I'll be right over."

"No, it's okay. The doctors said they should be fine in a few days. But they need to rest and stay near a bathroom. Erica, we have to cancel the campaign."

"We can't."

"Brett's ready to pull the plug. Listen, I've got to run. We should be back soon."

"Another chocolate martini," I order down at the bar shortly thereafter. "Make it a double."

"What's a beautiful woman like you drowning her troubles in chocolate for?" I turn to my right and find myself rubbing elbows (literally) with a guy that could pass for Nick's brother. He's a good half a foot shorter but he's got the same brown curly hair and eyes, olive Mediterranean skin, chiselled cheekbones, and lean, muscular frame. Same smooth talk, too.

I look him straight in the eye. "Bet you a drink I can guess your profession."

"You're on," Nick Jr. says.

"Shake on it," I say, extending my hand. He shakes my hand then proceeds to caress it, which only confirms my guess. "You're an attorney, aren't you?"

"Nope. Can't stand the law."

"Car salesman?"

"Nope."

I sigh. "I can't get anything right today." I take another sip and my head starts to spin. I should have scarfed down a few more party sandwiches.

"Tell you what, beautiful," Nick Jr. says, "drinks are on me anyway and I won't try to sell you a car."

"Deal." I nod and we shake again.

"What could be so bad that you're drinking this much this early in the afternoon?"

I wouldn't normally be so forthcoming with a perfect stranger in a strange city but at this point, I have little to lose. Not only that, I'm as drunk as the wine in *Sideways*. "So," I conclude, "we've indirectly poisoned our contest winners. There goes our photo op. Forget any press interviews. This whole women and technology campaign is blowing up in my face."

"You're not going to believe this, but I think I can help you, Erica."

"Not possible."

"Come up to my suite and I'll show you what I have in mind."

"Can I use your washroom? My bladder's going to explode."

"Beautiful, you can do anything you want." He smiles and leaves a C-note on the bar. As we get in the elevator and the door closes, the weirdest thing happens. I start hallucinating Teddy running toward us, shouting something, but it's all a blur. That's what I get for drinking on an empty stomach.

If you enjoy spam a lot, you no doubt:

(a) are a huge Monty Python fan

(b) also feast on other canned luncheon meat like corned beef
hash

(c) lead a very lonely life and enjoy receiving unsolicited junk
email

chapter
twenty-two

I rush back to the hospitality suite a couple hours later, applying some lip gloss and neatening my hair en route. Brett is in his own little world, slouched on the sofa with his shirt unbuttoned, viewing some sort of space travel research report on his laptop and talking to our lead attorney on his Rockit. Teddy's standing by the oversized window, looking out over the lush Central Park treetops. I walk up to him.

"How are the girls?"

"They're fine now," he says. "Back in their rooms, each with their own nurse."

"Of course. Must have been a big scare. Are you guys okay?"

"We're fine. And they will be too, in a few days. The food poisoning was only mild. We got lucky," he says, turning to me. "But not as lucky as you."

"That's what I wanted to tell you!"

"I kept racking my brain at the hospital, trying to figure out how to help save *your* women's campaign because I know how important it is to you. And then when I find you, you don't just ignore me, you let the elevator door shut in my face while you hang on to some creep you don't even know."

"What? No wait. He's not a creep. That's what I want to tell you."

Teddy turns away from me like he's pissed off or something. "I can't keep doing this. I'm not Sloane. I don't care about your soap-opera-name billionaire or latest conquest in New York. Enough already! All I wanted to tell you was that we saw Big, I mean Chris Noth, in the lobby on the way to lunch," he says, and then he walks out the door.

The confirmation that I wasn't hallucinating is of little comfort. I've just messed things up with Teddy yet again and his friendship means more to me than any campaign.

"Let me in, Teddy," I say a few minutes later through his hotel-room door. "I want to explain. I was tipsy and I thought you were a hallucination. You know what chocolate martinis do to me."

I wait for some reaction. A "leave me alone," a grunt, even a nasty note under the door would be nice. Only the waiter pushing someone's dinner past me pays my soliloquy any attention, if that's what you call the sorry look he's giving me. There's got to be a better way to get through to Teddy.

i have plan b
open up

Almost magically the door opens. Teddy is nowhere to be seen but I hear his voice coming from behind the door. "Whaddaya want?"

I march full speed ahead to the desk at the back of the room, explaining how I met Nick Jr. at the bar. "Funny thing about New

York. You never know who you're going to meet—like say, Chris Noth's good buddy. Chris himself might even be hanging out in his suite upstairs. It could happen," I say, turning around to face Teddy. He's standing behind the door. Hair dripping wet and a white towel around his waist.

"Oh. You were in the shower." Has he been working out or did he always have that body under his baggy clothes?

"It's been a long day and we need to regroup with Brett soon. What do you want?"

Want? What do I want? Oh my god. What the hell is wrong with me? Teddy's like a brother. Stop staring! If I'm not careful I'm going to risk our friendship—and a sexual harassment lawsuit. What am I thinking? I already have a boyfriend and another guy in waiting. I sit down at the desk, focus my eyes on the Bible fortuitously sitting in front of me and collect my thoughts.

"Erica." His voice is getting louder. Nearer. I feel a few drips on my shoulder. "What do you want?"

"I have a plan to save the campaign," I manage to say.

"And you need my help, right?"

"No," I say, my ego a bit wounded. "I've got everything under control. I just wanted to share my news with you first."

Need his help? I'm not some helpless little woman who can't make a move without him. Not anymore anyway. I don't know whether to feel more hurt or angry as I dash out of Teddy's room.

"Women everywhere will want to get their hands on a Rockit," I say to Brett a few minutes later back in the suite. "I'm telling you, this campaign could be bigger than we imagined."

"How much?" he asks.

"Hard to say, maybe 25 percent more news hits, not to mention more women in Central Park than the time Bon Jovi played there."

"How much?" he asks again. I'm ignoring the obvious and he knows it. "How much more money do you need?"

With less than forty-eight hours to make this happen, I call Tory on my way back to my room and book her on the next flight out. Then I start tracking down our advertising and events agency directors and hold an emergency conference call. Next I call room service. It's going to be a long night. Herbal lemon tea won't cut it. I need caffeine and plenty of it. A couple carafes of coffee should do it, plus a platter of chocolate biscotti.

"Yes, full-page spreads in the *New York Times* and the *Daily News*. Style and Lifestyle sections, respectively. I want online banners, too." I'm on the phone again with our media buyer when there's a knock and muffled "Room service" at the door.

Only when I open up, it's Teddy and Lasagna Express reincarnated. "Thought you could use some sustenance in the form of a cheesy apology." He wheels in a room service trolley cart, draped in white linen.

"Lasagna?" I laugh.

"Brett told me about the plan but I'd rather hear your version."

"Deal," I say, sitting down and cutting into my food, recounting how Perry once told me that women would read about technology providing you didn't label it tech. "So I started thinking of women's icons that we could camouflage and parlay into Techs and the City."

"If it looks like a duck and quacks like a duck…"

"Exactly. I decided there's no less techie and more sexy a women's institution than the *Cosmo* sex quiz. Then this guy I met at the bar introduced me to his friend Chris Noth and he said he'd help. Everything just gelled."

"Who was the guy in the elevator?"

"Forget about him. Be a woman for a second and answer me this: If you're running wireless you are: a) jogging without boob support; b) answering the front door in Velcro versus hot rollers; c) sitting on the toilet, doing your makeup, and answering email at the same time; or d) having a good time with your handy battery-operated vibrator."

"That's good," he says, getting up from his seat. "Only one problem. I'm not a woman."

"No?" I respond stupidly. Nervously but still stupidly.

"Nope," he says, wheeling the tray away from me. "And I don't have a boyhood crush on you."

"No?"

He shakes his head slowly and kneels in front of me, tracing his finger around the side of my face and down my neck as if he's done it hundreds of times.

"You know this is going to change things," I say, my heart racing.

"Not for me," he whispers. "I've wanted this forever."

I push my chair away and kneel down to him, my lips mere inches from his, and freeze. What if this is a mistake? What if this destroys our friendship? What if he thinks I'm a bad kisser? Oh God. I don't know what to do.

Then Teddy pulls me onto the plush carpeted floor.

calling all techs in the city!

are you a TECHNO virgin or DIGITALLY promiscuous?

TAKE THE QUIZ TO WIN 1 of 500 Rockit smartphones

MEET Chris Noth in Central Park!

PLUS play designer and create the perfect smartphone for women!

~~~~~~

1. If you have good bandwidth:

(a) the 3 mm diamond eternity ring on your left hand is the perfect complement to the three-carat rock on your right

(b) you can get away with not washing your mane for a day, especially if you got your hair band from Lululemon Athletica (along with a new hoodie and pair of yoga capris)

(c) you are part of a good band with, well, what every good band has—lots of drugs

(d) you can send loads of photos from the cam on your mobile without so much as a hiccup

2. If you're an expert in disaster recovery you:

(a) could replace Stacy and Clinton on *What Not to Wear*

(b) know the difference between a black box and a BlackBerry

(c) probably work in crisis communications

(d) are better than the guy who couldn't fix Carrie Bradshaw's MacBook

3. If you're running wireless, you are:

(a) jogging without boob support

(b) answering the front door in Velcro versus hot rollers

(c) sitting on the toilet, applying your makeup, and sending email at the same time

(d) having a good time with your battery-operated vibrator

4. If you need your handheld:

(a) you've been dealt a royal flush at Caesar's Palace but you have to pee

(b) you're giving birth but your partner is #!@&! stuck in traffic

(c) you electronically schedule your day to drive carpool, "bring home the bacon and fry it up in a pan," and still manage your family's social calendar without missing a beat (or appointment!)

(d) you are trying to whip up meringues but your prosaic whisk won't cut it

5. You are a product of social engineering if:

(a) your best friend set you up on a blind date with a billionaire

(b) a fraudster pretending to be your help desk fooled you into telling them your password

(c) your roots date back to Nazi Germany

6. In your world, patches are:

(a) very hip and retro fashion accessories in a Sonny and Cher kind of way

(b) the best cure for butting out your nicotine habit

(c) saviours when it comes to protecting your computer against viruses

(d) where you (and Linus van Pelt) wait for the Great Pumpkin to appear

7. If you've heard about Blu-ray:

(a) you'll be relieved to hear he's taking antidepressants

(b) wait till you see Red-ray

(c) you know it's the newest version of Bluetooth wireless technology

(d) you know it's the best format for watching action flicks

8. If you like to duplex, you:

(a) have a thing for small, low-rise buildings

(b) are one efficient, paper-saving tree-hugger

(c) probably also like Pyrex

9. If you contract viruses daily:

(a) horizontally speaking, you really get around

(b) you work with kids and should really think about taking a good multivitamin

(c) you are undoubtedly pissing off everyone in your email address book

10. *If you know all about Trojan horses, you:*
(a) know that next to Mongolian wild horses, they're the most challenging to ride
(b) could write a book on Greek mythology
(c) have been infected with a sneaky virus
(d) have been watching too much porn

11. *If you haven't heard about OLED:*
(a) you haven't looked through an IKEA catalogue lately
(b) your command of Spanish isn't as good as you think
(c) your co-worker might not have been rolling a joint after all

12. *Technically, if you're having a problem with cookies:*
(a) you should work out for an extra thirty minutes to compensate for the extra calories
(b) you may want to try using less baking soda and more chocolate chips
(c) there's a reason you keep getting Internet pop-ups about your favourite stores' holiday sales.

13. *If you can't get enough of SMS, you:*
(a) need more than basic S&M can provide
(b) probably love getting PMS too
(c) even text-message your friends on the toilet

14. *If you know about scalability, you:*
(a) know the score at Weight Watchers
(b) could have written Beethoven's *Fifth*
(c) know the rate at which a fish swims has nothing to do with its scales
(d) know when a salesman is trying to scam you into buying a new computer instead of just adding memory

15. *If you're reading about external media:*
(a) you know just how evasive the paparazzi can be
(b) you specialize in advertising on billboards, blimps, and bus placards
(c) your computer just told you it has no more room to save the digital photos you took at the nude beach

16. *If you've hit a dead spot, you:*
(a) have stumbled upon a nightclub filled with fifty-year-old computer programmers who still live with their mothers
(b) are likely cursing your cellular provider
(c) are probably using a wooden baseball bat with a hairline crack
(d) should try tilting your pelvis. If that doesn't work, fake it.

17. *If you have a FireWire drive, you:*

(a) have more speeding tickets than you can count

(b) have a stronger sex drive than a john cruising Hollywood Boulevard

(c) won't freak if your laptop runs out of space without warning

18. *If you received a false negative:*

(a) don't bother trying to sue the manufacturer. Home pregnancy tests are never 100 percent accurate. Save your strength for the baby.

(b) contrary to your email inbox, you didn't win that UK lottery windfall. Make sure someone shows you the money before maxing out your credit cards.

(c) you may have been *Punk'd.* That questionable photo of you and your best friend's husband was doctored and is a total fake.

19. *If you expect a token ring, you:*

(a) don't need the ceremony, just a sparkly symbolic gesture

(b) expect a courtesy call when he's going to be late

(c) know a lot of elves and hobbits

(d) might as well be working in Bedrock

20. *If you have BHO, you:*

(a) are a dyslexic couch potato and meant HBO

(b) have a rare type of BO called Body Hair Odour. Try a vanilla sponge bath twice a day to curb smell and dirty looks.

(c) do cool things on the web thanks to the Browser Helper Object mini-program you installed in your web browser

(d) have Bacterial Hepatitis Oxidation and should go to the ER pronto

21. *If you are a Black Hat, you are:*

(a) an artsy-fartsy Bohemian type with a penchant for ebony berets

(b) a sneaky devil who prefers the term to hacker or cracker

(c) a Hasidic Jew

22. *If you enjoy spam a lot, you no doubt:*

(a) are a huge Monty Python fan

(b) also feast on other canned luncheon meat like corned beef hash

(c) lead a very lonely life and enjoy receiving unsolicited junk email

chapter
twenty-three

It's only been a few hours since the event and our corporate phone lines are still flooded. Website traffic has gone through the roof. Thousands of women flocked to the park. So did the press. Brett's already talking about doing follow-up events in L.A., Chicago, and Toronto. Mom just called to say she saw me on the news. She tells me about Perry. About how they met at my loft warming and had instant chemistry. How he cooks her dinner, takes her to the theatre, and makes her smile.

As I listen, my nose starts to tingle and the tears come fast, tickling the pores on my cheeks. I resist the urge to wipe, and instead catch the tears on my tongue as if it were February 1981 and I'm catching acid-rain snowflakes drifting down to me.

Mental note: I'm not seven anymore.

I no longer wear a bright royal blue parka with embroidered polar bears. I haven't built a snow fort in almost a quarter century and, for the life of me, I can't remember what happened to that teeny red metal shovel Dad gave me to help him with the driveway.

I close my eyes and picture Dad and me in one of Tory's plastic snow globes. Leaning his shovel against his LeMans, Dad makes a snowball and readies himself on a bumpy mound of snow. I haul my shovel across my shoulder, wait for his pitch, and then blast the icy granules across the driveway. I run around the imaginary bases and slide headfirst into snowy home plate, licking the sweet snowflakes from my face, and smile.

I can almost feel Mom's heartbeat pulsating though the phone. She has someone who makes her happy again. And can you believe it—she's a cougar! I guess I shouldn't be so shocked. So am I if you count the five years I have on Teddy.

"Ready to check out?" he says as I hang up.

"Yep. But I'm not ready to go home." I gaze into his eyes in the gilded gold mirror. Not ready to return to reality and tell Sloane or Ren where my heart really lies.

"Me neither." He removes his glasses and wraps his arms around me from behind. His eyes are delicious: melting milk-chocolate-covered almonds. "Especially since we're only 200 miles south of Cooperstown," he says with a wink and plays with my hands. "I always knew you'd have great thumbs."

"Think I could win the National Texting Championships?"

"Don't push it." He smirks and sinks his face into the crook of my neck as if it were quicksand. I try not to laugh out loud but his lips may as well be feathers they're so ticklish. Don't ruin the moment, I instruct the woman in the mirror with the large, brown-curly-haired love growth on her neck. *Focus. You can do whatever you set out to achieve. You are Erica Swift, the quintessential modern woman—nothing has changed*, I tell her, spotting a faint smile line I swear wasn't there yesterday.

crib
notes

Are you a techno virgin or digitally promiscuous?

1. If you have good bandwidth:

d) you can send loads of photos from the cam on your mobile without so much as a hiccup

Generally speaking, when it comes to moving data from one place to another over a cellular network, the greater the bandwidth, the quicker the transmission. Think of the plumbing in your house: the wider the pipes, the more water can flow to the shower—so when you flush the toilet, no one gets scalded. Likewise, the greater the bandwidth of your network, the more data it can accommodate.

2. If you're an expert in disaster recovery, you:

d) are better than the guy who couldn't fix Carrie Bradshaw's MacBook

If your computer conks out or gets hacked (translation: major disaster!), data recovery specialists can help restore your files (and your sanity!). As wonderful as these folks may be, try to avoid them. Back up your data regularly on an external hard drive or secure storage website.

3. If you're running wireless, you are:
(c) sitting on the toilet, applying your makeup, and sending email at the same time

A growing number of homes and small offices are running wireless networks because they offer more flexibility and freedom than traditional wired (Ethernet) networks. Meaning you can work on your laptop or print to a printer up to 300 feet away from your wireless router. (Did someone say "Chocolate martinis in the backyard"?)

4. If you need your handheld, you:
(c) electronically schedule your day to drive carpool, "bring home the bacon and fry it up in a pan," and still manage your family's social calendar without missing a beat (or appointment!).

Handheld computers, these days more commonly called smartphones or Personal Digital Assistants (PDAs), combine a phone, calendar, phonebook, and a host of other technologies (even video and GPS!) in one mini-computer to help make managing today's busy lifestyles easier.

5. You are a product of social engineering if:
(b) a fraudster pretending to be your help desk fooled you into telling them your password

Social engineers are modern-day con artists who sneak around, eavesdrop, and impersonate others to obtain private information (i.e., passwords) to break into secure computer networks at banks and credit card and mobility providers. Don't fall into their traps. Be wary of giving out your personal data to an apparently friendly stranger.

6. In your world, patches are:
(c) saviours when it comes to protecting your computer against viruses

Similar to patches used to cover kids' (and hippies') torn clothes, computer patches are updates that software developers issue to help fix flaws (they call them "holes") and improve performance in their software. Operating system developers and programmers will sometimes automatically send registered users patches—but not always, so you may want to check their website and see if you need to update your system for optimum performance and security.

7. If you've heard about Blu-ray:
(d) you know it's the best format for watching action flicks
Forget DVDs. If you have a high-def TV, Blu-ray is the media platform for watching movies at home. That's because Blu-ray (which gets its name from the blue-violet laser it uses to read and record data; DVDs use a red laser) can store loads more data resulting not only in higher-quality video and audio, but also more bonus features. It can even be connected to the web and let you access current movie trailers, games, and updated language tracks.

8. If you like to duplex, you:
(b) are one efficient, paper-saving tree-hugger
Duplexing—also called two-sided printing—is a great way to save paper. Many inkjet and laser printers for the home and office offer duplexers as a standard or upgradeable feature. Printing multi-up (2, 4, 9+ pages on one page) is another environmentally friendly option that is a good idea for proofing and editing a wide range of documents. At the end of the day however, the best way to save paper is to print only what you need.

9. If you contract viruses daily:
(c) you are undoubtedly pissing off everyone in your email address book
Computer viruses are software programs that attach themselves to your software and duplicate without your permission or knowledge. Most people contract them by opening innocent-looking, infected email attachments and unknowingly passing them on to contacts in their address book. Think twice before automatically opening random email attachments. Make sure you're protected with trusted anti-virus software and back up your data regularly, just in case.

10. If you know all about Trojan horses, you:
(c) have been infected with a sneaky virus
A Trojan horse is a malicious type of computer program that fools you into thinking it's one thing (like a game) when it's really a program that's going

to erase your hard drive. Worms are another type of virus that travel across the Internet attempting to break into your computer. Millions of computers around the world—even within the supposedly most secure organizations—are affected each year. As smartphones become used more as computers in the future, there's a good chance they could be infected, too.

11. If you haven't heard about OLED:

(c) your co-worker might not have been rolling a joint after all
OLED—aka Organic Light-Emitting Diode—is a hot new flat-screen technology being introduced on TVs, computer monitors, and mobile phones. It's thinner than a supermodel. So thin, in fact, some screens can be rolled up as if they were paper!

12. Technically, if you're having a problem with cookies:

(c) there's a reason you keep getting Internet pop-ups about your favourite stores' holiday sales.
As fattening as they sound, cookies—the kind on your computer—are calorie-free and fat-free, though they can add a bit of weight to your hard drive. Many websites—especially shopping sites—use cookies (little text files they send to your computer) to keep track of your personal preferences, user history, and what's in your online shopping cart.

13. If you can't get enough of SMS, you:

(c) even text-message your friends on the toilet
SMS—or Short Message Service—is a techie term for texting and it's quickly become one of the most popular ways to communicate digitally between mobile phones because it's typically cheaper to use than email. Especially popular with kids, teens, and others who (like me) haven't grown up yet.

14. If you know about scalability, you:

(d) know when a salesman is trying to scam you into buying a new computer instead of just adding more memory
If a product is scalable, it has the ability to be scaled up—or upgraded— almost like Lego. Next time your computer maxes out its memory, think about adding additional RAM. It's a lot less expensive than replacing the whole system—and better for the environment, too!

15. If you're reading about external media:
(c) your computer just told you it has no more room to save the digital photos you took at the nude beach.
Even scalable systems can run out of space on internal memory drives. Don't automatically toss your computer out if that ever happens. You may want to consider simply connecting an external hard drive (these devices are also ideal for backing up your data).

16. If you've hit a dead spot, you:
(b) are likely cursing your cellular provider
There's nothing more frustrating than your cell phone conking out in the middle of an important call. Unfortunately, that's often the reality of chatting on the go. Calls can get dropped due to interference (anything from electrical issues to a large truck blocking your signal) or lack of free cell towers—even in densely populated areas where there's an abundance of them. Don't despair. As mobile communications continues to mature, the technology keeps getting better. In the meantime, if you hit a dead spot, move around until you find a spot that rings true.

17. If you have a FireWire drive, you:
(d) won't freak if your laptop runs out of space without warning
A FireWire drive is a type of external computer hard drive, designed to store video files and tons of data. Back in the dinosaur days (translation: less than a decade ago), external drives came with 250 MB (megabytes) of data storage. These days, that won't hold diddly—not with all the photos, MP3s, and video we put on our systems. Nope, better get a hard drive with two TB (terabytes)—that's over two million megabytes—to last you for a while.

18. If you received a false negative:
(b) contrary to your email inbox, you didn't win that UK lottery windfall. Make sure someone shows you the money before maxing out your credit cards.
It may sound riddle-like but receiving a false negative simply means you got legitimate-looking spam. If you get more than your share of junk mail, it may be time to look for a new spam filter. Same goes if legitimate emails are being blocked and tagged as spam (aka, wouldn't you know it, a false positive).

19. If you expect a token ring, you:

(d) might as well be working in Bedrock.

Token ring computer networks were popular in offices back in the mid to late 1980s. A decade or so later Ethernet networks took over as the wired network of choice with their ability to transmit data faster. They're still top dog—and not just in the office. A growing number of new homes have been prewired for Ethernet connectivity, though wireless is quickly becoming the way to work at home as it becomes more affordable and secure.

20. If you have BHO, you:

(c) do cool things on the web thanks to the Browser Helper Object mini-program you installed in your web browser

Okay, so Browser Helper Object isn't exactly a common tech term but hey, when have you ever heard of Body Hair Odour or Bacterial Hepatitis Oxidation either? Unlike the latter two absurdities (though it is possible for body hair to smell, I suppose), a BHO is a type of web browser plug-in—like a Yahoo or Google toolbar—used to enhance your surfing experience (some kinds are a snooping kind of program called spyware).

21. If you are a Black Hat, you are:

(c) a sneaky devil who prefers the term to hacker or cracker

It sounds so debonair—almost Fred Astaire-in-a tuxedo-like—but a Black Hat is actually techie slang for computer hacker. The term is said to have come from Hollywood where a Black Hat refers to a villain in a movie (think the bad guy in all the Westerns). The hero of the movie, not surprisingly, is called a White Hat, as is a hacker who uses his or her powers in a good way, like protecting computer networks from being compromised.

22. If you enjoy spam a lot, you no doubt:

(c) lead a very lonely life and enjoy receiving unsolicited junk email.

If you're like me, you hate getting spam almost as much as getting your period. Prescription drugs, porn, fake Rolex watches—it doesn't matter what's being peddled via email, it's spam and it's an invasion of your inbox. Just say no! Block spam using a good Internet security suite that includes a spam filter that blocks these pesky intruders.

acknowledgements

To thank someone for rejecting me seems silly yet somehow fitting. For, had one of my former editors at *Chatelaine* not advised me five years ago that women "aren't ready" for a feature on embracing technology, opportunity surely would not have rung in the form of this novel.

Backtracking, the recession of the early 1990s also seems an unlikely acknowledgement. But had it not hit, had I landed another job as an advertising copywriter, I would not have become a tech publicist/writer (no, really…) working on accounts like Lexmark, Palm, Microsoft, Symantec, Dell, NEC, and D-Link. Nor would I likely have turned to comedy.

Thanks to my Second City writing instructor, Jerry Schaefer, for teaching me I can always be funnier. To my gurus of geek: Andy Walker, Sean Carruthers, Jordan Silverberg, and Marc Saltzman. To Andy especially, for also being my sounding board, chief reader, and manuscript smiley-face maker. To all my friends for all their support and enthusiasm, including Julie Falconer, Judy Ranieri, and Lisa Nackan, my other trusted readers, for laughing in the right places (as well as the wrong ones).

To designer Marijke Friesen and illustrator Alanna Cavanagh for hitting the well-manicured nail on the head with their finger-licious front cover. To my editor, Jane Warren, for patiently putting up with this first-time author and making me seem not so neurotic on paper. (You can't tell, can you?) To my publisher, Jordan Fenn, for taking a personal interest in Erica's journey with only a hundred pages to go on. To Amy Moore-Benson, my make-things-happen agent, for all her sunshine, guidance, and the best birthday gift any writer could (and did) ask for.

To my family for their constant love, great sense of humour, and honesty. To Stephen for always being there and believing in me. To Erica, Teddy, Sloane, Dani & co., for being so flawed and yummy. And to my real-life children, Melissa and Turner, for making me smile even when there are no words.